Silent Crimes

ALSO BY MICHAEL HAMBLING

THE SOPHIE ALLEN BOOKS

Michael Hambling
SILENT CRIMES

Detective Sophie Allen Book 8

JOFFE BOOKS

Revised edition 2024
Joffe Books, London
www.joffebooks.com

First published in Great Britain in 2019

© Michael Hambling 2019, 2024

Cover art by Nick Castle

ISBN: 978-1-83526-860-5

FOREWORD

This is a work of fiction and none of the characters and situations portrayed bear any resemblance to real persons or events. That said, in the course of researching the novel, I came across several interesting snippets of information that I have referred to in the text. The Quantock Hills in Somerset were home to a Victorian-era religious cult. One of the lanes that cross the hills has a rough parking area next to a spot called "Dead Woman's Ditch." Make of this what you will.

CHARACTER LIST

Dorset Police Violent Crime Unit (VCU):
Detective Superintendent Sophie Allen
Detective Inspector Barry Marsh
Detective Constable Rae Gregson

Bournemouth CID:
Detective Inspector Kevin McGreedie
Detective Sergeant Lydia Pillay
Detective Constable Jimmy Melsom

Dorset Police Uniformed Officers:
Sergeant Rose Simons
Constable George Warrander
Constable Gerry Baldwin (dog handler) and Floyd

Avon and Somerset CID:
Detective Inspector Polly Nelson

Past members of the Heathfield Farm Commune in the Quantock Hills, Somerset:
Katie Templar
Paul Prentice
Timothy Brotherton
Andrew Atkins
Trent Baker
Catherine Templeton
Linda Brooker

Other witnesses and incidental characters:
Craig Millins (DC Rae Gregson's boyfriend)
Russel Poulter (would-be boyfriend of Catherine Templeton)
Judy Price (partner of Timothy Brotherton)
Babs Atkins (Andrew's mother)

Sandra Bulmore (Katie Templar's best friend from her university days)
June Brown (Katie's aunt)
Roger Brown (Katie's cousin)
Sir Roger and Lady Marion Prentice-Jones (Paul's parents)
Martin Allen (Sophie Allen's husband)
Jade Allen (Sophie and Martin's eighteen-year-old daughter)
Pauline Stopley (a member of a Dorset walking group who also appears in novels 4 and 6 of this series)

PROLOGUE

The western sky glowed orange, ablaze with the remnants of a glorious sunset. Was this the harbinger of a warm summer to come? Beyond the horizon, bats were already flitting between the trees, swooping on swarms of insects that had gathered in the fast-deepening dusk. The bats veered sharply, avoiding the small fire, despite the fact that it was now little more than a pile of smouldering ash. An unshaven, dirt-smeared tramp took a stick and poked the few remaining bits of branch into the embers, causing a myriad of sparks to fly into the air and a blaze of light to illuminate the small clearing. He placed the blackened pot on his dish, together with the spoon. He would rinse them in the morning when he went down to the shore to wash.

A sudden distant sound, maybe a dry branch snapping, disturbed the near silence. His small dog raised its head and growled softly, and the tramp reached down to stroke it. The dog, still alert, lowered its head. Were there animals in these woods heavy enough to snap a dead branch? A fox or a badger? He rose and moved slowly towards where he thought the sound had come from. The dog followed, sniffing.

The night was growing rapidly darker. Inside the woods, the dense overhead foliage blocked every remaining trace of light. Sounds were muffled. He waded through undergrowth up a gently rising slope. The dog had run off somewhere, probably chasing rabbits. The man heard a slight rustling behind him and half turned.

The darkness exploding into a million stars that blurred into streaks. A searing pain.

He crashed to the ground and lay still.

CHAPTER 1: IN THE WOODS

Friday afternoon

'Bye. See you later.' Jade Allen waved and turned away from her friends, towards the quayside and home. Today had been special, bringing relief together with sadness. Already she felt a bit wistful. She had just completed the last of her A level exams, a biology paper, surely a reason to feel cheerful. In a few hours' time, she and the same group of friends were to meet for a night of celebration, pubbing and clubbing. But right now she mostly felt nostalgic. The great change, the giant step, was now upon her. She'd be at school just once more, in a week's time, to return her books and attend a farewell tea with her teachers. And that would be the end of it. She'd be saying goodbye to Jade the schoolgirl, the carefree, fun-loving teenager. She frowned. That wasn't exactly true. She'd been aware of the weight of moral responsibility for a few years now, having developed too large a social conscience to be quite as "freewheeling" as many of her friends. This sense of social responsibility was the reason she had waved goodbye to them just now, instead of heading into town for a quick celebratory drink before going home to get ready for their night on the town. Something had been at the back of her mind for days, and if she didn't check up on it now, she might never forgive herself. She hurried home, collected some odds and ends of food from the kitchen, pulled her latterly underused bicycle from the garage and headed down to Wareham's riverside quay. She crossed the ancient river bridge and turned left onto a waterside path that led east towards the picturesque village of Arne.

It was a beautiful afternoon. Water birds frolicked in the reeds and swallows dived back and forth above the water, chasing insects. A few small boats nudged their way slowly upstream, their crews enjoying the June sunshine. A few of the women had even ventured out in bikini tops, hoping to catch an early summer tan.

After half a mile, Jade turned south, away from the river. She followed a track that took her through the hamlet of Ridge and onto a narrow road that headed towards the heavily wooded and somewhat wild countryside of the Arne Peninsula, which jutted out into the wide, watery expanse of Poole Harbour, the largest natural harbour in Europe. The single-track lane was busy with visitors to Arne's popular nature reserve. Jade wasn't going that far, however. Instead, she turned off into the woods a mile before the birdwatching centre. At one point, the roadside fence struggled to hold back a dense thicket of trees and shrubs. She brought her bicycle to a halt at a point where the copse thinned somewhat, and a faint path could just be discerned beyond the fence. Jade dismounted, hefted the machine over the fence and clambered across. She left the bike behind some trees and began to follow the path through the woods, heading towards a slight rise a few hundred yards ahead. On the far side of the rise stood an old ramshackle timbered structure, half hidden in the undergrowth. The small hut had no door, but someone had lodged an old sheet of rust-streaked corrugated iron against the opening in recent years. This was now lying on the ground, several yards from the hut. Jade walked to the edge of the small clearing and stood still. She couldn't make sense of what she was seeing. The small open area was strewn with bits of cloth, as if wild animals had entered the hut and pulled things out.

'Paul?' she called. 'Are you here?'

Silence. No birds. Had they been singing before she called out? She moved forward slowly. Inside the tiny hut his meagre belongings were spread randomly across the floor. Foxes? Badgers? Or had someone been searching the place? If so, what for?

'Paul?' Something was seriously wrong. She peered into the shadows beneath the surrounding trees. A rook squawked nearby, startling her.

'Paul? Algy? Are you there?'

Was that the sound of something small moving through the undergrowth? Jade made her way through the trees in the direction of the river, towards the top of the low ridge.

'Algy? Is that you?'

She heard a dog bark. It sounded muted and weak.

'Algy.' There was a rustle in the thicket ahead of her, and a small, filthy dog emerged and limped towards her. She bent down and ruffled its skinny neck. It whined at her.

'What's happened, Algy? What's wrong? Where's Paul?'

The dog barked again and limped back towards the pocket of shrubs. Jade followed, scrambling through the undergrowth, scratched by brambles. Algy's rear left leg was dragging on the ground. Had there been an accident? Why was the dog so thin and filthy? She rounded a clump of bushes.

On the ground in front of her lay a body, sprawled across the grass. She ran towards the motionless figure and bent down.

'Paul?' She was about to feel for a pulse, but a look at his face told her it would be pointless. The dog must have kept the rodents and other animals away, but it couldn't stop the insects. She staggered back, her gorge rising. Was there a mobile phone signal here? What had happened?

* * *

5

They sat on damp logs, waiting for a forensic unit to arrive. Jade was sipping from a water bottle that she'd brought in her backpack. Sergeant Rose Simons was asking questions and Constable George Warrander was taking notes.

'So, what brought you up here into the woods? I'm not clear on that point,' Rose asked the tall, dark-haired teenager.

'Paul's been missing from his usual places in town for days now, maybe weeks. He's usually either in the town centre or one of the underpasses.'

'What do you mean?'

'He's a beggar, a sort of tramp. He's here every summer. Surely you've seen him around town?' Jade said.

'We're not normally based in Wareham. We're over in Blandford or Dorchester. We're just doing cover over this way for a few weeks. What's your name by the way?'

'Jade.'

'Well, Jade, you'd better explain how come you know him so well, this Paul Prentice.' Rose was watching the young woman carefully.

'I bring him and his dog Algy some food a couple of times a week. You know, sandwiches, cake, maybe a pork pie. Sometimes I give him some money but not very often. He spends some of it on booze and I got a bit fed up telling him that it wasn't doing him any good. He used to try to kip overnight in the town centre but you lot moved him on when some of the locals complained. He had nowhere else to go so I told him about this place.' She waved towards the old hut. 'And if he had some food, he'd sometimes make a fire and cook it here.'

'Have you ever come up before to visit him?'

Jade regarded the police sergeant warily. 'Yes, but not very often. It was just that I hadn't seen him in town for a while. I wanted to know he was alright.'

'Why?'

Jade's voice rose. 'He had no one. Don't you see? If I didn't do it, who else was there? I mean, what kind of world is it when someone has nobody to take care of them? We're lucky. We all have someone, but people like Paul, they don't.'

'What else do you know about him?' Rose asked.

Jade sighed. 'He was about thirty-six, but he looked a lot older. He didn't come from around here originally, he was from the Somerset area, I think. In the winter he used to go to Poole, to spend the coldest months in one of the hostels. He told me he hated being cooped up with others and was much happier being out in the open. He didn't like being "caged in," as he put it. And he had his dog, Algernon Fortescue Blythe — Algy for short.' She paused. 'The thing is, he wasn't stupid. He used to work in an office somewhere, but he'd had some kind of breakdown or seizure. That's what he told me.'

'He never caused you any bother? He never tried anything on with you?'

Jade's reply was abrupt. 'Of course not. Do you think I'd have stayed on good terms with him if he had? Do you think I'm weak-minded or something? For pity's sake.'

'Look, I have to ask these questions,' Rose said. 'This is an unexplained death, and you might be the person who knows him best.'

Jade snorted. 'Well, I can believe that. No one else seemed to give a toss about him. He was either totally invisible or some kind of public nuisance. That's how he was treated. Take your pick.'

'Okay, I take your point. I'm not the totally cold-hearted bitch I might appear to be.' Rose glanced at her colleague's notes. 'We don't have a record of your surname or address, Jade. Apparently, you didn't give it when you phoned in.'

'No, I didn't.'

Rose waited, but the young woman said nothing further.

'Do I have to ask you more forcefully?'

'Please don't,' Jade replied. 'Is there any way you can avoid identifying me? Please?'

'No. You found a dead body.' Rose was growing increasingly exasperated. 'At the moment, you appear to know more about the deceased than anyone else, so we'll need some written statements from you. Of course we'll need your full name and address. What did you expect? What's the problem anyway?'

Jade looked at the ground. 'This is just what I was worried about,' she said. 'I'm Jade Allen. You know my mum. In fact, everyone in Dorset police knows my mum.'

'Oh shit,' Rose said. 'Sorry. Did I say that out loud? Can you conveniently wipe it from your mind?'

Jade smiled for the first time in several hours. 'Of course. And if I get a bit senseless in the town centre tonight, can you just deliver me home rather than throwing me in the cells?'

'It's a deal,' Rose said. 'Are you having some kind of celebration?'

'End of A levels,' Jade said. 'I had my last one this afternoon. We all had a big night planned but I really don't feel like it now, not after this. I might give it a miss.'

Rose nodded. 'I can understand how you feel, but to be honest, it might be better if you stick to your plan. You may not enjoy it much but at least it'll take your mind off all this.'

'Can you tell how he died?'

'Not me, no. But it'll all come out in the post-mortem.'

* * *

Rae Gregson was the first detective to turn up. She crossed the clearing and looked askance at Jade.

'What's the boss's daughter doing here? Don't tell me . . .'

Rose pulled a face. 'Exactly. It was her that found the body. She's fine. George has been looking after her, giving her the five-star treatment. Actually, she's a really public-spirited young lady. How do you know her?'

'Just a couple of social events,' Rae said. 'I'd better phone and let Barry know. He'll hit the roof if I don't tell him, what with the boss being away in London at a conference today. We just thought it was a tramp found dead of natural causes and I only came because I was fairly close by. But you look a bit concerned. Is there something else I need to know?'

Rose pursed her lips. 'Maybe the fact that he's been hit over the head with something heavy? The skull wound is pretty severe. It doesn't look accidental, not to me. We haven't mentioned it to young Miss Social Conscience over there — she's upset enough as it is. I'm telling you, if my snotty son grows up to be remotely as caring as she appears to be, I'll be over the moon. So far, his emotional attachments seem to extend only as far as the person who's gonna supply him with his next dose of pizza and chips.'

DS Barry Marsh arrived at the same time as the forensic team. He organised a search of the immediate area and conferred with the pathologist when he arrived. He exchanged a few words with Jade before getting George to take her home in a squad car, her bicycle loaded into the boot. Rose had been watching all this carefully. She'd heard that Barry had recently passed his inspector's exam and hoped this didn't mean he'd be looking for a transfer to another county. In Rose's opinion, Barry Marsh was the best detective she'd ever worked with — apart from her ladyship, of course. When she saw that he'd finished his various discussions she sidled across to him.

'Was he hit with a slab of wood?'

'Looks like it,' Barry said. 'The doc thinks there are splinters in the head wound.'

'Thought so. You'll still be organising a fingertip search of the area, I'm sure, but I don't think you'll find it anywhere out there.' She took his arm and pointed to the ashes of the dead fire. 'See that central line of ash? It's from something that was added after the rest of the fire died down.' She pointed to the rim of the fire. 'And look there. One end unburned. Here's hoping someone forgot to wear gloves, eh?'

9

CHAPTER 2: BACKGROUND

Saturday morning

Benny Goodall, Dorset's senior pathologist, was speaking to a woman standing opposite him. She was tall, blonde and smartly dressed. 'I'd say about a week, judging from the state of skin deterioration and the insect activity. Maybe we'd be able to pin it down a bit more precisely if we could get one of these forensic entomologists in to have a look. Can you afford that?' He raised his eyebrows.

Detective Superintendent Sophie Allen made a face. 'Of course not, Benny. This is the age of austerity, as you well know. I have to beg, borrow or steal to get anything I need. In this case, I'll beg. I have a couple of contacts at the local universities who owe me some favours. If the worst comes to the worst, I'll offer to do some kind of talk at their graduates' careers convention.'

Benny smirked. 'How could they refuse you after an offer like that? Here, how about making it a double act? *The Detective and the Pathologist — Solving Crimes Together!* What a title for a lecture. Maybe we could charge for entry. Maybe we could hit the road and go on tour.'

Sophie Allen rolled her eyes. 'This is all because you failed to make it as a rock star twenty-five years ago, isn't it? I don't think your idea quite matches up to the reality, Benny. You wouldn't get flowers and underwear thrown on stage at a lecture with that title. Or any lecture, come to that. You've got to move on in life and put these adolescent disappointments behind you. Let's get back to business. How did he die?'

'It looks as though he was hit from behind with a log or something wooden, judging from the splinters embedded in the wound.'

'Nothing of that description was found nearby, nothing complete anyway,' she said.

'Doesn't that tell you something? You're the detective.'

'Did he die quickly, or could he have crawled to where he was found, maybe trying to get back to his shelter?'

'No, not with a head wound that serious,' Benny said. 'Chances are he was dead within a minute or so of being hit. The injuries are pretty severe. Is it true that Jade found him?'

'Yes. Apparently, she befriended him without telling anyone. She used to take him food. She hadn't seen him around town for a while and decided to check up on him. I'm quite proud of her, actually.'

'Well, it's good to know that my goddaughter has grown up the right way, despite the somewhat slapdash parenting she's had.'

Sophie gave an exaggerated scowl. 'I'll rise above that comment. Anything else I ought to know?'

'He was ill, though he probably wasn't aware of what was lying in wait for him. Cirrhosis of the liver, lung damage and he had a small tumour behind his left eye. All treatable in someone with a more orthodox lifestyle, but living the way he did, it probably wouldn't have been picked up in time. Everything else was pretty much as I'd have expected. He'd chosen a hard life and had the bruises and scars to show for it. So Jade never told you about him?'

Sophie shook her head, frowning. 'No, and it makes me feel a bit inadequate. As a mother, I mean. Why didn't she ever mention him? Does she think I'd have been so lacking in understanding? It shakes me up a bit that she didn't feel able to talk about what she was doing.'

'You're taking it the wrong way, Sophie. Don't you think we all need to keep some part of our lives private? Particularly from our parents. Why do you think you should know everything about Jade's life? Did you, do you, tell your own mother everything? Of course not. Well, Jade's her own person. She's making her own way in life, and jolly good for her. Anyway, she told me about him. Not much, mind you, and it was only once. Just that she was keeping her eye on a tramp.' Sophie stared at him, her mouth open to speak. 'Listen, just leave it. Don't mention it to her, it would only cause friction. Who's been interviewing her? Barry?'

'Yes, up to now.'

'Let him get on with it and don't interfere. Just be Mum, not the police bigwig. I'll be meeting her for lunch in a few days' time, so I'll do a bit of gentle probing and maybe let her know your feelings.'

Sophie sighed. 'Okay, bossy-boots. But what's this lunch about?'

'Just me performing my godfatherly duties like the responsible person I am. It's all very informal. She sometimes brings along a friend or two, particularly if they're gay. She introduces me as her gay uncle figure, and they use me as a sounding board. I've even visited her school for an official session on LGBT and personal relationships.'

Sophie raised her eyebrows.

'No need to look so surprised, Sophie. I am a doctor, you know. Jade is a brilliant organiser and very socially aware. You should be proud of her. I know I am.'

* * *

By the time Sophie returned to Wareham police station, Barry and Rae were already setting up an incident room. Computers

12

had been trucked down from county headquarters and Ameera Khan was directing her team of technicians who were networking the machines together. She was gone within an hour, leaving one resident technician behind. Sophie scanned the information board. The word "sparse" hardly did it justice. She'd never seen one with so little information on it. Her two junior detectives stood beside her, all three staring at it despondently.

'Sorry, ma'am, but that's all we have,' Rae said. 'It's a pig of a business trying to find out anything about him. I never realised how easily people can disappear off the record when they go walkabout like this man. It's as if he never existed. He didn't work in any organised way. He didn't pay tax. He wasn't on the voters' roll. He doesn't seem to have been registered with any doctor in the area. As far as I can tell, he didn't even claim any state benefits. He must have lived a real hand-to-mouth existence, which ties in with what Jade's told us.' She glanced at Barry.

'What it means, ma'am,' he said, 'is that Jade seems to have known him better than anyone else around. She'll have to be questioned again, until we've made more progress. It's not what we want but that's the reality. Which one of us would you like it to be?'

Sophie passed a hand across her forehead, unconsciously brushing away the headache that had been threatening for a while. 'Rae, I think. Jade knows you too well, Barry. I'll stay well clear, so that there's some chance of the mother-daughter relationship surviving this lot.' She shook her head slowly. 'Bloody hell. And I've just had to endure a lecture from Benny Goodall about Jade's laudable sense of social responsibility. What a day.' She turned and trudged from the room.

'How carefully do I have to tread?' Rae said.

Barry shrugged. 'It's your baby, Rae. You rarely get these things wrong.'

Rae rolled her eyes. 'Gee, thanks for your help, boss.'

* * *

Rae was at the Allen house, sitting on a couch with a mug of coffee. Jade sat facing her in an armchair, legs tucked underneath her. A cleaned-up Algy lay with his head on her lap, a small splint strapped to one of his back legs.

'Tell me how and when you first met Paul Prentice,' Rae said, notebook at the ready.

'About three years ago? It was spring, and I was on my way home from school with some friends. Paul was in the doorway of an empty shop in West Street looking cold, wet, hungry and ill. Even Algy here looked a bit pathetic.' She tickled the small dog's neck and it whined contentedly. 'Some louts from the year below me at school were giving him a hard time so I told them to get lost. They'd have probably gone for me if I'd been on my own, but I was with a bunch of my friends, so they thought better of it and wandered off. There was a café nearby, so I went in and bought him a coffee and a ham roll, plus a pork pie for the dog. I don't normally do things like that, but he looked so vulnerable. He didn't look as though he was in a fit state to be living rough like that. Anyway, I came here to drop my stuff off, then I went back on my bike to see if he was still okay. But he'd gone.'

'Did you try to find him?' Rae asked.

Jade shrugged. 'I cycled around the town centre for a bit but didn't spot him. The next time I saw him was a couple of days later, on the Saturday morning. He was back in the same doorway, wrapped in an old sleeping bag just like before. I couldn't stop to check up on him 'cause I was on my way to hockey practice. He was gone when I came back, but this time I found him. He'd shifted around the corner to North Street, to get out of the wind. I got him a carton of hot soup from the café, along with another pork pie for the dog. The thing is, even in April it can get really cold if someone's stuck outdoors all the time. He had to spend time in the town centre because he wouldn't pick up any begging money otherwise. He told me that he was spending his nights in the old wooden stand at the cricket club, but the groundsman kept chucking him out.'

'When did you tell him about the place in the woods?' Rae asked.

'It must have been a few months later, in the summer. Dad and I stumbled across it by accident when we were out bird-watching one day. It was ramshackle even then, and it smelled disgusting. Paul cleaned it out a bit, so it wasn't so bad. I never told Dad what I'd done.'

'I suppose I can understand that, but I'd have thought your dad, of all people, would have been sympathetic. And your mum, come to that. Aren't I right? Maybe I shouldn't ask you that. She is my boss, after all.'

'It's not that. Once you tell someone who's in an official position like they are, they feel duty bound to do something about it. Which means calling in some authority or other. Paul just wanted to be left alone. So I decided to just keep an eye on him myself. He turned out to be a really nice man. He was intelligent, and he had a wicked sense of humour once you got to know him.'

Rae thought back ten years to when she'd been eighteen. Of course, she'd been a young man at that age, some six years before she transitioned, and bound up in her own mental anguish. But even taking that into account, would she have had the same degree of social awareness Jade had shown? Hardly. That younger Ray, and all his friends, would have seen some old tramp sleeping rough in a shop doorway and begging, and he'd have been just about invisible to them. They might well have made fun of him. It had taken Rae until she was twenty-eight — thirteen years older than Jade when she'd first encountered Prentice — to get to the same level of human understanding. It made her feel inadequate.

'What else can you tell me about him?' she said, moving on quickly. 'You must have picked up something if you've been seeing him for a couple of years. Anything would help, Jade. He dropped off the official radar years ago and we can't find a thing about him.'

'All I know is that something happened to him way back. Someone close to him walked out or vanished, and it totally shook him up. He decided to become invisible and that's why he ended up here. There's no point in looking for him in any local records 'cause he originally came from somewhere in Somerset. You see, Rae, he wasn't stupid. I got the feeling that he'd had some fairly high-powered job but left when the bad thing happened. And he was worried or scared about something, as if he still felt threatened. He asked me once to let him know if there was anyone asking around after him. He wouldn't explain why, he just clammed up when I asked.'

'Did you ever pick up any clues as to what this high-powered job might have been?'

Jade shook her head. 'It must have been a long way back. After all, I've only known him for the past couple of years. I got the impression he'd been tramping around this area for a lot longer than that. He used to spend the worst of the winter in a hostel in Poole. Maybe they can help?'

'I've found three that he might have used,' Rae said, 'but the most likely one closed down at Easter when the parent charity folded. I'm trying to trace the warden who was there most recently, but it isn't easy. Apparently, he moved to one of the big cities, but no one seems to be sure which. It's a pig, to be honest.'

'He seemed to know about the law, and not just his own legal rights. And he was well-spoken, articulate. We once had a chat about local bylaws, and he really seemed to know his stuff. He explained it really well. He knew a lot about the land. I don't mean as a farmer or anything, he seemed to know about the way boundaries and roads originally followed the landscape. You know, contours and stuff.'

Rae nodded slowly. 'Could he have been a surveyor? That would explain both of the things you mentioned.'

Jade shrugged. 'Could be, but he never said. We mostly talked about more general things — wildlife, the night sky, human behaviour, that kind of stuff.'

'Sort of philosophical? Is that what you mean?' Rae said.

'Partly. He seemed to have thought a lot about why people behave the way they do. Maybe that was connected to whatever happened to him. I did wonder a couple of times

16

whether he'd been badly let down by someone. You know, got into some kind of trouble because of someone else. But that's just me speculating. I never asked him about it.'

'Is there anything else you can think of that might help us?'

Jade tickled Algy's neck again and shook her head. 'Not about Paul, no. But there is something about Algy. Ever since I've known him, he's always had a collar on. It had a little silver canister attached to it. You know, the type that unscrews and has the owner's address on a bit of paper inside. It's gone missing. The thing is, Algy doesn't let strangers get near him, not willingly. Whoever took it either knew Algy or got hold of the collar by force. And I've puzzled over how he got his leg injury. I wonder if someone had to wrestle with him to get the collar off, and that's how he got hurt. If Paul was lying badly injured or already dead, Algy would have fought like a wild thing.'

'So whoever it was might have suffered bites and scratches? Is that what you're saying?'

'Could be. The vet thought that Algy's leg injury was consistent with a blow from a stick. That's what the X-ray showed. Maybe it was the same stick that was used to attack Paul.'

'Do you think Paul Prentice was his real name?' Rae said. 'If he was on the run from someone or something, he might have adopted a false identity.'

'He never gave me any reason to think that, but I guess it's possible. If so, that would leave you with nothing to go on, wouldn't it?'

Rae nodded. 'Dead right. And it's a spot-on description of the state we're in. But don't worry, we'll get there.'

CHAPTER 3: GOSSIPS

Late Saturday morning

'Have forensics found anything useful, Barry? I don't hold out much hope, but you never know.'

Sophie had returned to Wareham police station in time to join her second-in-command for coffee in the incident room.

'I was on the phone to Dave Nash just now, ma'am. They've completed the search of the immediate area, but nothing's turned up yet. That bit of branch poking out of the embers didn't produce any useful fingerprints but it's being forensically wiped to see if it has any traces of DNA. It'll be ages before we get the results and I don't hold out much hope. It looks to me as if this was planned. Someone travelled down here specifically to kill Prentice, and they made sure not to leave any evidence. It backs up the idea that they knew what they were doing, doesn't it?'

Sophie shrugged. 'It may look premeditated, but we can't be sure at this stage. Let's head off and join the group in town. I want to know if anyone's been asking around after Prentice in the last couple of weeks. According to Jade, he was getting to be a well-known figure around the place. The locals are a nosey lot. I know because I'm one of them. Someone wandering around asking dubious questions is likely to have come to the attention of the local nosey-parker league, as we call them. Nothing escapes the attention of old Mrs Denhay and her friends in the pensioners' coffee group. Maybe I'll speak to them while you check on the official door-to-door squads. Apparently, they consider me an honorary member for some reason, particularly since I got my recent promotion. They've asked me to be a guest speaker at one of their official morning get-togethers and give a talk about modern policing methods.'

'Will you do it?'

'I'll have to. Turning them down would result in the whole family being sent to Coventry for a year. Their memories are long, and the old dears can be quite vindictive. Small-town life.'

* * *

Mrs Denhay and her friends weren't able to offer any help, but a uniformed officer out on a house-to-house enquiry did discover from a local shopkeeper that a slightly suspicious-looking individual had been seen hanging around the town centre a week or so previously. The problem was, of course, that it was the start of the summer holiday season, and large numbers of dishevelled people could be seen hanging around Purbeck. It was a favourite area for camping, trekking and beach holidays, not to mention the regular jazz, folk and blues festivals. And the country's favourite nudist beach on Studland certainly meant that, during the summer months at least, the area was crawling with keen disciples of alternative lifestyles.

Barry went back to visit the shopkeeper in question, the manager of a hardware store conveniently situated on a corner of the High Street and an equally busy side road. The views out onto the main thoroughfares were particularly good.

'This man you saw last week — what raised your suspicions?' he asked.

'He just didn't seem right,' said the manager, a middle-aged woman wearing blue shorts and a loose cotton top.

Barry looked with fascination at her toenail varnish. It spanned the colours of the rainbow, starting with a deep red on the small toe on her left foot and ending with violet on her equivalent right toe. He looked up to find her watching him, her eyes sparkling with mischief.

'Um, what do you mean exactly?' he asked, embarrassed to be caught staring at her feet.

'He gave the impression of being a dozy tourist, but he was definitely after something. He asked some questions about facilities for tramps and travellers in the area, but the way he said it made me a bit suspicious, so I watched him after he left. He spoke to several other people outside and kept looking around as if he was expecting to see someone. He was kind of furtive. Does that make sense?'

'Of course. And thanks for bringing it to our attention.' He noted her name and said that they might have to contact her again. 'And I really like your toenail colours,' he added. 'I might mention it to my fiancée. They look great.'

She frowned. 'Why? Is she gay too?'

He made a hurried retreat from the shop and ran into Sophie leaving a café further down the road. He repeated the shopkeeper's observations, adding the story of the toenails.

She roared with laughter. 'Barry, you really are priceless sometimes. The rainbow flag? No? You really need to brush up on your LGBT culture, you know. Let's find Rae and get some lunch. I'll take you to my favourite local café. I have to be sure to avoid the ones used by Jade and her friends, though I expect they'll all be nursing hangovers this morning. And, luckily, it's also one that Mrs Denhay and her gang tend to avoid. The owners come from Turkey.'

'Closet racists, are they?' Barry asked.

'Not all of them, just a few of the worst and most malicious. Jade had a go at them a few months ago because of it. I expect there was blood all over the floor — metaphorically speaking, of course. The old biddies have kept quiet since then, but they still don't visit that café. Good thing really. It means I can get a peaceful snack or coffee when I need one, without them pestering me about local crime and what am I doing about it.'

* * *

Rae was conducting interviews with the rangers at the Arne nature reserve, but so far nothing of note had come up. She was standing in the small outdoor centre, looking at the large-scale map on the wall and listening to the senior ranger point out the boundaries of the reserve.

'You can see the three main zones,' Petra Smith said. 'Two south of the road, and this single one to the north-west. Your crime scene is way over here to the north-east, a good mile beyond our boundary. I know you have to interview all of our staff members, but we've discussed it among ourselves and no one remembers meeting a tramp. We were vaguely aware of someone sleeping rough in the woods, but it wasn't happening on our land, so we didn't go poking our noses in. And I don't think he was there during the daytime. Wasn't he usually around Wareham town centre, begging?'

'Yes, we think so,' Rae said. 'But I have to check with everyone who lives or works in the area, to help build up a picture. What about on the road? Did you ever pass anyone of his description when you were travelling to and from work?'

Petra shook her head. 'No. But he'd have been using the footpaths, wouldn't he? I tell you what. Lynette, one of our volunteers, comes in on her bike. She sometimes uses the paths. Maybe she might be able to help a bit more than the rest of us. She's not in today but I can give you her phone number. Oh, and don't forget the café staff, though I think they all drive in and out. The café is open at the moment, so you can see them right now if you want.'

None of the other centre staff could help, so Rae crossed the narrow lane to the café. Three staff were in the building, either preparing food or serving, and none had known about Paul Prentice's life in the woods until news of his death had filtered into the local community. None could remember seeing a man of his description on the road. Rae ordered a sandwich for her lunch, then sat down and phoned the number the senior ranger had supplied for the volunteer, Lynette. She had more to offer than the full-time staff, so Rae arranged to see her after lunch, at her home in Stoborough, a small hamlet a mile south of Wareham on the other side of the river.

Lynette Brown was a trained telecommunications engineer in her early twenties with a passion for wildlife photography. She invited Rae into the tiny house she shared with her partner, where she told her that living so close to one of the country's top bird and nature reserves was like a dream come true. Her freckled face lit up as she spoke about the wildlife, while Rae looked at the shelves in the small downstairs room filled with books on animal life. Photoprints of birds covered the walls.

Lynette introduced her partner. 'This is Eddie. He's pretty keen too.'

Rae wasn't surprised. The young dark-haired man was dressed like Lynette in combat trousers and outdoor boots.

'We've been discussing it since you phoned. We both think we've seen the man you're asking about, but only a couple of times. Eddie is more observant than me when it comes to people, so he can tell you more. If you wanted to know about a bird, then it'd probably be me who'd have noticed more.'

Eddie rolled his eyes at his girlfriend, then smiled at Rae. 'She's always on the lookout for birds or lizards, all that kind of thing. If she was more interested in people, she'd remember them. I like wildlife too, but I find people even more fascinating. Don't you?'

Rae laughed. 'I have to. It's my job. I have to interview all kinds of people, from innocent onlookers like yourselves, who might have witnessed something, to the worst kinds of human lowlife. And I have to be observant. So, what can you remember, Eddie?'

'I think I've seen him about four times. Twice on the riverside path, heading in or out of Wareham, and maybe twice in the town centre, sitting in a doorway. I think it was probably his dog that got my attention. Beggars often have aggressive, snarling dogs, or that's what I imagine, but his little terrier was very inquisitive and friendly. It used to trot across to me and wag its tail like mad. It looked well cared-for.'

'Did you ever speak to the man?' Rae asked.

'Only to say what a nice dog he had. He just nodded at me and smiled. But he seemed wary, as if he didn't trust people in general.'

'What did he look like? The man I mean, not the dog.'

'Sort of middle-aged? Maybe in his late forties or fifties.' Eddie frowned. 'It's so hard to be sure with a tramp, isn't it? They have such hard lives, and they always look weather-beaten and a bit grubby. Maybe he'd have looked younger after a good wash, a shave and a change of clothes.'

'Is there anything else you remember about him?' Rae asked.

'Not really. But there was someone else asking about him last week. I was in town at the time, just coming out of the supermarket, and a guy stopped me and asked if I'd seen a tramp around.'

Rae looked up from her notes. 'Could you describe him for me?'

Eddie shrugged. 'Pretty nondescript really. Fairly tall and thin, I guess. He was wearing jeans and trainers, and a thick lumberjack-type shirt. I can remember thinking that I could do with a shirt in that style.'

'So did the conversation last long?'

'No. As soon as I said I hadn't seen anyone of that description, he was gone, just like that.'

Rae was puzzled. 'But you had seen the tramp — hadn't you?'

'Yeah, but I wasn't going to tell him that. Even though I hadn't talked to the tramp much, I felt he was a decent bloke.

This one made me wary. I don't quite know why, maybe it was something about his eyes.'

'Can you remember when this was?' Rae asked.

'On the Saturday? Must have been. It would have been about eleven in the morning. I sometimes do the food shopping then, after Lynette's left for the reserve.'

'Did you see the tramp in the town centre that same day? Please try hard to remember.'

Eddie frowned. 'I didn't see him in the shopping area, but it's possible he passed me down by the bridge when I was on my way home. I was on my bike at the time. Can't be sure, though.'

CHAPTER 4: GOING NOWHERE

Monday morning

'We're in a very different situation here compared to most of our previous cases,' Sophie said. The three detectives were gathered around a table in the incident room at Wareham police station, attempting to formulate a plan for the murder investigation. 'Usually by this time we've garnered a fair bit of background about the victim, but not in this case. For reasons known only to himself, Paul Prentice deliberately dropped out of the public eye years ago. He doesn't seem to have sought help from the state. There are no local medical records for him. He wasn't registered for state benefits of any kind. He never shared information that would identify him with any organisation, even the hostels he might have used in Poole during the winter months. There's always the possibility that he went further afield than that, so we have to keep checking, but my gut feeling is that he was deliberately secretive about his background. But why? Ideas, anyone?'

Barry tugged at the ends of his ginger hair, a sure sign of unease with him. 'Could he have been on the run from someone or something? Nothing has shown up on the database yet, so Paul Prentice might not have been his real name. What I'm saying is, he might have been involved in something criminal in the past, and he's been down here in hiding. If so, he'd take on a false identity, wouldn't he? After all, the way he was living, who would ever know? Or he was on the run for some other reason. Doesn't that tie in with what we found over the week-end? That someone was in Wareham last week asking around after a tramp? The two events must be connected, surely? He's lived here quietly for a couple of years, suddenly someone appears asking around, and then he's murdered. So what was he running from? A financial scandal? Could he have cheated someone? Or maybe it was something more personal than that. Maybe he hurt someone who's come looking for revenge?'

'Jade doesn't seem to think he was the kind of person who would have been involved in serious criminal activity,' Rae said. 'According to her, he had a clear sense of right and wrong.'

Sophie frowned. 'Yes, but she knew the current Paul Prentice, not the one from years ago. He's had years of a soli-tary existence. People choose that for a reason, and it's often to escape something from their past that's troubling them. Day after day alone with their thoughts can give someone a differ-ent slant on things. What I'm saying is, people can change. I've seen it happen. Given time and the right environment, problematic, antisocial people can alter their perceptions of life. There are enough reformed criminals touring the youth clubs and welfare groups in this country to show that. As far as his past is concerned, we can't rule anything out.'

'This kind of speculation isn't going to get us anywhere,' Barry said. 'Maybe we ought to change tack and go back to the facts. I'm wondering why the dog's collar and identity tag were removed. We got the area checked again and nothing's been found. So whoever took the collar may have kept it. Could that mean that it contains some important informa-tion? A contact phone number or an address?'

'It's always possible,' Sophie replied. 'It confirms that there was more to this than an act of random violence, but it's of limited use beyond that. We don't have the thing so we

26

can't make use of it. And if Prentice's murderer targeted him specifically, either in revenge or to silence him, then there won't be other victims, so we can't go looking for patterns.'

Rae looked pensive. 'But what if there are others? I don't mean other tramps, because I've searched the records and no similar cases have shown up. But shouldn't we consider the possibility that there are other victims? I don't know how we'd tell, though. Not without more evidence. And how do we get that?'

'We have to keep looking,' Sophie replied. 'Paul Prentice is the only name we have to work with, so we keep digging into anyone with that name, anywhere. I hate this situation as much as you do. It's like stumbling about blindfolded at midnight in a coal-cellar. But we have to do what we can until we're convinced there's nothing to find. We just have to hope that something turns up. If it doesn't, this'll become an unsolved case, and I bloody hate those. We all do.'

'Have you had many, ma'am?' Rae asked.

'Not here in Dorset, no. But I've been involved in a few, both in London and in the West Midlands.' Sophie looked down at the tabletop.

There was a sudden charged silence. Rae glanced across at Barry, who was looking at her and shaking his head slightly. She realised that she'd unintentionally stumbled into forbidden territory.

'Maybe we should just get back to work?' Barry suggested. 'We might be in a better position in a couple of days if something turns up.'

Sophie came out of her reverie. 'Of course. No sense in prolonging this meeting if there's nothing to say. It's nearly coffee time, anyway.'

* * *

Rae caught up with Barry as they made their way back to their desks. 'What happened just then?' she asked. 'I obviously triggered something. What was it, boss?'

27

'Her father's murder was an unsolved case for forty years,' Barry said. 'It was a strange one because no one even knew he was dead until his body turned up. I've avoided giving you the full details and just warned you not to mention certain names, but maybe you need to know the full story. Now might not be the best time, though. I'm still wondering about that dog's collar. If it was taken off just to get at the message capsule, then wouldn't whoever took it discard the collar itself?'

Rae shrugged. 'It'll have been dumped in a bin somewhere, surely? Nothing's been picked up at the scene, so how likely is it that we'll ever find it? But if we find the container, that would be a real bonus for us. It's a small, stainless steel one according to Jade. Maybe the killer took it away with them.'

'Yes, but what you say about the collar is also true for the container. Once they unscrewed it and took the contents out, they'll have gotten rid of it. It'll be the bit of paper we want, and whatever was written on it. That's probably also been destroyed by now. Let's contact the local A & E units to see if they've treated anyone for injuries that might have been caused by a dog struggling to escape. Hands, arms and faces.'

After a fruitless hour on the telephone, the two detectives sat in silence. No hospital casualty department in the county had any record of such injuries to a recent patient, nor had there been any in the nearby major units at Southampton and Salisbury.

The day finished with the team even more despondent than before. They'd found nothing of any consequence. All they could do was hope that something would crop up soon, though they weren't holding their breath.

CHAPTER 5: HURRY!

Tuesday morning

Jade had another restless night, disturbed by a sequence of particularly vivid dreams. That evening she'd been out clubbing in Poole with friends but had felt slightly distant from the swirl of chatter, music and flashing lights that formed the backdrop to their favourite dance venue. The uneasy feeling had remained with her on the journey back to Wareham in the early hours, and she'd tossed and turned for a long time before eventually drifting into a light slumber. Then the dreams started, with colours, sounds and words coalescing and then fragmenting again, repeatedly. Was she being followed somewhere? Why did she feel the need to hurry? The disco lights faded to be replaced by darkness. An image of the small clearing in the woods appeared, dimly lit by the flickering of a fire, but no one could be seen. The sound of a dog whining and barking carried through the dark foliage of the trees. She still felt a driving need to hurry.

The scene shifted and it was now early afternoon, the sun bright in the sky. She was with Paul and they were walking along a narrow track away from his small camp and towards

29

the riverbank. They were passing one of the oldest trees in the wood, a huge gnarled oak that was set back a few yards from the faint track. The pressure to hurry towards something unknown was still growing.

Jade woke and sat up with a start, her eyes wide open. She'd forgotten. The memory of that walk and Paul's brief mention of the tree had somehow gone from her memory. And no wonder. She'd been totally preoccupied with revision for her forthcoming exams and had only half listened to his words.

She felt too alert to return to sleep now, so she slid out of bed, put some clothes on and tiptoed downstairs to the kitchen. It was four thirty, the only sound the quiet ticking of a clock. She made some tea and toast, trying to get her thoughts in order. What had Paul said? Something about the old tree and the fissures in its trunk making an ideal hiding place. That was it! A great hiding place for bits and pieces. What should she do? Surely there wasn't much chance of actually finding anything in that tree trunk? Wouldn't it already have been examined during the forensic team's search of the area? She slurped down the last few mouthfuls of tea, gathered a few things together and headed out into the early morning light. She still felt a driving need to hurry.

Half an hour later, Jade was hauling her bicycle over the fence and hiding it in a thicket, as she had done the previous week. She looked around her. The sun was starting to climb, and the air was alive with the sound of birdsong. Maybe now was the time to stop hurrying. She needed to be cautious. She took a circuitous route towards the clearing, moving as quietly as she could. And was glad she did. As she approached, she could hear faint sounds of someone moving about ahead. Who or what would be here this early in the day? Surely not a police officer? According to her mother, the search had been completed days before and night-time security was no longer required. Jade edged closer to the old hut and watched from behind a clump of bushes. A man was poking around the ramshackle structure with a stick, probing into the gaps between the half-rotten planking, clearly looking for something. And he wasn't a police or forensic officer. That much was obvious from his manner. He kept casting nervous glances around him. What should she do? If she took the time to return home and report the man's presence, he might have found the tree and recovered anything Paul had hidden there long before the police arrived.

Jade made up her mind. She backtracked a hundred yards and circled around the area, hoping to reach the track that led from the clearing to the riverbank, at a point close to the oak tree. She'd calculated her route perfectly. Here was the spot. The ground fell away gently towards the Wareham Channel, the small estuary of the River Frome. Its waters glinted in the sunlight just four hundred yards ahead. She glanced around, assuring herself that she wasn't being watched, and then made for the tree. She put on a pair of rubber gloves and pulled a torch from her bag, shining the beam into the three largest fissures in the trunk. They all seemed to be empty, full of nothing but leaf mould. She thrust a hand into each one in turn, rummaging around and running her fingers through the damp matter. She reached the last and most awkwardly situated hole without having found anything. Yes! She took hold and pulled, and out came a small, grubby plastic bag which she pushed hastily into her rucksack. Another glance around — no one in sight, thank God. She took a wide arc back around the wood and made for her hidden bicycle. Where was it? Think. Hadn't she left it pushed up against a tree in this very copse? Panic started to seep into her mind but she forced herself to think rationally. Get yourself oriented, she mouthed silently. Are you in the right place? She looked south to where the roadside fence should be. It was there but it slanted off at an unexpected angle. Maybe this wasn't the right copse. She clambered over the fence onto the road and looked around her. No, she was a good twenty yards short of her normal entry point into the woods. She hurried along the narrow lane and clambered back over the fence. There was her bicycle. She was beginning to shake, imagining eyes upon her and a violent assailant about to leap out of the trees brandishing a thick bludgeon. But all was quiet. She almost threw her bicycle across the fence and climbed over after it. Once she was on the move she'd expected to calm down, but the release of tension caused a feeling of intense nausea. She was halfway along the winding lane when she was forced to stop and vomit into the undergrowth at the side of the road. She stood, feeling faint, trying to take some deep breaths.

As she climbed back onto her bike a small car approached, heading towards Wareham, the only vehicle she'd seen since setting out from home an hour earlier. Had she passed it on her outward journey, parked close to the wooded area? She wasn't sure. She averted her face as it went by, although this meant she couldn't see the driver. It was only a few hundred yards to the junction where she turned off through Ridge, so she cycled as fast as possible. She felt safer once she was off the Arne road and on her way through the small hamlet, and even more so once she reached the riverside path. Then the next worry hit her. Would someone be watching the bridge, the only crossing point into Wareham from the south, or was she being ridiculously paranoid?

It was no longer a case of hurrying in search of something unknown. She needed to be careful.

* * *

Sophie woke with a start. Someone was in the room, yet she could feel Martin beside her, asleep and still breathing heavily. She heard a slight clunk as someone deposited a mug on the small shelf beside her. She turned to see her daughter standing beside the bed.

'Mum?' whispered the figure. 'Can we talk? Once you've drunk your tea? I'm really sorry it's so early, but I think I've created a problem for you.'

Martin grunted, turned over and spotted the mug of tea beside him, next to the clock. 'What's going on?' he said, yawning. 'It's only six thirty. Great to have tea in the morning, but does it have to be this early?'

Sophie shifted sideways and patted the bed, sufficiently alert to notice the worried look on Jade's face. 'Alright. What have you done now?'

She listened in disbelief as Jade's story unfolded. 'It was a murder, Jade. Killers don't play games. What on earth caused you to deliberately walk into danger like that?'

'I never thought there'd be anyone there. I mean, wouldn't anyone have assumed the same thing? After all, I did find something hidden in the tree, something Paul put there. If I hadn't gone, that man would probably have found it, and then where would you be?'

Sophie shook her head, speechless. Martin said, 'To be honest, I think I'd have done the same as Jade, but then I'm half loopy too. Let's have our tea and think things through. Are you sure he didn't see you, Jade? I mean, if it was the killer driving that car?'

'I turned away, but that meant I didn't get a good look at him or his car. I don't think he saw me earlier — I was really careful.'

'It was pretty clear thinking, getting one of the boats to take you across the river. You were lucky to find someone awake that early. If the driver of that car was the same man, he might well have waited at the bridge for a second look at you.' Martin reached across and patted Jade's hand. 'Eggs and bacon in half an hour? I think you deserve a good feed. I'll cook.'

Sophie shivered at the thought of how close to danger Jade had come. From a rational point of view, Martin was right. But in her job she had often come across the violence criminals used against potential witnesses. She couldn't bear the thought of her own daughter becoming a victim, just because she had helped a tramp in difficulties. Where was the justice in that? Better to stay quiet about it now though.

'This Paul Prentice,' Sophie said. 'He never gave you any idea of what he might have hidden in that tree?'

Jade shook her head.

'So you don't know what's inside that plastic bag?'

'No. And in case you're wondering, I haven't looked. It's well wrapped up. It could be anything.'

'And this man you saw poking around, you didn't recognise him? He wasn't a local?'

'I don't think so. Do you think he might be the killer, back for another look, something he missed first time?'

'I don't know, Jade. But we'll need to sit you down in front of one of our artists so you can produce a rough photofit image.'

'There's no point, Mum. He was wearing a hoodie and he had his back to me. I didn't hang around long enough for a better view of him.'

* * *

A forensic technician worked her way through the contents of the package, all of which were spread across a bench. She was examining them for fingerprints and DNA samples. The items included a passport, a small notebook, a collection of photographs in a clear plastic wallet and an old library card that looked as though it originated in an era before computerisation. Hovering over the bench, Sophie eyed the card with interest. It bore the handwritten label *Taunton Library* and was made out in the name of Paul Prentice. There was no other information on it. Didn't libraries always put full contact details on their tickets? And weren't they printed rather than handwritten? She tried to remember her own library card from childhood. This one didn't look right. She could just make out the two book cards it still contained.

'It'll take me another hour or so before I finish checking the outer surfaces,' the technician said, looking nervous and guarded. 'That has to be done before we can open them up and look inside.'

Sophie took the hint. 'Sorry. I didn't mean to put you off. I'll go and get a coffee and come back later.'

She climbed the stairs to her office, annoyed at herself. She could be too impatient, she knew. After all, forensics was the future of crime detection, and it wouldn't do to alienate the staff by making excessive demands. She sat at her desk, drumming her fingers on the surface. There was no point in returning to the incident room at Wareham police station — by the time she got there, she'd have to turn around and come back. She extracted a sheaf of documents from her bag and had just started to read when her mobile phone rang. She glanced at the caller display and sat staring at it for a few seconds before answering.

'Hello, Pauline. What can I do for you?'

'Well, Chief Inspector, it's not so much what you can do for me but rather what I might be able to do for you. You remember my walking group, the Chatty Ramblers? I'm currently the organiser while Flick Cochrane is recovering from surgery. I read about the discovery of that tramp's body in the local press. We've had a couple of walks at Arne recently, and, well, we may have seen something.'

Sophie closed her eyes and took a deep breath. What was it about this woman that set her on edge? It was always the same — a mixture of annoyance and a strange fascination. What made her tick? She thought hard. There was no way she wanted to meet Pauline Stopley, not at the moment.

'Can you tell me over the phone?'

'Not really,' Pauline replied. 'I think it would be better if we met.'

Sophie thought carefully. 'That might not be possible, Pauline. I've recently been promoted to superintendent. I'm busier than ever and have this investigation to run on top of the rest. I'll send one of my team, either DS Marsh or Rae Gregson. You remember them, don't you?'

There was a pause. 'Yes, sort of. Well, I suppose it can't be helped. It's just that I saw the tramp and may have seen someone else. It would have been about ten days ago.'

'I'll get someone across. Are you still in Dorchester?'

'Yes. I'm working from home this morning, at the vicarage. It's great for a day or two each week. Tony appreciates it, I think.'

'Have you moved in then?' Sophie wondered what some of the more strait-laced parishioners made of their vicar's fiancée and her history of moral flexibility, not to mention her penchant for playing the teasing seductress at social events. Had she changed her ways, as she'd claimed when they last met? Sophie had her doubts. Pauline simply oozed mischief from every pore.

'Not officially, no. But I'm here more often than in my own flat. It's quite a cosy arrangement really. It suits us both. We get to see more of each other.'

Sophie couldn't help but think that this throwaway remark contained a hint about the couple's sex life. Sophie made a face. Better not to pursue that line of thought.

'I'll see if Rae is free to come across. In about an hour maybe? She'll have to drive from Wareham.'

'Okay. And congratulations on the promotion. I'm sure you deserved it.'

Sophie ended the call. Why did she suddenly feel so uneasy?

CHAPTER 6: ANOTHER WITNESS

Late Tuesday morning

Rae steered her small car through the open gates of the vicarage, glad not to have to hunt for a parking bay on the street. The team had visited St Paul's manse in Dorchester several years before, during an earlier investigation, and she remembered the spacious driveway and the creeper-clad building. The old Victorian vicarage had been divided into two flats, with the vicar's residence occupying the ground floor. Even so, it still had a spacious interior if her memory was correct.

She clambered out of her car and was greeted by a distracted-looking Tony Younger, standing on the doorstep and hurriedly adjusting his dog-collar. 'I was just on my way out,' he said. 'A meeting about local drug problems. I've been asked to chair. We'll probably end up going round in circles again. It seems to be an issue that can't be resolved.'

'I don't envy you,' Rae answered. 'I'm here to see Ms Stopley?'

'Yes, she mentioned that someone from the police would be coming. She's in the back room, working her way through some Arts Council bids. Tearing her hair out, as far as I can tell. Well, I'd better run.'

And he was off. Rae entered the hallway and pushed the door shut behind her. 'Hello?' she called. 'It's me, Rae Gregson, from the police.'

The familiar head, still blonde, appeared around a door at the far end of the narrow hall. 'I'm in here. You're just in time for coffee. Give me a moment to tidy my paperwork away.'

Rae stepped into a spacious, airy room. Pauline was at a table, collecting papers together and sliding them into folders. Rae just managed to stifle a gasp. Pauline was wearing tight-fitting brown leather trousers, an ivory silk blouse and wedge-heeled summer sandals. Her hair was cut shorter than Rae remembered, with flecks of ginger highlights. She looked stunning.

'Done,' she said as she packed the last folder into a bag. 'Let's go through to the kitchen and get some coffee. I'm gasping.'

'I love what you're wearing,' Rae said tentatively. 'I don't think many of us could get away with it, but on you it's fabulous.'

Pauline smiled. 'Never knowingly underdressed, that's my motto. Or, to use an old actors' phrase, "knock 'em dead, honey."' She laughed. 'I've got a lunchtime meeting with a banker in a posh restaurant. I'm hoping this'll land us a bigger donation than he intended to give. Besides, Tony loves it when I look like this, he can't keep his hands off me.' She took two mugs from a nearby shelf and started to fill them from a coffee machine. 'It's all ready. Tony made it just before he left. He says he didn't really believe in the devil until he tasted council chamber coffee. Let's go back through.'

They sat in two easy chairs looking out through a bay window onto flower beds filled with colour.

'It's beautiful,' Rae said. 'Who does the gardening? Do you pay someone?'

Pauline shook her head. 'No, it's me. I like getting down and dirty, to borrow a well-known phrase. It plays havoc with my skin though. I get through gallons of hand cream.'

Rae took out her notebook. 'We'd better get started. So, when were you on this walk at Arne?'

'A week last Saturday. It was one of our monthly rambles. I've stood in as organiser since Flick's surgery, but that afternoon we were led by Derek, one of our members who's also a keen birdwatcher. That's why we were at Arne, although he took us on a walk around the northern bit of the peninsula rather than the southern side. Most people visit the southern route when they're looking out for birds.' She opened out a footpath map that had been lying on the table and traced a route with her finger. 'We left our cars in the RSPB car park and took an anti-clockwise direction. The problem with the north section of Arne is that it's not all nature reserve, but Derek knows the landowner and had got permission for us to walk along the edge of the mudflats. It was near a marshy area that I saw the tramp and his dog, coming down to the shoreline. It was about here.' Her finger paused on the map. 'I was quite a bit behind the others at that point because I'd stopped to retie a shoelace. I think he'd been waiting in the trees for us all to pass before he moved out into the open. Then I blundered along and nearly bumped into him. I said sorry, and he replied that I wasn't to worry and that it was a beautiful evening. What struck me was the way he spoke.'

'What do you mean?'

'Well, you imagine that a tramp is going to be a bit, er, rough, but he sounded quite cultured and intelligent. Anyway, that was it. I hurried on to catch up with the others and he disappeared in the direction of the shoreline. It's the Wareham Channel there, as you can see.' Pauline's finger rested on the map.

Rae produced a small head and shoulders photofit. 'Was this him?'

Pauline stared at it. 'Yes, I think so. He had a crinkled kind of face, whereas in this photo the skin is smooth. But everything else is similar.'

'You told the super that you saw someone else. Is that right?'

Pauline nodded. 'That was about an hour later. We were heading home, and I'd just turned into the road from the nature reserve car park. A small car was parked at the side of the road, half on the verge. The lane's narrow at that point and I can remember wondering what idiot would park in a spot like that, right on a bend. There was a guy clambering over the fence. He was heading into the woods.'

'Did you get a good look at him?' Rae asked hopefully.

'No. The sun was in my eyes. I think he had a hat on and his jacket collar turned up, but I can't be totally sure.'

'And the car?'

'It was small and white. That's all I can tell you.'

'Would some of the other members of your group have seen him too?'

'Possibly, but I was the last to leave the car park, I think. I went to the loo when we arrived back from the walk, then had a chat with one of the rangers. He might have only just arrived when I passed him.'

'We'll need to check, so I'd appreciate a list of everyone who was on the walk. Were there still rangers on duty?'

'It looked as though the one I spoke to was tidying stuff away. I think it was about four thirty or so. Maybe they close up at five.'

Rae nodded. 'So, what time do you think you bumped into the tramp near the shoreline?'

'Maybe an hour or so earlier?' Pauline said after a pause. 'Difficult to be sure.'

Rae finished making her notes. She didn't tell Pauline that her description of the car matched Jade's exactly. Could she have sighted this man on the evening Prentice was killed, or had he been scouting the place out? She did share one detail with Pauline. 'Your description of the tramp as sounding educated matches what we've learned from another witness, so it would appear to be the same man.'

Pauline smiled at her. 'Why did your boss send you to interview me? Didn't she want to come herself?'

'She's very busy,' Rae replied. 'She always was, but since her promotion it's gotten even worse. She works too hard.

Anyway, she trusts us to ask the right questions. We've been thoroughly trained.'

'Us? We?'

'Well, there's still the two of us. Me and DS Marsh. Although he's passed his inspector's exams, so he'll be promoted soon. And she's pushing me to sit my sergeant's exam. She's always encouraging us to get experience, build up our knowledge and go for promotion. She supports everyone who works for her.'

'So she looks after you, does she?' Pauline sounded genuinely interested.

'Of course.' Rae looked at her watch and finished her coffee. 'Well, I'd better be off.'

'Okay. Will you remind her that we never got around to having that meal we talked about? Tell her the offer's still open.'

CHAPTER 7: THE LETTER

Late Tuesday morning

The contents of the package had all been dusted for finger-prints and carefully swiped for DNA testing. Now Sophie could go through them.

She was mildly disappointed. There was a lot less than she'd hoped for, and she wondered if the items would add anything to their knowledge. The old-fashioned library ticket was interesting. The dark blue card was made out in the name of Paul Prentice and contained two book slips. The first was for a book entitled *Religious Cults: A Modern Scourge?* The second was for *The Commune in the Hills.* She looked closely at the card. It seemed almost homemade. Hadn't libraries computerised their issue records several decades ago? It was almost as if this card was a copy of an official library record. She picked up an old photograph, curled at the corners. It showed a young couple with their backs against a tree, arms around each other. Sophie looked at it closely. Could the young man have been their victim, Paul Prentice? It was difficult to say because the photo had deteriorated with age and use. It would need further examination with a magnifying glass. A second photo lay beside it. Another outdoor shot, it showed two men smiling at the camera. Neither of the men looked like Prentice, but it was difficult to be sure. She turned it over. A few faint words could be seen written in pencil on the back, but they were almost impossible to decipher. Could they be names?

Next, a handwritten letter taking up two sheets of paper. The writing was small, spidery and badly faded, making it difficult to read, but it started with the words *Dear Paul*. It looked as though it might be a love letter, but it was difficult to make out the faded wording. It ended with a simple but plaintive message: *I will always love you, Katie.*

The next-to-last item was a recent bus timetable for the Taunton and Bridgwater area of Somerset. Beside it lay a bus ticket, which had been found tucked between the pages.

'Everything's been photographed or scanned,' Dave Nash said, anticipating her next question. 'You'll find all the images waiting for you in an email attachment. The letter will be easier to read on a backlit pad or screen.'

Sophie nodded and turned her attention back to the bus timetable for west Somerset — last year's.

'Why would he keep something like this?' she mused. 'Wouldn't you replace it with this year's?' She looked more closely at the towns covered: Bridgwater, Taunton and the small towns in the area around the Quantock Hills. 'Unless, of course, it has a significance beyond the mere bus times. Nothing else?'

The forensic chief shook his head. 'That's your lot, Sophie. Nothing's yet shown up on the fingerprint check, and any DNA matches should be with us by early next week. Don't hold your breath, though. The team who did the check didn't think there was anything to find.'

'These faint words on the back of the photo, Dave. Is there anything you can do to make them legible? If they're names, that would be a massive boost to the investigation. Can you do what you can? And with this letter?'

He gave her one of his spine-tingling smiles. 'Anything for you, Sophie.'

* * *

43

My darling Paul,

I'm writing this in the odd spare minute when I am alone in my room. I'm trying to keep it secret. You can guess why! God knows how I'm going to manage to post it without arousing suspicion. Maybe the woman who comes to collect the craft stuff from us to sell in her shop could post it for me.

Timothy is getting worse. He was bad enough before, but your leaving has made him paranoid. He wants to introduce a new ethos in our group. I don't comment on any of this, so I think he wonders what my views are. I feel isolated. I sometimes feel I'm being watched everywhere I go.

One of the children was ill last week but Timothy wouldn't get a doctor. He insisted that we rely on our so-called medical expert, but she's not even a qualified pharmacist, just an assistant in a chemist's shop. Luckily the child recovered but it makes me wonder what he'll do if someone gets seriously unwell. Surely we'd have to get a doctor in then? How has it all gone so wrong? I keep thinking back to the summer before last, when we were setting the place up and everything was so perfect. We all believed what he said, that the right spirit would see us through. Even you believed it, didn't you? So when did it all start going wrong? I don't know. Maybe you've had time to think things through now you are out of it. Maybe it was always going to end this way.

I don't know what he's going to do next. He had a go at me again yesterday, saying that I was having negative thoughts. I was afraid that he could read my mind, but I tried to stay calm, just like you said, and didn't reply. He was looking for a commitment from me, but I refused to give it. I wonder if that made him even angrier. He could always browbeat me in an argument and leave me feeling down. But with me staying silent he couldn't do that. And he seems to be even more reliant on that twisted viper, Trent Baker, who's wormed himself into a position of power.

They both really hate you, I suspect. If you do come back for me, you must take care. They could resort to violence.

Are you planning something? I hope so with all my heart. I can't bear to be here much longer without you. But you must plan it all carefully, my darling. How can I just walk away, with my responsibilities? I feel so trapped. But always remember: no matter what happens, I will love you forever after what you did for me when I needed your support.

I will always love you, Katie xxx

* * *

'Well, what do you think?' Sophie asked.

The three detectives sat in a darkened room, looking at the letter projected onto a screen in front of them.

Rae spoke first. 'What physical state was the letter in, ma'am? That's the one thing we can't tell from the display. But it would help if we knew.'

'Old, by the looks of it,' Sophie said. 'The paper was thin anyway, torn from the pages of a cheap notebook, and it hasn't aged well. A sample of the paper is still away for analysis in the hope of getting an accurate date, but Dave Nash thinks it's at least ten years old. What you're looking at is an enhanced copy of the letter. The writing on the original is almost too faint to read.'

'Could we be looking at a cult of some kind?' Barry suggested. 'The two library ticket stubs suggest so, and this adds weight, don't you think? The mention of a group ethos, and then the leader-guy, Timothy, who's clearly started to bully people and lay down the law about how they should behave. This Katie is clearly worried that Paul's life is in danger. Now here we are, some ten years or so down the line, and Paul Prentice has been murdered. Could all of this be connected?'

'What about the wording? Does it tell us anything about the writer, Katie, and her relationship with Paul?' Sophie asked.

'I'd guess they were lovers,' Rae said. 'He left for some reason but she's still there at the time of writing the letter.'

Sophie thought for a moment. 'That's how it looks. But in that case, why didn't they leave together? Wouldn't most couples have done it that way? Why leave her behind?'

'They could've had their reasons,' Barry said. 'Maybe she had more ties to the place than him. Maybe this Timothy guy was a relative of hers, like a brother or cousin. She mentions her responsibilities.'

'What about the style of writing?' Sophie asked. 'Does that give us any clues about this Katie?'

Rae spread her hands. 'Ma'am, you're the expert there. I'm an engineer and Barry's from a farming background. We're still learning from you about behavioural stuff.'

Sophie sighed loudly. 'Okay, point taken. It's well written, so she's well educated. Look at the language and the sentence structure. It wouldn't surprise me if she was an arts graduate of some kind, or at least someone with an A level in English or history. The punctuation is near perfect, despite the letter probably being written under stress. She uses the word *darling* at the start. To me, that implies a middle-class background, although I might be wrong there. She's apparently in distress. Even so, she manages to keep her feelings sufficiently under control to write a letter as factually clear as this, yet carrying all the emotion you see in front of you. She's one heck of a woman, in my opinion. Strong and usually in control. I wonder if she might have been the real threat to this Timothy character, and that's why she felt she was being watched? It's all conjecture, of course, but how does it sound so far?'

'Can't fault your reasoning, ma'am,' Barry said. 'I've been wondering why he kept this stuff all together. Maybe it was deliberate because he knew someone was likely to come after him at some point. He put it together and told Jade about the hiding place as a precaution. So if everything is linked, what could it mean? Some kind of commune maybe? It could have been somewhere in Somerset, if that bus timetable fits into the scheme. Somehow Prentice was involved with this Katie, and she was also important to this Timothy guy who might have been the leader. Do you think one of the men in the other photo might be Timothy?'

Sophie shrugged. 'It's possible, but that particular photo looks more recent than the other stuff. Though, if your theory is right, it must be connected somehow.' She changed the image onscreen to the photo of the couple, then clicked over to the two men. 'Is that Prentice in both? If it is, his age is different in the two shots. Ten years or more, don't you think?'

Rae stared hard at the two images. 'I'm not sure it is him. It looks a lot more than a ten-year difference to me. I know he was living rough and that would have altered him, but I'm not convinced. The other thing is, if he was in a relationship with that woman and something terrible happened to her, it would affect him, wouldn't it? What if he didn't manage to rescue her, something awful happened, and she died as a result? That would traumatise him, wouldn't it? Isn't that exactly the kind of thing that would cause someone to drop out of society and choose to live alone in the woods, just like he did? Jade told us that he drank heavily. If that had been going on for years, then he'd have aged really quickly. He might be younger than we think.' She paused. 'That younger guy, the one on the right, looks as if butter wouldn't melt in his mouth. Kind of angelic. What do you think?'

Barry shook his head. 'Hard to say.'

Sophie moved on to the library ticket. 'What puzzles me is why this is in the bag at all. It's not a real one. Is it some kind of clue, deliberately put in to tell us something? Why Taunton Library? Maybe you can follow that up, Barry. Get in touch with the library to see if they can help. Rae needs to be pursuing the commune or cult idea and trawling through any records that we have access to.'

She picked up the bus timetable. 'This also mystifies me. Why is it here? It's last year's winter timetable, much more recent than any of the other items. Dave said there are some pen marks on a couple of pages, the timetables from Taunton to Bishops Lydeard and Nether Stowey.'

She opened the timetable at these pages. Each of the services had been circled in blue pen.

Rae said, 'Do you think he might have travelled to those places?'

'It's a possibility. Jade said that he headed off to a hostel every winter, but what if this year he didn't stay in Poole? What if he went to Taunton instead? Maybe we've been barking up the wrong tree by concentrating on the hostels in this area. Any other ideas, anyone?'

The other two shook their heads.

'In that case, let's get busy. Oh, and don't forget tomorrow morning.'

Rae looked blank, so Barry reminded her. 'It's Lydia's first day back at work. Remember? We're all going to Bournemouth to welcome her. I hope Jimmy hasn't forgotten. He's meant to be buying the bubbly.'

'I don't think Kevin will have let him. He can be a bit like a mother hen at times like this,' Sophie said, laughing. 'I know he wants to keep this one low-key, though. She'll be getting an official welcome back from the chief constable sometime next week, and we'll probably be expected to be there for that, too. Why are you looking so preoccupied, Rae?'

Rae forced a smile. 'Oh, no reason.' In truth, she was thinking of a conversation she'd had with Lydia only a day or two before she was nearly killed by a psychotic criminal. The throwaway comment had left Rae with very mixed feelings about her.

CHAPTER 8: BELLIGERENCE AND BUS QUEUES

Tuesday evening

'Do you fancy a week's holiday down on the south coast, Tim? My sister has the chance of a cottage in Dorset for two weeks but can only make the first one, so it's free the week after next. We can have it if we want, and it's a good bit cheaper than they usually are. I know it's less than two weeks away, but I could get the time off and your diary looks pretty clear.'

Judy Price, thirty-two years old and chocaholic, was slicing tomatoes for the salad that would accompany their evening meal of lasagne, currently cooking in the oven. The aroma was making Judy feel hungry, but she resisted the urge to nibble on a few nuts. It wouldn't do to reveal too many of her bad eating habits to her partner this early in their relationship, especially this one. Tim Brotherton was proving rather more uptight than most of her previous boyfriends. She waited for an answer, but none was forthcoming. Had he even heard the offer? She tucked some stray locks of her chestnut hair behind her ear and turned to look at him. He was no longer in the room. He'd been there when she first started talking, she was sure of it. Maybe that was another aspect of his character, not liking things being sprung upon him out of the blue. Well, he'd have to get used to it. Judy liked spontaneity. She and Jen, her sister, had the same approach to life, of which the proposed holiday was a perfect example. Her sister's friend had originally booked the cottage many months earlier at a discounted rate but had only recently found that she couldn't make use of it. On hearing this, Jen had snapped up the chance of a holiday and paid for both weeks, then found that she couldn't get the second week off work.

Judy frowned. She'd thought Tim would jump at the chance. He probably knew Dorset, having been on the south coast a couple of times recently on business. After all, hadn't he brought her back some tasty treats as a trade-off for his absences? That Blue Vinny cheese was lovely stuff. And didn't the area have some great pubs as well as the beaches? Come to think of it, he hadn't actually said that he'd been in Dorset, but those cheeses were a bit of a giveaway. Why was he being moody?

'Dinner ready in ten minutes,' she called, and listened for a response. Should she assume that the faint grunt was an acknowledgement? There was no other sound, so she'd just have to go with it.

Judy and Tim had been together less than six months and were now living in her house, close to the centre of Weston-Super-Mare in Somerset. She was a senior ward sister in the large Weston General Hospital, and he was a graphic artist, specialising in book and magazine covers. His work took him all over the country, following up on contracts. Not only were their personalities different but their jobs were too. Hers was regular, with a reliable income, even if it was a relative pittance for the huge weight of responsibility it carried. His was erratic, with bouts of tense and frenetic activity counterbalanced by periods when he was short of work. But the relationship seemed to be working, in Judy's opinion anyway. It was hard to pin Tim down on how he saw their future together. She had recently begun to wonder if he lacked commitment.

If that was the case, she'd have to make some hard decisions, and soon. She was all too aware that the years were ticking by and she would have to start planning for babies. Was Tim the right person to be a father to her children? At first, she'd thought he was, but now she wasn't so sure. If she brought the topic up, he'd do exactly what he'd done just now, slide quietly out of the room, leaving her talking into an empty space. They were the same age, so it couldn't be that. Maybe he was afraid to commit. Added to all this, she still knew very little about his background. He listened attentively enough when she chattered about her own childhood and adolescence, but he never reciprocated by telling her about his own formative years. Nor had he mentioned his past relationships. There must have been some, surely? Was he hiding something?

She sensed his presence in the room again, so she turned and found him thumbing through a guidebook. It wasn't for Dorset.

'So, I take it you're not keen on that idea?'

He looked up. 'What?'

'Going to the coast in a few weeks' time? Even if it would help my sister pay the bill she's landed herself with.'

Tim shook his head. 'Fine, but not Dorset, not just now. I can't explain why, but it's just not possible for me to go there at the moment.'

'Can't or won't?'

He came across and massaged her shoulders. 'Look, don't take it that way. It just holds some bad memories for me, things I haven't processed fully yet.'

'So where did the Dorset cheeses you brought back for me a couple of weeks ago come from then? Yorkshire? Come on, Tim. Don't pretend you weren't there.'

'Just because I was there briefly doesn't mean I enjoyed being there or want to go back. If you must know I hated every bloody minute of it.' He sounded almost angry.

'How can you dislike a place so much? It doesn't make sense.'

'Memories. It reminds me of people that caused me pain, and I get tense and irritable, so I don't want to be there unless I have to. Now, can we pick somewhere else to go?' He handed her the guidebook. 'How about the Channel Islands?'

She gave him a contemptuous look. 'You're seriously suggesting that we should go away the very week my sister has paid for a holiday, but not where she's booked? Leaving her stuck with the bill for an empty cottage? Are you mad? This is my sister we're talking about, the only close family member I have left. She's done me hundreds of favours over the years and has never asked for anything in return. She's been good to me, Tim, and I don't intend to let her down. So I'm going. You can come or you can piss off somewhere else if you prefer. Honestly, I don't understand your mind-set.'

Tim sat down and held his head in his hands. After a while he looked up. 'Okay, you win. We'll go.'

'It's not a question of winning, Tim. It's not some kind of competition we're in. I'd go to the Channel Islands like a shot at any other time, but this is a favour to the one person who's always been there for me in recent years. Surely you can see that?'

He gave her a faint smile. 'Yes, I can. It's just that I've never had close family, not for years anyway. I suppose I'm just too set in my ways.' He ran his hand through his sandy hair. 'I promise to be more cheerful and understanding in future.'

'Just be yourself, alright? Though a few more smiles wouldn't do any harm.' She sniffed. 'I think dinner's ready. Pour some wine, will you? I could do with a good slug.'

She opened the oven door. Interesting. He'd caved in far more easily than she'd expected.

* * *

Some twenty miles further north in Bristol, Trent Baker was making his way from the city centre to the Bedminster area, warily scanning the faces of the people he passed. The street was busy — there were far too many faces passing by too quickly for him to see if one of them recognised him. Nevertheless, he couldn't get out of the habit of checking. Someone, somewhere, might notice his cherubic features and start to think. He needed to be on his guard, prepared, in case he became the object of a revenge attack. Maybe he was already on someone's list. If so, he was probably safer here in a big city than out in some rural hamlet, working on an isolated farm like that one on the Quantocks where the problems had got too much. Wouldn't somewhere like that be where they'd expect to find him? And what is more, where he'd stick out like a sore thumb. Here, in these hordes, he was just another mister nobody, a face in the crowd, a stranger in the bus queue. As long as he kept sliding through life with the minimum of friction, he should be okay. He looked up at the sky. It was starting to rain again, which was always a blessing. He wore long sleeves all the time to cover the scars on his arms, and he knew how out of place they looked on warm sunny days.

Trent joined a bus queue, ducking as the lady in front of him put up her umbrella. She must have spotted his sudden movement because she turned and apologised for her clumsiness.

Trent smiled at her. 'No worries.'

'Want to share?' she said. 'There's room for two.'

He looked her up and down. She was attractively dressed for an older woman. Might he be in with a chance? He could do with some comfort after all these empty years. He pulled up his jacket collar. 'No, I'm fine.'

Her smile faded and she turned her back on him. He wondered what it would feel like to slide a long, slim knife into that back. Pity that he was no longer in possession of his favourite one. The police would have gotten rid of it by now, melted it down for scrap in a furnace somewhere probably. Just then a bus appeared and began to slow down. Umbrellas were being lowered and the people in the queue began to push forward, rooting around in their pockets and purses for tickets, passes and money. Trent suddenly changed his mind and walked away. Did he really want to be trapped inside a crowded bus with a load of tired, irritable commuters? Better to be out in the open air. It was only a fifteen-minute walk, after all. And the rain was easing off. Good. He had a busy evening ahead of him.

* * *

Catherine Templeton was in the bedroom of her flat in Bath, trying to decide on a suitable outfit for a first date. She was standing at the wardrobe, sliding dresses and skirts aside, pulling out the occasional item and tossing it onto the bed. This pesky rain! She'd decided days ago on a thin, strappy dress in a wheat colour, along with a matching cardigan, but that might not be a good idea in this cooler, wetter weather. She suffered from cold legs at the best of times, and maybe this wasn't the ideal night to show them off. Would Russell be offended if she turned up in jeans? Even with a sparkly top? *Oh, sod it. I can't be arsed with all this.* Would *he* be worrying about what to wear? Not bloody likely.

She replaced the skirts and dresses, and pulled out her tightest, sexiest jeans along with a blue silky top. They would do. She knew she looked good in them, particularly with a pair of attractive ankle boots. After all, it wasn't as if they were going to the Ritz, just the Italian restaurant close to where Russell lived. She glanced at her watch. Perfect. Just enough time to get made up and changed. She could then arrive a reasonable few minutes later than they had arranged, allowing Russell time to get settled in, ready for her.

Catherine made her entrance precisely eight minutes late. She'd noticed a number of admiring glances on her way from the bus stop, and not all of them from men. She looked around. *Shit*. No Russell. The manager eyed her with a raised brow.

'A reservation for Poulter? For two? At seven o'clock?'

'Ah, yes,' he said. 'Let me show you to your table. Mr Poulter isn't here yet.'

Catherine ordered a gin and tonic, and sat for twenty minutes sipping it. Where the hell was the man? She tried calling him several times but there was no answer. She was ravenous by now, having skimped on her lunch. She waited another half hour then ordered a starter. She was tucking in to king prawns in garlic butter when Russell wandered in. He looked flustered when he saw her eating. Before he sat down, the manager drew him aside and whispered in his ear. He listened with a look of embarrassed horror on his face.

'I'm so sorry,' he said as he sat down. 'I thought I'd booked for eight thirty.'

Catherine seethed with anger. 'I've already ordered my main course, so I'll eat that, then you can pay the bill and fuck off for all I care.'

And that was just what she did. Studiously ignoring Russell's confused pleas and entreaties, she ate steadily then stood up and walked out, still furious. She hadn't felt so enraged since that business with Trent Baker more than a decade earlier. Who the hell did Russell Poulter think he was to treat her like that?

CHAPTER 9: MISCHIEF-MAKING

Tuesday night

Judy woke with a start. She looked at the clock beside the bed. It was twelve fifty, only an hour and a half since they'd come to bed. She turned over and found she was alone. Where was Tim? He'd come to bed at the same time as her. In fact, she'd been a few minutes after him, but she'd fallen asleep quickly. Maybe he hadn't. Had it been him getting up that had disturbed her sleep? She listened for the sound of water running or the toilet flushing, but there was just silence.

She thought she heard a rustling outside. She rose, went to the window and pulled the curtains gently aside, peering out. Nothing seemed to be moving but she kept watching. After a few moments a shadow seemed to detach itself from behind a bush and slide into the deeper shadows at the side of the house, out of her view. Could it be Tim? If so, what the hell was he up to? She watched for a further couple of minutes but saw nothing else. Maybe she'd imagined the movement.

Judy went out to the landing. The bathroom was in darkness, the door open. There was no sign of Tim. Where was he? She looked down the stairwell and spotted a faint glow coming from the lounge. Could he be watching television? Maybe he hadn't been able to fall asleep. She walked silently down the stairs and peered around the lounge door. Why was she nervous?

And there he was. He seemed to be dozing in an armchair, his eyes closed and an open book on his lap. She walked forward, stepping on a floorboard, and he opened his eyes wide.

'What's going on?' he asked.

'Why on earth are you down here, Tim?'

'I couldn't sleep, so I got up to read for a while. I must have dozed off.'

'Were you outside? A couple of minutes ago?'

'Outside? No, of course not. Why?' He certainly sounded as if he'd only just woken up.

'I thought I saw a movement in the back garden just now.'

He shrugged. 'Maybe it was a cat or a fox. Whatever it was, it wasn't me.'

'I thought it was taller than that, about the same height as a person. Maybe it was just a trick of the moonlight. Are you coming to bed?'

He yawned. 'I guess so. I'm sleepy enough now.'

As he stood up she glanced at his pyjamas. Was there a patch of damp at the bottom of the left trouser leg? It was difficult to be sure. But why would he have been outside, prowling around in the bushes at this time of night? She shook her head wearily. Now wasn't the time to follow this up.

* * *

Russell Poulter stayed up into the early hours, in utter despair. What had gone wrong? His world had turned upside down in the space of twenty minutes and he was at a loss as to how it had happened. He'd booked the restaurant for eight thirty, he knew he had. So why were both Catherine and the manager convinced that the reservation had been for over an hour earlier? After the pithy comments that she'd flung his way, he was in little doubt that their relationship was over before it had even begun. Ignoring all his apologies, she'd eaten her food quickly, gathered her jacket and bag, and flounced out.

The problem had been compounded by the fact that Russell never reacted well in emotionally charged situations. His mind always went blank, as indeed it had on this occasion. He'd panicked and kept muttering apologies when he should have been trying to find out the cause of the mistake with the table reservation.

At least he could check now. His phone had gone missing somewhere at work, which is why he'd missed Catherine's calls, but he could use his tablet to check back through his emails. He switched on and sat back, scrolling through the screen. There it was — his original reservation for eight thirty, made at the start of the week. But there was another message in his inbox, received at midday and as yet unopened, stating that the restaurant had agreed to his phoned request to alter the booking to seven o'clock. Russell frowned. What request? He hadn't made any request for a change in the time. It couldn't have been a simple mix-up because Catherine had somehow also been informed. What was going on? Come to think of it, how had his phone gone walkabout at work? He rarely took it out of his pocket and had hardly used it at all today. No, something odd was at work here and Catherine needed to know. The problem was, how best to go about the task of winning her round? She hadn't left him in much doubt that she wasn't keen to see him or speak to him again. Ever. He looked at the time. Maybe the best thing to do was go to bed for a few hours and sleep on it. He was dog-tired, and it wouldn't do to turn up to work tomorrow feeling like hell. He had another meeting with his software team scheduled for nine o'clock. Some of them were just not pulling their weight and needed to be warned that times were getting tougher.

* * *

Meanwhile, Catherine had calmed down somewhat and was mulling over what had gone wrong. After leaving the restaurant she'd taken a taxi to a bar close to her home. There, she'd ordered several glasses of chilled white wine, rebuffed an attempted pick-up by a fat bloke wearing a hoodie (really! Even if she was angry, frustrated and approaching middle age, she still had some standards), and finally taken a taxi back to her flat just before midnight.

None of it made any sense, she could see that now. She'd had coffee with Russell Poulter several times at the fitness club where they'd met, and he'd always seemed so sensible and organised. Shy, of course, and a little slow to latch on to her hints about meeting up for an evening out, but he'd come across as thoughtful, if a bit on the dull side. So what had gone wrong? She tried to remember what he'd said during the ten minutes it had taken her to devour her cannelloni, but she'd deliberately closed her ears to his pleas. She did remember now that the date had originally been fixed for eight thirty, despite her own preference for an earlier time. Hadn't Russell said that he couldn't make it any earlier because of a visit to see his mother in hospital? Yes, that was right. So she'd been pleasantly surprised when the text message had arrived at midday telling her he'd rearranged the time. This was all too weird. He'd acted exactly as if he wasn't aware of the change that he himself had initiated. It was laughable, really — as if anyone else would gain from spiking their date and ruining their relationship before it had even begun.

Catherine froze. Trent Baker. Wasn't he due out of prison about now? That evil, scheming, twisted bastard, that angel-faced, poison-dwarf. Had he traced her somehow, even though she'd moved here to Bath, while he was inside? Oh, Christ.

* * *

At home in Bristol's Southside, Trent Baker shook the water from his raincoat and hung it in the hallway. Two o'clock.

59

Bloody hell. It was late for him, but he wasn't working tonight, and the time had been well spent. Sowing seeds of discord was more satisfying than he'd anticipated. Maybe he was in the wrong job. Working as an office cleaner, he didn't get much chance to make use of the human interaction skills he'd developed in prison and he'd wondered how his little scheme would work out in practice. As it happened, it had gone like clockwork. Nothing like a spot of mischief-making to keep the world moving forward. It was a shame that he hadn't actually been present in the restaurant to witness the results of his machinations, but he had waited across the road and watched her storm out. Had she hit the poor sap? Had she cursed and stamped her foot like the Catherine of old? Maybe both, if her temper hadn't mellowed during the intervening years. Oh, this was such fun. Was there time for a quick cele-bratory glass of Scotch before he went to bed? You bet! He'd nicked the Scotch in question from an easily distracted shop-per in the car park of the local Tesco. He looked at the label. Fine single malt. Way beyond his slender means and tasting all the better for it.

CHAPTER 10: PROBING THE PAST

Wednesday morning

Detective Constable Jimmy Melsom had a reputation for being slapdash and forgetful, but not on this very special occasion. Today, he'd done them proud. All the detectives invited had chipped in and he'd bought a range of breakfast foods, champagne, and even some decent tea and coffee. The office of Bournemouth CID was festooned with *Welcome Back, Lydia* banners in red and black — Lydia's favourite colours. The group of detectives stood about, chatting quietly until Lydia's immediate boss, DI Kevin McGreedie, alerted by a phone call from reception, looked around at the expectant faces.

'She's here!'

The door opened and a slim figure with jet-black hair cut in an elfin style hopped into the room on elbow crutches. She waited until the whoops and cheers had died down before attempting to speak.

'I wondered if you'd do something like this. I'm feeling really nervous but it's great to be back.' She accepted the plastic tumbler of bubbly that Jimmy thrust into her hand, as well as the short embrace that went with it. Grinning broadly, she leaned back against her desk, took a sip and raised her cup. 'Hmmm. I could get used to this.' Kevin McGreedie, then Matt Silver and Sophie Allen all hugged her warmly.

Soon, she was asking about their current cases. Fraud and money-laundering provided the current focus for the local Bournemouth CID, but she was intrigued by the VCU's investigation into the "tramp murder," as it had come to be called.

'Sadly, we don't need you on this one, Lydia. Not at the moment anyway,' Sophie said. 'But you never know what might crawl out from under the stones we turn over. If we do find something financial, would you be happy to get involved? That is, if Kevin doesn't mind?'

'Of course I'd want to be in. I can't get out of the office much, not like this. I've been told to ease myself in,' Lydia said. 'This week I'm here mornings only, then I have to review things with the boss.' She nodded towards Kevin. 'He'll fuss over me far too much, I know. He's worse than my dad.'

Sophie noticed that Lydia was holding herself stiffly. 'Still sore?'

Lydia nodded. 'I'm still on painkillers but at a low dose. I'll be off them completely by the end of the month. That's the plan, anyway.'

'We'll be off shortly, Lydia,' Sophie said. 'But maybe I'll see you next week at the chief constable's tea party. Look, don't try to do too much too quickly, will you? I know what you're like. Kevin doesn't want to lose you again for any length of time, so just do what he suggests. Okay?'

'Sure thing, boss.' Lydia grinned.

Sophie caught the eye of her own boss, DCS Matt Silver. He cleared his throat. 'It's great to have Lydia back with us but in fact, just by chance, we have two other things to toast this morning. Kevin's been under a lot of strain in recent months, but we're hoping that today will be a bit of a turning point. He mentioned to me just now that his wife's cancer seems to have gone into remission, and if that isn't a cause for celebration, I don't know what is. So here's to Laura. Long may she remain in good health.'

The group raised their plastic cups.

'And finally, a bit of news that we've been anticipating for some time. Confirmation only arrived this morning. Raise your glasses everybody and drink a toast to Detective Inspector Barry Marsh, a sergeant no longer.'

More cheers and clapping. Barry looked bemused. 'I didn't know,' he said. 'Why didn't someone warn me?'

'Because it all fitted in so well,' Sophie said. 'Don't you just love it when a plan comes together?'

* * *

They had been back in the Wareham incident room less than an hour before Barry made the first real breakthrough. He'd given up on tracing injuries that might have been caused by an aggressive dog and switched his attention to the only name they had, other than Paul Prentice himself. Within a few seconds of entering the words "Trent Baker" into the main PNC, his computer pinged and a set of records came through. He stared at the screen for some minutes and then called to the other two.

'Look at this lot. Assault, criminal damage, affray, attempted murder, arson. It goes right back to when he was a teenager.'

Sophie leaned forward, peering at the screen. 'Doesn't he look a bit like one of the men in the photo? The one Rae described as angelic? He certainly doesn't look like the photofit that Jade produced. Rae, you find out where he is now and what he's doing. That's if he's not still locked up somewhere. Barry, work your way through all of these cases. Check who his victims were. We guessed our man Prentice had hidden that pack of stuff for a reason. Well, it looks as though it might all connect. Look for anything that might provide a link to that area of Somerset, around Taunton and the Quantock Hills. Cults. Someone called Katie. Someone else called Tim.

63

While you're doing that, I'm going to see if those two books are still available anywhere — the ones in the library ticket. And great work, Barry.'

As the records had shown, the charges for affray and assault dated back to when Trent Baker was sixteen, with drunkenness seeming to have played a part. The arson charge involved a disused warehouse that had gone up in smoke only a few weeks after he'd escaped a custodial sentence for the earlier crimes. No one had been in the building at the time, but it looked as though that had been due more to luck than judgement. He'd served a short spell in a young offenders' institution, but clearly it had not done him any good. Within a few months of being discharged, he was back in trouble for wrecking a corner shop after the manager refused to serve him anymore because of his constant belligerence and routine petty theft. After this, he seemed to have stayed out of trouble for several years, until his trial for attempted murder, which took place at Exeter Crown Court. He'd attacked a young woman by the name of Catherine Templeton as she'd left a pub in Taunton. A knife had been his weapon of choice. He'd received a fifteen-year sentence, with the provision that he should serve a minimum of ten. Barry took note of the dates. That ten-year spell would have run its course some six months ago, giving him ample time to settle a few old scores. This needed looking into.

Starting with the court case, it quickly became apparent to Barry that the victim, Catherine, had been lucky to escape with her life. She and Baker had both been at a pub on the outskirts of Taunton but not together. Witnesses said that there was obvious rancour between them dating from some time in the past, but that Catherine had tried her best to stay out of Baker's way during the evening. He'd consumed a great deal of alcohol and had become belligerent and confrontational. Annoyed by the continued friction, Catherine had left the pub early, slipping out quietly in the hope that Baker wouldn't notice. Trent Baker followed her and attacked her on an unlit section of footpath, leaving her for dead. Luckily a friend had seen her leave. He'd also seen Baker follow her a minute or two later and decided to check up on her. He found her lying under a bush, fast losing blood. The medics who attended reportedly said that another fifteen minutes and it would have been too late.

Barry was intrigued by the fact that the pair knew each other, yet the details of their prior relationship — if, indeed, they'd had one — were vague. Maybe he should visit Catherine Templeton. The other interesting fact was that Baker had used a knife, not some piece of wood, as in the tramp killing. Clearly the attack was premeditated, and the judge had referred to this in the course of sentencing him. In Barry's experience, killers tended not to change their weapon of choice, although this wasn't always the case. As the boss often said, keep an open mind and don't make assumptions. He told Rae what he'd found and asked her to do some further digging.

Rae soon found an address for Trent Baker. As a recently discharged inmate of Devizes Prison in Wiltshire, his release under parole meant that his whereabouts had to be logged. He was living in Bristol, a mile or two south of the city centre. He was also recorded as working for an office cleaning company based in Weston-Super-Mare that had contracts throughout north Somerset. Rae pondered this. So were there some Bristol cleaning contracts on the company's books? It seemed unlikely. Rae checked Google maps. Yes, it was a good twenty miles between the city and the much smaller coastal resort town, although much of the route followed the fast M5 motorway. There was also a good train service, according to the regional timetable.

Rae visited the cleaning company's website. CleanStyle seemed to specialise in the upkeep of modern high-tech offices. She found something else of interest: an employment policy statement hidden away in the depths of the site. It stated clearly that the company contributed to the social rehabilitation of recently released prison inmates by offering them suitable employment opportunities, but that such employees would not be deployed at sensitive locations and would be monitored constantly. Rae wondered what the company meant by "sensitive locations," and how the monitoring was done. In her experience, most cleaning companies were so short-staffed that the cleaners were merely dropped off at an office block and told to get the job done as quickly as possible. Maybe a visit was called for, but she'd need to consult the boss first. It wouldn't be a wise move to make the company aware of their interest until they had more facts.

The boss had also asked her to look into the area in west Somerset covered by the old bus timetable and had mentioned the Quantock Hills. She'd never heard of the place. Maybe she could pay a visit with her boyfriend, Craig. He'd just bought a new car and was keen to show it off to her, along with his imagined skills as a rally driver. She looked at the map again and then did a search for background information. The Quantocks were a small range of hills only fifteen miles or so in length, running south-east to north-west towards the Bristol Channel, with views across twenty miles of sea to South Wales. Apparently the Quantocks had been designated England's first Area of Outstanding Natural Beauty in 1956. Why had she never heard of them? She supposed that people from Bristol would visit the better-known Mendip Hills instead, with their famous caves and gorges. Did that mean it would have made a good place to establish a commune? Maybe the local press would have archive records of such a group. She couldn't make any headway in identifying who Katie and Tim might be until she'd found evidence that a commune had indeed existed.

Sophie was sitting at her desk, frowning over one of the books on the library tickets. Thanks to modern technology, she'd downloaded a copy of *Religious Cults: A Modern Scourge?* to her tablet. The second book, *The Commune in the Hills*, seemed to be out of print and had never been published in electronic format. She'd have to trace a paper copy, which could take days. It couldn't be helped.

She skimmed through the book on cults. An academic work, written by a social historian, it wasn't easy reading. The study looked at the incidence of cults across the world and throughout history, starting with examples recorded in classical literature and the Bible before moving on to medieval times and into the modern era. The last quarter of the book dealt with the twentieth century and included a few well-known examples such as the Branch Davidians in Waco. There was a short section on the incidence of cults in Britain. Sophie sat up with a jolt. There had been one in the west of England, situated in a quiet valley in the Quantock Hills. It had come to a sudden end in the latter part of the twentieth century amidst tension and infighting, although no details were provided.

* * *

'So that makes it doubly useful for me to pay a visit, I guess,' Rae said. 'I was wondering about it when I had a look at the area on the atlas. Maybe the local paper might hold some records?'

Sophie smiled. 'My thoughts exactly, Rae. I've been trying to track down a copy of the second book and can't find any trace of it. I'm beginning to wonder if it wasn't published but is some kind of small monograph. And if that's the case, the only libraries likely to hold a copy would be the ones in Somerset. You could call in while you're in the area and see what they have. Maybe they've got a copy squirrelled away in their archives. We also need to check up on hostels for the homeless in the area, in case Prentice ended up in one this winter.'

'Craig's off work this week, ma'am,' Rae said. 'He's been decorating our new flat and has nearly finished. We could head off to the Quantocks, have a short break and I could do a bit of digging around. Just an idea.'

Rae saw the look of concern flicker across Sophie's face. Of course. The last time she and Craig had made a similar visit, to Exeter that time, someone had ended up dead.

But Sophie said, 'Good idea. Would tomorrow and Friday be okay? But isn't it a bit manipulative? Will Craig agree?'

'Oh yes,' Rae replied breezily. 'It's right up his street, driving around country lanes. He'll love it.'

CHAPTER 11: THE QUANTOCK HILLS

Thursday morning

Rae held onto her seat as the small car hurtled around another tight bend, and then climbed a steep incline.

'Craig, slow down, for God's sake. It's not a bloody race. I want to enjoy the scenery. I can't do that if you're scaring the wits out of me like this.'

He laughed. 'Sorry. It's got such a great engine in it. Wow, look at that. Some view, eh?'

They'd taken the last bend up through the heavily wooded slopes and had just emerged close to the summit of the hills. Craig turned into a small parking area and they gazed onto an open, sunlit, heather-clad vista. The view to the north-west encompassed the hilltop ridge and stretched across the sparkling waters of the Bristol Channel to the Welsh coastline, visible some twenty-five miles away.

'Isn't it peaceful? There's hardly anyone about. I bet it's busy at weekends, though.' Rae got out of the car and walked a few yards to a knoll. The place had an almost otherworldly feel. Many of the trees clinging to the hillsides looked ancient. Gnarled trunks, split boughs, ivy and mistletoe. Leaf-litter that looked six inches deep and decades old. A group of horses ambled across the grassy glade, and one of them lifted its head and whinnied.

Craig joined her. 'So, here we are. What now?'

Rae took a walkers' map out of her bag and opened it out. 'Let's just walk along the ridgetop a bit, then circle around on this lower path and get back here in an hour or so. We can leave those sandwiches we brought in the car and have them when we get back, then go on to the inn this afternoon. I just want to get a feel for the place. Is that okay?'

'Fine by me.'

They set off past the horses, heading west, following the top of the ridge. The whole area was owned by the National Trust and the major paths were way-marked. Rae checked she had a compass in her pocket. Not that you could really get lost on hills as benign and compact as this. After all, the Quantocks were a far cry from the Scottish Highlands, although they probably became bleak and treacherous during winter snowstorms. On a bright summer's day like this, walking across the hilltop would be a gentle stroll, and a beautiful one. She breathed deeply. For several days she'd spent her spare moments decorating, and the penetrating aroma of paint seemed to have sunk deep into her head. That had now gone.

She grabbed Craig's hand. 'This is lovely. The view's lovely, the air's lovely, and you're lovely.' She spread her other arm wide.

Craig looked at her in amusement. 'What are you up to?'

* * *

The inn they'd chosen as their base was nestled in one of the deep, sheltered coombes that cut into the hills. The Waterside Inn was a nineteenth-century building, not as old as others in the area but comfortably furnished and inexpensive. As the name implied, a stream trickled down from the hillside past the pub's garden. They arrived late in the afternoon and were shown to their room by a young woman who introduced herself as Eliza. She was dressed in a smart black uniform and spoke in a Somerset accent.

'Do you know much about the history of the area?' Rae asked as Eliza turned to leave.

'Nah, not really. I'm looking for another job down in Taunton,' she said. 'There's nothing goin' on here. 'S all a bit dead, really. But some of the locals'll be in later. They know a bit.' She left them to unpack.

'So, what's the plan?' Craig asked.

'I thought we could get some food here tonight and have a few drinks. Maybe someone can tell us about the area, but I don't want to let on what I'm after. I haven't really thought through my angle yet. I may have to make it up as I go along.'

They visited the bar in the middle of the evening and as Eliza took their order, she pointed out several villagers who might know about the local history. One was an older woman, Babs Atkins, who, Eliza explained, ran the local historical society. She was having a meal with a well-dressed, gaunt-looking man.

'She lost her husband a couple of years ago,' Eliza whispered conspiratorially as she brought them their meals. 'She's just started dating again. He's someone new, not seen him before.'

'Oh well, I couldn't possibly spoil a first date,' Rae said. 'I don't want to interrupt someone's romantic night out.'

Eliza rolled her eyes. 'I don't think it'll be a problem. He's hardly said a word so far and they're already on their desserts. It's obviously not working, so I wouldn't worry if I were you. Do you want me to have a word? It'll be fine, honest.'

'Well, only if you're sure.'

Within a couple of minutes, Babs came across to their table and sat on a spare seat. She was a small, grey-haired, vivacious woman.

'Eliza told me you were interested in local history,' she said. 'What do you want to know?'

'I'm really grateful but I hate to spoil your date. I told her to leave it if you'd rather not talk now.'

Babs smiled broadly. 'That girl. She's got the wrong end of the stick, as usual. This isn't a date. That's Brian, my older brother, he's just visiting for a few days. He lives in London. Mind you, I have started doing this internet dating business and I've had a couple of interesting evenings.' She winked.

Rae laughed. 'Well, if you're sure it's alright.' She looked at Babs, at her sparkling, intelligent eyes, and decided to be straight with her. 'I'm trying to find out if there was a commune near here a decade or two ago. It might have had a religious slant to it. Were you ever aware of one?'

Babs suddenly looked uneasy. 'Why would you want to know about that?'

'I'm a police officer, a detective from Dorset. I'm just being nosey, I suppose, but it might link to a case I'm investigating. Craig here is just my boyfriend. He isn't with the police.'

Babs was silent for a while, frowning. 'I see. Well, there was a place like that, quite a long time ago now. It's something we never talk about much, not to outsiders. Even among the locals it's never spoken of. I don't want to talk about it here and, anyway, I'd need a bit of time to remember everything. How long are you here for?'

'A couple of days, but I've got a few other places to visit. Would tomorrow morning be convenient?'

'I think so,' Babs said, rather hesitantly. 'Make it about half past nine. I've got a sewing group after coffee time. I live in Holly Cottage, it's just five houses down from the pub.'

Rae smiled at her. 'I'm really grateful.'

Babs rose from her seat. 'You've got quite a deep voice, dear. I bet men find it alluring. Not like mine — I've always been a bit squeaky.'

'I wouldn't have said so. You sound fine to me. And thanks again.'

Rae watched Babs return to her table and pick up her coat. She turned to Craig. 'Is my voice still too deep?'

He smiled. 'I like it. As she said, it's alluring. Don't get paranoid about it.'

CHAPTER 12: THE DERELICT FARM

Friday morning

Looking out of the rear window of Babs's sitting room, Rae could see the hollies that had given her cottage its name. A row of the prickly shrubs lined the rear lawn. The ground rose steeply beyond the end of the garden, where it merged into the heavily wooded lower slopes of the Quantocks.

'It's a lovely view,' she said to her hostess. 'I bet you get all kinds of wildlife here.'

'I can't keep the deer out.' Babs grimaced. 'It's impossible to grow flowers or vegetables here. A couple of deer can eat the lot in a single night. So I have to stick with the orchard — apples, pears and plums, plus a few gooseberry and black-currant bushes. I grow some salad stuff in the greenhouse, so I get by. But I don't mind really. How many people can say they have wild deer wandering through their garden? My grandchildren love it when they're here. Where's your young man, by the way?'

'Craig? He's back at the inn, reading. He likes detective stories. Maybe he thinks they'll give him an insight into the work I do. Though most of them are just a load of nonsense

— you know, those moody, maverick cops solving complex crimes with a whisky glass in hand and fractured marriages. I ask you.' Rae rolled her eyes in mock disgust and sat down. 'Anything you can tell me about the commune will be a help, Babs. I'll take notes, if you don't mind.'

Babs looked into space, the corners of her mouth turned down. 'Their place, Heathfield Farm, was across on the southern slopes of the hills and over to the east, up one of the coombes. The valley splits there and they were up the smaller cut. It was a bit out of the way. Still is, to be honest. I don't think anyone goes up there much, even now. They took over a farm that was already struggling 'cause of its small size and the steep slopes, which make it difficult to grow crops there. The valley kinks at that point and gets quite steep-sided so a lot of the ground is in the shade and doesn't get a full day's sun. Some of the young folk there worked hard for the first year or two and got some good harvests but then we had a wet summer and they began to struggle. I think it all went downhill from then on. Some of them left and most of the ones who stayed on didn't have a clue about farming — not as far as the locals could tell anyway. That's what I heard. They started falling out with one another. Some of the villagers said there were fights and arguments. I never saw any, since I'm right over here on this side of the hills.'

Rae looked up from her notebook. 'What's it like now?'

'Derelict. I don't know of anyone who goes up there much. I expect some of the local kids wander around the place, breaking things up even more, but that's just me being old and grumpy. They're probably not as bad as us oldies think, not most of them.'

'So there were reports of violence?'

Babs shrugged. 'There's always gossip, isn't there? But it wasn't obvious. Just before they all left, there was a rumour that a young woman had gone missing. But then someone said she'd turned up. It was all hearsay and rumour, and we never knew what was true and what wasn't. Then all of a sudden, one morning we heard that the place was empty. As far as I know, it's been empty ever since and has gone to rack and ruin.'

'Did they ever come over this way? Maybe to the pub or the local shop?'

Babs shook her head. 'It was just as easy for them to get to Bishops Lydeard from where they were, and it's always had a good minimarket, better than what we had along here. But I don't think they used that much either. It was easier to drive into Bridgwater and get it all from the cash and carry, or Tesco. From what I heard they all ate together, so it would make sense to buy in bulk. In the summer and autumn, of course, they'd be eating their own produce so they wouldn't need the shops.' She frowned. 'Though there was one of them I did see a couple of times in our local bookshop, along in Nether Stowey. A young woman. Quiet, she was. Never said much. I used to work part-time in the bookshop, you see. I did afternoons.'

'Would you be able to pick her out in a photo?' Rae asked.

'I doubt it,' Babs replied. 'It was ages ago and my memory's not what it was. I can't even remember what some of my old neighbours used to look like and I spoke to them most days.'

'How long have you lived in this area, Mrs Atkins?'

'All of my life, just about. We moved into this house after our older two children left home. That's about twenty years.'

'You must like it, living in the Quantocks?'

Babs nodded. 'Oh yes. It's lovely. Mind you, the hills are a bit Jekyll and Hyde. The weather's usually good enough for the visitors. But just occasionally, when the weather turns, it can get a bit nasty up there. People have died.'

* * *

The smallholding was exactly where Babs had said. A narrow lane threaded into a valley at the south-east corner of the Quantock Hills. This soon became an overgrown, muddy track curving into a deeply shadowed dell. After half a mile Craig was forced to pull over at the edge of a field. He and Rae got out of the car and set off on foot. There had been a light shower of rain as they had driven across the high ground and the overhanging trees were dripping water onto the track, which was pitted with potholes, some of them pretty deep. Rae could imagine how dark and dreary it would be here on an overcast day in winter. The thought made her shiver.

'It's a bit brooding, isn't it?' she said. 'Normally I like walking in woodland, but this place seems to have a peculiar atmosphere. It's so quiet, so silent. Or is it just me being over-imaginative?'

Craig shook his head. 'No, I feel it too. Sort of sinister, though I was half expecting that from what you told me in the car.'

'Are you pulling my leg?' Rae asked.

He grinned. 'Would I ever?'

At that point they rounded a corner and the valley opened up in front of them into a pretty, sheltered coombe, about half a mile across. In the middle lay Heathfield Farm, a collection of ramshackle buildings, most lacking a serviceable roof. The whole place was overrun with brambles and weeds. Doors sagged, tilting at crazy angles, and only a few of the window-panes were still intact.

'What a sorry sight,' Rae whispered.

They drew nearer.

'Hallo?' she called out. 'Anyone here?'

A group of rooks, startled by the sound of her voice, flapped away, cawing in protest. There was no other sound and little movement, other than the gentle swaying of branches in the slight breeze. They entered the farmyard.

'Don't we need permission for this?' Craig asked.

'I couldn't find who owns the place. But there's no need to worry, Craig. Technically, we're within our rights to be here because a public footpath runs through the yard. While we're on that path there isn't a problem. Anyway, I'm an officer

75

of the law, concerned about reports of rural theft across the region. This place is totally insecure.'

Up close, the small farm was in an even more pitiful state than had been apparent from a distance. Nettles, brambles and other weeds seemed to spring out of every crevice and even the remaining bits of gutter were weed-infested. The very air carried an aroma of mould and mildew. Everything made of iron or steel was broken and rusted. Bits of rotten wood were hanging off the outhouses, covered in a coating of slimy green.

'Surely someone could have made something of this place?' Craig said. 'It looks beyond repair now, but ten or twelve years ago it wouldn't have been anywhere near as bad as this. Why didn't the owner do something while there was still time? The area's a favourite haunt of walkers, so why not do it up for holiday letting? It makes no sense to let it get into this state.'

'Maybe that's one of the things I need to find out about,' Rae said. 'You're right. It doesn't add up. I'm going to have a poke around inside. You stay out here and keep watch.'

The ground floor of the main farmhouse was divided into two large rooms, one a spacious kitchen and the other an equally large room that ran the length of the building at the back. Both were empty of furniture and fittings, although a broken sink hung off the kitchen wall beneath the window.

Part of the upstairs area showed signs of having been partitioned into small sleeping cubicles, although there was also a larger room that could have been a dormitory for children, judging by the odd bits of bed and cot frames that were spread about. Rae poked around the remains, all broken, filthy and damp. Just as she began to descend the stairs she spotted something that caught her attention. Set high and flush in the hallway wall opposite the stairwell was what appeared to be a small cupboard, discernible only to someone standing on the top two stairs. It lacked a handle or doorknob, and it was set too high to be reached without standing on something. She went blinking out into the sunshine.

'Craig, have you spotted a stepladder or anything that I could stand on? I need to reach a cupboard. And I'll need a thin bit of metal to lever it open. Something like a screwdriver?'

Craig went into one of the sheds and returned with an upturned crate, some three feet high, that was not too rotted with damp. He had also found a rusty screwdriver. He helped her manoeuvre the crate into position on its end and held it while she clambered onto it.

'Okay?' he asked.

'I think so. Can you pass me the screwdriver, please?'

At first the cupboard door refused to budge but, after an extra strong push, it swung open on stiff hinges. Inside were several small, thin folders, stacked on top of one another. Rae pulled them out, passed them down to Craig, and then jumped off the crate.

'Well, who would have thought it? All the trespassers who must have been through this place over the years, and none of them spotted that cupboard in the wall. I was lucky. The light was bright enough for me to see the edge when my eyes were level with it. The sun just caught it. It's impossible to spot from down there, isn't it?'

'Can't see a thing,' Craig said.

Rae put on some thin latex gloves and sifted through the contents — an assortment of letters, notebooks and several pamphlets. 'I'll wait until we're back at the pub before going through it properly.' She put the folders into her shoulder bag. 'Let's wander round a bit before we head back to the car.'

There was little else of interest on the farm. They could make out the small fields that had once been worked for vegetables and other produce, although all were now overgrown and weed-infested. A couple of pigsties were situated at the edge of the yard, but with their timber sides largely gone.

'The place needs to be demolished and rebuilt from scratch,' Craig said. 'Except for the house. That looks okay — a new roof and some basic work and it could be a nice place.'

Rae looked at her watch. 'Let's get back to the car. I'll need to report what we've found to Barry. Then we can visit Taunton, pop into the library and get a quick lunch. Alright?'

Craig nodded cheerfully. 'Sure thing, boss.'

* * *

The assistant librarian at the county library in Taunton couldn't have been more helpful. 'We do keep an archive of local interest material, some of it dating back almost a century, so you might be lucky. Let me have a look.'

He spent several minutes at the computer going through lists of titles before pausing at one. 'According to this, there was a small booklet published locally about fifteen years ago, entitled *The Commune in the Hills*. It's only thirty pages long. We've got a reference copy downstairs in a storeroom. Do you want to see it?'

'Please,' Rae said.

'I'll be back in five minutes,' he said, 'that's if it's where I expect it to be. You never really know.'

He was away for more than fifteen minutes, returning without the book but with a perplexed look on his face. 'It's not there,' he said. 'I've no idea who's taken it out.' He looked again at the computer record. 'No. Sorry. No record of anyone borrowing it.'

'Do you know if the author, this Timothy Brotherton, ever wrote anything else?' Rae asked.

He spent a few minutes searching the catalogue. 'It doesn't look like it. Nothing's showing up here.'

Rae and Craig made their way back to their car. 'There is somewhere else we can try,' she said. 'As we drove through Nether Stowey this morning, I noticed an old second-hand bookshop. I wonder if it might be worth asking in there to see if they know anything about it?'

Towards the end of the afternoon they entered a dimly lit shop that smelled of old paper and musty books. Once again,

Rae explained what she was looking for. The bookshop owner, an elderly, stooped man wearing a grey cardigan with patches on the elbows and a bow tie, listened with a glint in his eye.

'I know exactly where you mean,' George Biddulph said. 'That place was somewhat notorious. Maybe Babs Atkins didn't tell you but there were all kinds of rumours doing the rounds about drugs and wild parties and the like. I don't know whether any of it was true. But I did used to have a leftover copy of that booklet. It was written by one of them, I seem to remember. One of the leaders. Let me have a look.'

He rooted around in some low cupboards at the back of the store and finally emerged with a look of triumph and some dusty smudges on his face.

'The last copy,' he said. 'It's a bit grubby and it's got a tear in the cover, so it's yours for half price.'

'When did you sell the previous one?' Craig asked.

The bookseller screwed up his face. 'About five years ago?'

Soon they were back in the car, heading towards the motorway and the trickiest part of the visit. They had to investigate the cleaning company where Trent Baker worked — without giving the game away.

CHAPTER 13: WHAT A DAY!

Friday morning

Several days after Tuesday evening's escapade, Trent Baker was still cheerful. He'd been back on the night shift at work, but his tasks weren't exactly onerous, and he'd had plenty of time to scheme, plan and plot while flicking a damp mop across floors that were already perfectly clean. He was back in the premises of the company in Bath that employed Russell Poulter, so he'd need to be careful. Not that there was much chance of the poor sap coming in to work this early, and he would be finished by seven, before the first workers turned up. It was very useful knowing the entry codes for the various office doors. He'd managed to slip Poulter's phone back into his office drawer early on Wednesday morning, having deleted all trace of the text messages he'd sent to dear Catherine Templeton. The guy probably hadn't even noticed that it had gone missing.

It still gave him a thrill to recall the way Catherine Fuckface had stormed out of that restaurant, slamming the door behind her. What a display of rage. What a picture she'd been in full flight! It was hard to resist the temptation to follow her into the wine bar. When she reappeared several hours later, she was looking extremely pissed and wobbly on her feet. It had taken all of his self-control not to approach her. *'My, my. If it isn't Catherine. What a coincidence, meeting you like this. And with you looking your usual cheerful self!'* He probably wouldn't have escaped the encounter intact. Not only was Catherine a good six inches taller than him, but she had made her feelings about him perfectly clear during the court case all those years ago. The parole board would have a field day if he confronted her.

He laughed. Had she really thought that his ten-year spell in prison would cool his hatred of her and the others? He felt even more bile than before. He intended to dedicate his days to making her life a misery. The restaurant incident was only the beginning, but it wouldn't do to follow it up too quickly. No, he'd let things settle for a while. Once she had recovered and was back enjoying her usual social life, he'd pick his moment and strike at the bitch again. Of course, what he really wanted to do was to smash an iron bar into her face but, sadly, he'd have to forego that pleasure. The cops would know it was him. Hadn't he already done ten years in a stinking cell for the earlier assault? Maybe he should have killed her when he'd had the chance. He'd fucked up big time by holding back. But he could still make her suffer. She'd pay. Over and over again, for the rest of her measly life. But it would need a lot of careful thought to do it right. Just like chess, this game was totally absorbing.

Meanwhile, as soon as this shift was over, he needed to make a trip to CleanStyle's offices in Weston to sign his end of week timesheet and collect his payslip. After all, there were more important things in life than a simple need for simple revenge. A complex need for complex revenge, for example. He laughed.

* * *

Something was going on. Tim Brotherton knew it. It was as if the smooth flow of the universe had shifted, just slightly, but nevertheless it felt significant. He sensed that he was no longer in control and it worried him. What worried him more was that he couldn't quite put his finger on what had changed. What had managed to free itself from his influence?

He looked down irritably at the magazine cover designs he'd been working on for the last few days. They didn't look right somehow. They seemed to jar slightly, but he couldn't put his finger on what was wrong. He stood up and walked to the window. Maybe he needed some fresh air. A short walk and a light lunch in a café somewhere, rather than working solidly here and getting nowhere. He really couldn't face beans on toast in the silent kitchen. Pity Judy was out at work. He missed her presence on days like today when he was feeling out of sorts. In her own way, she was kind of inspirational. Maybe part of the tension he felt was the fact that his work-related problems were so trivial compared to hers. If he made a mistake, a magazine might sell fewer copies. If she made a mistake, people died. He felt inadequate in comparison, and he hated feeling that way. It just wasn't him to feel less important than the people around him. He'd gotten used to being top dog early on in his life and felt uncomfortable in any other social arrangement. But Judy was such a good person, and she had an awe-inspiring sense of judgement. He'd never yet known her make a duff decision. Him? Even as a child he'd believed he was indestructible. Well, events had proven him wrong, big time. Quickly, he grabbed a jacket and made for the door. Rain or not, a walk along the seafront would do him good.

Two hours and several pints of beer later, he emerged from a town centre pub and made his way back to the seafront, woozy in the warm sunshine. He got as far as an empty bench and sat down. His head drooped, and he fell into a deep sleep.

* * *

Trent Baker couldn't believe his luck. Having left the CleanStyle office, he decided to take a short walk along the promenade and plan his next move when he spotted a familiar figure fast asleep on a seafront bench. He stopped dead. Tim bloody Brotherton! Unbelievable. The gods were surely on his side. Now, how best to make use of this chance encounter? Could he throw a rope over that nearby lamppost, slip a noose around Tim's reptilian neck and haul him kicking and gasping into the air to die in agony? What a lovely thought. Too many people around though, and he did lack the all-important rope. Pick him up, sling him over his shoulder and throw him into the sea? Hardly. Tim was a good five inches taller and several stone heavier than him. Trent stood and thought. *Come on! You have to do something. You can't let this opportunity slip away.* He noticed that one of Tim's shoes had slipped off and was lying on the ground below a dangling foot. He lunged forward, grabbed the shoe, ran across the beach and hurled it as far as he could into the water. Small victory, but it was something. He hurried off towards the car park and set off up the M5 to his home in Bristol. What a day!

CHAPTER 14: AROUND SOMERSET

Late Friday afternoon

Also in Weston-Super-Mare, Rae was sitting in a bare, functional office talking to the manager of the CleanStyle Contract Cleaning Company. She noted with some amusement that the carpet needed hoovering and the walls could have done with a wash.

'Has there been a problem with Trent?' the manager, Caitlin Beckett, asked. 'Should I be worried about him?'

Rae shook her head. 'No, not as far as we're aware. We're investigating a recent serious crime, but we have no reason to believe that Trent Baker was involved. His name just turned up in an old document that was found. We'd let you know straight away if we found something that connected him to it.'

Caitlin frowned. 'You see, what we do, cleaning commercial premises, is ideal for people just out of prison. That's why we have this agreement with the remand service and take on a handful every year. I tend to use them in places where they won't come across anything valuable, but I can't guarantee that's always the case. In the end I rely on their honesty and their wish to stay on the straight and narrow.'

'Have you any cause for concern with regard to Mr Baker?' Rae asked.

'Well, not really. He's a reasonable worker and none of the people at the premises he cleans have made any complaints.' Caitlin was still frowning.

'But?'

Caitlin pursed her lips. 'It's just something about him. I sometimes wonder if there's a different man lurking underneath the cooperative and polite Trent Baker I see. He was in just half an hour ago to collect a few documents and sign off for the week's work. I know I shouldn't really judge him. I mean, ten years in prison would make anyone behave differently, wouldn't it? The thing is, if there's ever the slightest hint of trouble from anyone, I have them out in a flash. With Trent there's just something a bit off about his attitude but I can't put my finger on what it is.'

'Can you give me a list of the places he's been cleaning?'

Caitlin looked uneasy. 'Look, the cleaning contract business is cut-throat. I can't afford to lose any customers. If some of them got wind that ex-cons out on remand have been cleaning their premises, they'd hit the roof.'

'I wouldn't be that insensitive, Caitlin. I just want to look around, see where they are. Will he be at the same places next week?'

Caitlin nodded, still looking uncertain. 'Yes, he will.' She scribbled some company names and addresses on a sheet of paper and pushed it across the desk. 'I'm trusting you not to get us into hot water here.'

Rae picked up the paper and glanced at the list. 'Do the cleaners have any say in what premises they work in? Or are they just allocated by you?'

'I allocate them, but I try to take into account the distance from their homes.'

'It's just that this one here is in Bath. Trent lives in Bristol. Why's he been given that job?'

'He did ask for that one,' Caitlin said. 'Apparently it's round the corner from his aunt's, so he can get breakfast when he's finished.'

'Right. Maybe that's the one we'll need to keep an eye on. Listen, I'd appreciate it if you didn't let him know I've been here. Don't do anything or say anything unusual to him. Not yet. I'll keep you in the picture if I find anything suspicious. That's a promise.' Rae stood up to leave.

She was aware of Caitlin watching her as she made her way out. She still looked unhappy. Maybe she should ask the boss to phone and reassure her. She walked down the road towards the car park and looked at her watch. Maybe there would be time for another visit to the tumbledown farm later this evening before it got too dark.

'Where to now?' Craig asked as she climbed into the car.

'Barry's arranged for me to visit a retired bobby who used to work at Bishops Lydeard nick before it closed. I'm hoping she was around at the time of the commune. It shouldn't take long. If you drop me off, you can go for a coffee or something. Then I think we should head back to the hotel to get something to eat before the bar gets too busy. Oh, and I may need to talk to that bookshop owner again. I think he might remember more than he told us, but I just didn't ask the right questions. If we step on it, we should get there before he locks up for the day.'

* * *

Rae knocked at the door of a small terraced house in Bishops Lydeard. The woman who answered looked to be in her late fifties. Her greying hair was pinned up, she was wearing slacks and a baggy shirt several sizes too big for her, and she had a smile like a Cheshire cat.

'I've been expecting you,' she said, holding out her hand. 'Sue Penny, police constable, recently retired. And you must be Rae Gregson.'

Rae shook her hand. 'That's right. I'm really grateful you found time to see me. I could do with a bit of local insight from someone who was in the force and I'd like to pick your brains.'

She followed Sue Penny into a small sitting room that looked out onto a tiny garden packed full of flowers in early summer bloom. Sue poured tea from a china pot into two flowery mugs and handed one to Rae.

'Your boss told me why you wanted to see me but I'm not sure how much I'll be able to help. The people up at that commune kept themselves very much to themselves. We didn't see a lot of them down here in the village and they rarely caused any trouble, so I didn't have much to do with them. I did call in once or twice just to show my face, but I didn't see anything to arouse concern. There weren't any obvious signs of serious drug abuse, the place seemed reasonably well run and the children looked clean, happy and cared-for.'

'I heard that they may have struggled to grow enough food. Is that right? That would be a problem if they wanted to be self-sufficient.'

'Well, there's truth in what you say. It was never one of the most productive farms in the area. I don't know exactly why. I think the soil was a bit poor and the drainage was wrong. But it wasn't a huge problem. They made things to sell at the local markets, you know, arts and crafts, jewellery, knitted clothes and the like. Someone even ran a poetry workshop up there for a while, had classes one afternoon a week. They made some extra cash that way.'

Rae took a sip of her tea. 'I'm trying to find out whether there was any coercion — if people were ever kept there against their will. Also, whether there was any violence towards the end.'

Sue shook her head. 'I was never aware of anything like that. But then they were stuck up in that valley by themselves, so I suppose we wouldn't ever have known if there was. We had reports of some heated arguments just before they finally left, but when I went round to check, it all seemed okay. I went up because of something someone overheard in the local pub, a punter claiming that a young woman had gone missing. I think the name Katie was mentioned. When I arrived, the atmosphere was a bit tense, but the people recorded as living there all seemed to be present. A very vivacious woman called Catherine confirmed her identity to me — Catherine Templeton, it was. She stuck in my mind because of her dark, Mediterranean looks, just like a gypsy. A few weeks after that, they all left. One day they were there, the next they were gone. The place has been empty ever since. It's almost derelict now.'

Rae took out the photo of the couple from the package Jade Allen had retrieved from the crime scene.

'Could this be her?'

Sue looked, shook her head. 'Absolutely not. Wrong colouring, wrong face shape, wrong hair, wrong everything. The woman I met had a really upfront personality. That one in the photo looks a bit mousey.'

'You can't recall any other names, I suppose?' Rae asked.

'You're asking a lot, aren't you? We're talking about twelve years ago here. No, it's just the name Katie that I recall, and the leader, a man called Tim. He had a bit of a messiah complex if you ask me.'

'There wasn't anyone called Trent — Trent Baker — as far as you recall?'

'I don't remember the name. There was one man lurking in the background all the time I was there. I reckon he was keeping an eye on me. A short bloke with a face like a choirboy. But he'd vanished by the time I left so I didn't get to speak to him.'

Rae finished her tea, thanked Sue and rose to leave.

'How are things for you, Rae? I see that you're trans. How is the system treating you?'

Rae sighed inwardly. Did she really want to answer yet more questions about her life from well-meaning people? Still, Sue's interest seemed genuine, and she had tried to be helpful.

'It's been really good, at least since I've been in Dorset. I'm in the county's top team, the violent crime unit, and it's just fantastic. I could never have believed it a few years ago. And the boss wants me to sit my sergeant's exam. Sometimes I have to pinch myself. It's bloody hard work, though.'

'That's modern policing for you, isn't it? There's no room for passengers anymore. I miss it occasionally, though I wasn't a detective like you. So this case you're on is serious stuff?' Sue said.

Rae nodded. 'There might be a link to that commune or there might not. But we have to follow the lead. Right now I'm meant to be tracing hostels for homeless men in the Taunton area. Do you know where I might make a start?'

'There's a personal crisis one in Southburn Street, run by a local charity. It takes people in on an emergency basis, with no questions asked for the first couple of days. It may be a good place to start.'

Rae looked at her watch. 'Thanks for that. I'd better be off. I want to make one more visit while there's still time.'

Sue's description of a short man who looked like a choirboy fitted Trent Baker exactly, if the photo of him on the PNC was at all accurate. Very interesting. And hadn't Barry mentioned the name Catherine Templeton as being somehow involved in the man's criminal history?

She made her way along the street and was pleased to see Craig just leaving the café where he'd been waiting. They'd need to move quickly if they were to visit the bookshop owner before he closed up for the day. They were in luck.

George Biddulph stood at the door. 'I wondered if you might be back at some point, but I didn't think it would be this soon. You're only just in time. I was about to lock up.'

'Sorry,' Rae said. 'We left in a bit of a hurry earlier because I had to see someone else. But it occurred to me that you must have met the writer of the leaflet if he published it himself and gave the copies to you.'

George nodded. 'Yes, I did. I've been thinking about it since you left, trying to picture him. I can't remember many details, but he seemed a bit driven, if you know what I mean.

He seemed just the type you'd imagine to be running a group of that sort. Quiet but totally determined. Ruthless, maybe?' He shrugged. 'Maybe that's reading too much into the few minutes we chatted.'

'Was there anyone else from the group with him, or was he alone?'

'No. Now you come to mention it, he had a woman with him. She'd written part of the pamphlet. Blonde, she was. I think her name was Katie. She might even be mentioned as one of the contributors.'

Rae took out the leaflet and paged through it. Sure enough, someone called Katie Templar had written the chapters on craft-work and poetry. A vague suspicion began to form in her mind.

'She was blonde, you say?'

'Yes. Slightly built. She was very quiet and hardly spoke, probably a bit of a shy type.' He paused. 'It's funny how things can pop back into your mind, even after so many years.'

'She wasn't dark and vivacious?'

'No, absolutely not. The exact opposite.'

Rae frowned. There was something odd here. Rumours that someone called Katie had gone missing. A witness who'd described Katie Templar as being slightly built, blonde and quiet. A police check which had been called off after a Catherine Templeton, dark and vivacious, was confirmed as being alive and well. Katie and Catherine. Similar names but different peo-ple? And the fact that there was history between Trent Baker and Catherine Templeton was important. It would all need checking once she was back in Wareham. She took her copy of the photo out of her bag and showed it to George.

'Could this be her? The blonde woman who came into your shop?'

'It was a long time ago, but it might be. If not, it was someone very like that. I remember thinking that she looked a bit like my daughter, and I thanked God she wasn't in a commune. Some of them can be a bit, er, ropey, can't they?'

* * *

90

It was mid-evening by the time Rae and Craig drove back up the narrow lane towards Heathfield Farm. This time Craig took the car much closer, steering it carefully between the potholes that scarred the surface of the lane. The farm buildings and surrounding fields were in deep shadow, the high ground to the west blocking out the evening sun. 'I don't want to go into the buildings again,' Rae said. 'I just want to wander about a bit and get a feel for the lie of the land.'

The pair walked through the farmyard and followed a path up to a hillside field that sloped steeply towards the higher ground of the Quantocks. From the top they had a view across the coombe. The sight of the deeply shadowed valley and the half-rotted buildings and tumbledown fences gave Rae an uneasy feeling. Was there a malignancy still lurking here or was it her over-active imagination, stimulated by the fact that she hadn't eaten since a hasty lunch seven hours ago? They stood looking down, and then made their way back towards the buildings. Rae took out her copy of one of the photos that Jade had found. It showed a couple sitting with their backs to a tree. Had it been taken around here somewhere? She looked around. There was a solitary tree at one end of the field below her. Could that be it? She took Craig's arm and walked back down the slope towards the farm buildings and the tree. Yes, it looked similar, but larger.

'What do you think, Craig? Is it this one?'

'A sycamore. I'd say it was the one in the photo. You can see the start of the woodland beyond the top of the field.'

Rae tugged at Craig's arm and led him off the path and round towards the derelict pigsties. If there was a body buried here, where would it be? This could be the place, down under several feet of earth and muck. She shivered.

'Let's go back,' she said. 'I've seen enough. And I'm starving.'

She resisted the temptation to look back. There was something about the place that gave her the shudders.

'Did you know that a few miles away, up on the top of the hills, there's a place called Dead Woman's Ditch?' Craig said. 'I was looking at the walking map and spotted it. One of the stories about it says it marks the place where a woman was murdered by her husband a couple of hundred years ago. The story's a bit morbid.'

'Thanks very much, Craig. I don't think I wanted to know that.'

CHAPTER 15: CATHERINE'S STORY

Saturday morning

Early on Saturday morning Sophie and Barry met in the incident room to discuss Rae's findings from the Quantocks. She'd phoned Sophie the evening before and Sophie had told her to stay put on Saturday, as search teams were organised for that afternoon. Meanwhile, Sophie and Barry agreed to make a start on tracing and interviewing the people who had cropped up in Rae's enquiries, particularly Catherine Templeton and Katie Templar. Were they one and the same person, or had the local police become confused by the similarity of their names and merely assumed that they were? It would have been an easy mistake to make, particularly if all evidence of Katie Templar's existence had been deliberately covered up by the group leaders.

'It's possible that this Catherine Templeton might be in some danger, so we need to see her today,' Sophie said. 'As for Trent Baker, well, it's about time we took a look at him. Agreed? We can't let Rae do all the leg work.'

'Absolutely,' Barry said. 'I've been stuck in here far too long, staring at that screen. I think I might be going mad.'

Sophie looked at her number two in surprise. 'Should I be worried, Barry? It's not like you to make that kind of remark. I'll message a few contacts in the Bath and Bristol area, then we'll get going. Do you want to drive? It might help to get rid of some of that pent-up frustration.'

* * *

They drove to Bath and found Catherine's home address easily, drawing up outside her end-terrace house in the middle of the morning. Barry rang the doorbell and stood back, admiring the door's glossy red paint. The woman who answered his knock was tall, dark-haired, rather gypsy-like and she looked wary. Barry introduced the two of them and asked if they could come inside for a moment.

'You are the Catherine Templeton who lived in a commune near the Quantock Hills about twelve years ago?' he asked.

'God, that's going back a bit. But yes, I was. Why do you want to know?' she said.

'We're investigating a probable murder in Dorset that might be linked to it somehow, but we're not sure what the link might be.'

'A murder? In Dorset? Christ.' Catherine looked shocked. 'You'd better come in. I think I need to sit down. Who was the victim?'

They followed her into a sitting room furnished like a Spanish villa, the walls painted terracotta. The décor matched the owner.

'Did you come across a Paul Prentice in the commune when you were there?' Barry asked.

Catherine shook her head. 'No. I heard the name, though. He was one of the people that set it up, but he fell out with the others and left. That's all I know about him. How did you find out that I was there?'

Barry decided to keep the explanation simple at this stage. 'One of my colleagues has been in that part of Somerset for a couple of days and I think your name cropped up when she was talking to some of the locals. Could you give us a run-down of the place and the leading figures involved? It will help us decide whether it'll be worth following up.'

Catherine gestured to a settee and took a chair facing them.

'I may not be the best person to ask about the place. I was only there for a month or so before it fell apart and everyone left. As soon as I arrived, I could tell something wasn't right. There were tense faces all the time and loads of arguments. It wasn't what I expected. But some of the others said it had only recently got like that. They said it had been brilliant at first with everyone so happy. It was run on Buddhist principles, and everyone was supposed to muck in and do their bit. That's why I joined them. But by the time I got there, things had gone wrong. I thought the leader, a man called Tim Brotherton, seemed a bit of an autocrat, but some of the other women said that hadn't always been the case. I think he had a messiah streak, if you know what I mean. Anyway, I arrived at a time when a lot of the crops had failed, and the group was struggling to keep everyone fed and clothed. There had clearly been some kind of dispute, because I found out that a couple of the original members had left, your Paul Prentice among them.'

'Do you remember a local police officer visiting?' Barry asked.

Catherine frowned. 'Vaguely. She asked a few questions and took a look around. She was interested in the children's health, I think, but also whether anyone had gone missing. I said I didn't know because I was fairly new. The leaders were adamant that everyone was accounted for, but they couldn't vouch for those who'd left.'

Sophie broke in. 'You said "leaders," plural. Who else had influence, other than this Tim Brotherton?'

Catherine sighed. 'I can guess who you're interested in. There was someone there called Trent Baker, an evil little bastard as far as I was concerned. He was manipulative and nasty. He'd arrived some time before me and, according to some of the other women, quickly wormed his way into a position of power. That was when one or two of the originals left and after that the group was never the same, according to what I heard.' She stopped.

Sophie looked at her closely. 'Was this the same Trent Baker who assaulted you not long afterwards? Who nearly killed you?'

Catherine looked at the floor. 'Yes,' she said quietly. 'We had a fling just after I arrived, although it only lasted a few weeks. Just enough time for me to realise what a total creep he was. He never forgave me for giving him the elbow so publicly. We had some big arguments while the place fell apart. He accused me of stirring up trouble, but it was him, really. I refused to toe the line and do what I was told just because I was a woman. I mean, where are the principles and the equality in that?'

'And was that the cause of the later murder attempt, do you think?' Sophie asked.

'Among other things,' Catherine said. 'He thought he could have any woman he wanted just by clicking his fingers. I told him where he could get off. The problem was, I said it in front of the group and he felt I'd humiliated him. It didn't occur to him that he was demeaning all the women there by trying to force through his misogynist views. Most of the other men there were unhappy with him too. That's what led to the big break-up. I suppose he saw me as a troublemaker, but I was speaking for most of the people there, men and women alike. They were all unhappy with him. Really, the place had outlived its sense of direction anyway, but he hurried it along towards its collapse. Nasty piece of shit.'

'You don't think anyone ever went missing from the farm, Catherine?'

She shrugged. 'In the end, how would anyone know? People left when they'd had enough. Some told Tim or left a message. Others didn't and just cleared off in the night.'

Barry broke in. 'Did you ever hear the name Katie Templar mentioned?'

'That was what that policewoman asked me. I hadn't heard it then. It was a bit later, when I was asking around, that I found out there had been someone there with that name. She'd arrived at the start with Tim but had broken up with him and started a relationship with someone else, and they left together.'

'Do you think that was before Trent Baker arrived?'

'No. It was after. I know that because he talked about the pair of them once.'

'Could Katie's new man have been Paul Prentice?' Sophie said.

Catherine shrugged. 'I don't know. I don't think he was ever mentioned by name.'

'Is there anything else you want to tell us?' Sophie said quietly.

Catherine said nothing.

Sophie leaned forward. 'Catherine? Is something worrying you? You look a bit anxious.'

Catherine sighed. 'Yes. Trent's just got out of prison. And something happened recently that I can't explain. It was just weird.'

She told them about the ruined date and the mixed-up text messages.

'There'll be a court order banning him from coming near you or contacting you. That'll be part of his parole conditions and it includes sending messages using someone else's phone. If we can prove he did that, then he'll be back inside. We were planning to see him later today, so a word of warning may be in order — if you agree.'

'I want him locked up again or deported to the Antarctic or somewhere equally far away.' Catherine looked straight at Sophie. 'He won't let things rest. Not him. I know what I'm talking about. He's a snake and he's got a long memory.'

* * *

From a secluded corner of the children's play area at the end of Catherine's street, Trent Baker watched the two visitors leave her house. His face was dark with anger.

'Fucking cops,' he muttered. 'Spot them a mile off. Always sticking their noses in.'

He slid out from behind the climbing frame, stuck a finger up at a couple of the children hanging around and returned to his car. Time to go home.

CHAPTER 16: MEETING THE SNAKE

Saturday morning

'What do you think, ma'am?' Barry asked. They were on their way across Bath to the premises Trent Baker cleaned. Wessex Data Analytics was based in a modern office complex, close to the main Bristol road.

'Same as you, I expect. Trent Baker could well be flexing his muscles and deliberately creating mischief. But we need to be careful with him. I'll let the local force know about the threat to Catherine. They can keep an eye on her, but I'm inclined to stay back and watch what he does next. Here we are.'

Sophie looked around her as they approached the reception desk. The building looked secure enough, but she knew it wouldn't take a determined individual long to identify the weak spots, particularly if they already had official access.

She introduced herself and Barry to the receptionist. 'It's a nice, clean building,' Sophie said. 'It makes a difference, doesn't it?'

'Do all the companies based here use the same cleaners or do they hire their own?' Barry asked.

'It's a central contract,' she replied. 'It works out cheaper that way.'

They took the stairs up to the second floor. Always using the stairs was a habit they'd adopted several years earlier to offset the hours they were forced to spend sitting in front of computer screens or behind the wheel of a car.

The stairway opened onto a carpeted foyer. Sophie did a slight double-take. The young man behind the reception desk bore an uncanny resemblance to Clark Kent.

'I love that we're in the era of male receptionists,' Sophie said quietly. 'They sometimes wear such amazing shirts and ties. Look at that one, in gold and red. I pick up ideas for Martin's birthday presents from them.'

Barry fingered his own rather drab tie absentmindedly.

'We're here to see Gloria Brookman,' Sophie said as they approached the desk. 'We're from Dorset police. I'm Sophie Allen and this is Barry Marsh.'

The young man's smile was guarded. 'She's waiting for you. Her office is the first one along that corridor.' A middle-aged woman in black trousers and a loose top appeared and waved at them.

'I'm not entirely clear why you're here,' she said as they sat down in her office. 'It's fortunate that I happened to drop in this morning. I'm not usually here on a Saturday.'

Sophie smiled. 'We're grateful for the opportunity to meet you. And to be honest, we're not entirely sure why we're here either. I have some general questions to ask of you about one of your staff members, but he's not suspected of involvement in any crime. He may have been a victim without realising it, but I don't want him to know about it. Russell Poulter?'

Gloria Brookman looked surprised. 'It would astonish me if Russell had been up to no good. He's a lovely guy, and so reliable. He's one of our best team leaders.'

Barry said, 'You're a contract company, aren't you? Producing bespoke software to order?' Gloria nodded rather cautiously. 'What's Russell Poulter working on at the moment?'

'I can't give you the full details because of client confidentiality, but it isn't anything that would generate any security concerns. He's working for an agricultural agency on monitoring the salinity levels in estuary water.'

'So it's not contentious in any way?' he asked. 'No one's got hot under the collar about it?'

Gloria shook her head. 'Not at all.'

'Has he reported any worries or issues during the past week? Any security concerns of his own?'

'I'll check.' Gloria swung her chair round to her computer. Her long nails tapped at the keys. She shook her head. 'No. Nothing on the system.'

'Who's his line manager?' Sophie asked.

'My colleague, Frank Scalton, director of software development. Do you want me to phone him?'

'Please.'

The two detectives waited while Gloria made the call. She replaced her mobile in her bag with a puzzled expression.

'Apparently Russell told Frank that his mobile phone went walkabout for several hours a few days ago but it turned up again. He wondered if he'd left it in the loo. That sounds very unlike Russell, I must say.'

'When was this?' Barry asked.

'Frank thinks it was Tuesday. And he said Russell was very edgy on Wednesday, which is also unlike him.'

'Who has access to these offices, apart from your own employees?' Barry asked.

'Well, visitors like yourselves, of course. But they're always signed in at the desk and accompanied. Clients. Maintenance people. Delivery. Cleaners. We've had some decorators in, but that was last week. We sometimes see staff's family members, although not in Russell's case. He's single — a very eligible bachelor, in fact.' She looked more human when she smiled.

'Would regular visitors, like decorators and cleaners, know the entry codes to get in?' Sophie asked. 'After all, they may need access outside your normal office hours.'

Gloria frowned. 'Yes, they do. Why? Do I need to be concerned?'

'I don't think so,' Sophie said. 'Your procedures seem pretty sound to me. We had to go through two identity checks and sign in twice. That's a lot better than many organisations.'

Gloria's puzzled look deepened. 'So, what's the problem?'

'There may not be one,' Sophie said. 'I know it all sounds a bit enigmatic, but I can't tell you any more at the moment. Russell may have been the victim of a bit of personal manipulation — nothing to do with his work. But he doesn't know it, and I don't want you to mention it to him. We'll try to see him later this week.'

'This is all very curious, I must say.'

'Well, that's the nature of the work we do. It can throw up all kinds of odd situations. Most don't go anywhere or mean anything. Coincidences and dead ends.' Sophie sat back.

'What's your role in the police?' Gloria asked suddenly. 'You didn't say.'

'I head up the violent crime unit. Keep that to yourself for the time being, if you could. I don't want Russell unduly worried. And, please, don't change any security procedures yet. I promise I'll provide a fuller explanation once I've gotten to the bottom of it and will give you some advice then.' Sophie and Barry stood up to leave.

* * *

Back in Bristol, Sophie and Barry stood at the door to a small flat and looked down at the man who had answered their knock. Sophie recalled some of the words people had used to describe him. Twisted viper. Evil bastard. Snake. Nasty piece of shit. The terms were hard to square with the blue-eyed, soft-featured, smiling face turned up at them. He even had dimples, for goodness' sake! Despite the fact that he couldn't be any taller than five four, with looks like that he probably

102

found it easy to worm his way into the lives — and beds — of plenty of soft-hearted women. As arranged, she let Barry make the introductions and followed the two men into a small sitting room. She wanted to listen and observe for a while, get a feel for this man and see if she could spot what made him tick. His criminal history suggested that a violent and manipulative monster lurked below the surface of the angel-faced charmer.

'Dorset, eh? What brings you to my door?' The little man was twinkling with bonhomie.

'We're investigating a suspicious death and a possible link to a commune near the Quantock Hills a decade or more ago,' Barry said.

'Aren't they in Somerset?' Baker replied. 'I thought you said you were from Dorset.'

'The death occurred in Dorset, about two weeks ago. I understand you lived at the commune for a spell. Is that right?' Barry asked.

'Um, yes. For a short while. I wanted to try life in a commune, but it didn't really work out for me. And the place was starting to fall apart.'

He sounds relieved, Sophie thought. What did he think we were here for?

'What do you mean, it was falling apart?' Barry asked. This was something they'd discussed on the way here: query everything Baker said. Force him to do some explaining and see if he might trip himself up.

'Too many chiefs and not enough Indians,' Baker said. 'Discussion groups for everything. Too many middle-class softies who didn't want to get their hands dirty. All they wanted to do was the arty-crafty stuff, and that didn't get people fed. They should've been out in the fields.'

'Who was the leader?' Barry asked.

'Some guy who thought he was spreading God's word. He was into eastern religions and all that stuff. So were some of the others. Hippy gypsies, living off the land. Earth mothers, trying to be at one with the universe or so they claimed.' He was openly sneering now. How quickly that angelic face twisted into a contemptuous smirk!

'Why did you join them if you didn't agree with what they stood for?' Barry asked.

Sophie could see that Baker was momentarily at a loss for a reply. As with many loudmouths, his words had gone further than his thoughts.

Baker finally shrugged. 'I didn't find out till I got there. Then I thought I'd give it a go even though it wasn't my thing.'

'What was the leader's name?' Barry asked.

'Tim something or other.' Baker looked down at the floor.

'Do you remember any other names?'

He shook his head. Sophie guessed he was thinking hard, wondering what line to take.

'Katie Templar? Blonde and slightly built? Do you remember her?' Barry began to pick up the pace.

'Vaguely. It was a long time ago. There were a lot of people there.'

'Paul Prentice?'

'Sort of rings a bell. I can't picture any of them though.'

'Catherine Templeton?'

The whole room seemed to freeze. Baker shrugged. 'Yeah. Her.'

Sophie broke in at this point. 'We know about Catherine, Mr Baker. We know you attacked her with a knife and nearly killed her. We know you're only recently out of prison. On early release and on parole.'

Baker said nothing. He looked like a child with the sulks.

'Have you broken the terms of your parole, Mr Baker? Have you been watching her? Have you been trying to meddle in her life?' Sophie said.

'No,' Baker protested. 'Do you think I'm mad? Do you think I want to go back into that hellhole?'

'So why did you specifically request the cleaning job at Wessex Data?'

'What do you mean?' He looked confused.

'It's in Bath, only a few minutes' drive from where she lives. All your other jobs are on the south side of Bristol, around here. Why ask for that one if it wasn't to keep an eye on Catherine?' Sophie stared hard at him.

'I didn't know she lived there. It just looked a good place to clean and I remembered the area from when I was a kid. One of my aunties used to live in a street close by. It only takes me half an hour to get there. It's always the last job I do.'

'Let me tell you what I want you to do, Mr Baker. Phone your boss, Caitlin Beckett, at CleanStyle. Tell her you wish to be taken off that particular job as of now and ask her to allocate you somewhere closer to home.'

He continued looking at the floor, sullen. 'Okay. I will.'

'I don't think you understand, Mr Baker. I mean right now, while I can hear you. Here, I'll get her number for you on my phone.'

She waited for Caitlin to answer and handed the phone to Baker.

'Well, I'm happier now,' Sophie said once the call was over. 'Where were you at the weekend two weeks ago?'

'Here. I don't go out much, apart from work.'

'So you weren't in Dorset that weekend or at any other time recently?' she said.

'No. Why would I be?' Baker said. 'It's a bit of a trek, isn't it? And I don't know anyone there.'

'You own a car, Mr Baker. What model and colour?' Sophie said.

'It's a blue Ford Focus. Why?'

'Just so we know. By the way, did I say who I was?'

He shook his head sullenly.

'I'm Detective Superintendent Sophie Allen. I head Dorset's Violent Crime Unit. I may need to speak to you again. Better bear that in mind, just in case you're thinking of doing anything stupid.'

CHAPTER 17: THE BODY UNDER
THE BEECH TREES

Saturday afternoon

Sophie and Barry arrived at the farm soon after lunch and were greeted by Polly Nelson, Sophie's opposite number in the Avon and Somerset force. Rae was already there, wearing jeans and walking boots, and talking to a group of local Somerset officers kitted out in search gear. The weather was still fine, thankfully. Wind and rain could make a search in countryside like this a nightmare. A van drew up behind their own vehicle, and they watched the dog handler climb out and make his way to the rear doors. Sophie and Barry went across.

'Great to see you again, Gerry, and Floyd of course. His reputation still goes before him.'

'Thanks, ma'am. It's a great area for dogs, the Quantocks. Once we're finished here, I'll take him up to the high ground and give him a run-around for a while so he can relax.'

'You don't think he'll need the whole afternoon, then?'

'What? Floyd? Nah. If there's a body here, he'll find it within a couple of hours.'

'Rae thinks we should start at the site of the old pigsties. She reckons that's where she'd bury a body.' Sophie pointed to the derelict timber enclosures.

Gerry Baldwin shook his grizzled head. 'We can start there if you want, but that's not where the body'll be. Too close to the buildings. If anywhere, it'll be up in the woods, somewhere free from prying eyes. There would have been too many people around the farmyard area if this was a commune at the time.'

He took Floyd across the farmyard to the derelict structures, gave him a pat and let him off the lead. The dog nosed around for a few minutes but didn't show a great deal of interest. They then visited the remnants of the old kitchen garden but, again, drew a blank.

'Well, so much for my sense of judgement,' Rae said, looking mournful.

The others laughed. 'It was logical, Rae,' Barry said. 'Gerry and his dog are moving into the fields now, so let's get the teams organised.'

Once the dog had examined an area and passed on, it was free for a search team to have a closer look, peering in the undergrowth for anything that seemed out of place and might be relevant. Within an hour, the dog team had given the all-clear for the fields near the farmyard and had moved behind the treeline to the slopes of the hills. It wasn't long before Floyd stopped in a tiny clearing in a dense area of beech woodland and began pawing at the ground, whining. Gerry Baldwin blew a whistle and the main search unit assembled around him, standing on the rich brown soil, the result of years of accumulated beech nut debris.

'Something here,' he said. 'And, from the way Floyd's behaving, I'm guessing it's what you're looking for.'

'Can he distinguish between the remains of humans and other animals?' Rae asked. 'What if it's a deer or something?'

'A deer doesn't get buried, does it? Just covered by leaves and other debris. The decomposition is different several feet under, because of the lack of oxygen. Floyd can tell the difference. He's a wonder dog,' Gerry said proudly.

A Somerset forensic team started to dig while the dog team headed back into the woods to continue their search. The detectives stood back, watching in silence. After less than fifteen minutes one of the forensic officers suddenly stopped.

'I have something,' she said.

Within another hour the full skeleton lay exposed. Whatever clothes this person had been wearing were almost rotted away to nothing.

'What's that?' Sophie pointed down at the groin area.

'I think it's a rotted tampon,' the nearest forensic officer replied, looking grim. 'Poor sod.'

'Any sign of what killed her?' Sophie asked.

'There's a nick on one of the ribs just above where the heart would be. Could be from a knife wound, but we'd need to look at it more carefully back at base.'

They watched the body being carefully lifted and carried back to a specialist van that had driven up to the nearest access point. It was driving off just as the dog team returned.

'Floyd's been quiet since that find,' Gerry said. 'I don't think there's anymore, ma'am. Is that what you expected?'

'To be honest, I didn't know what to expect. But we're only aware of one person going missing, and even that wasn't definite. Thanks, Gerry. Floyd's certainly earned his run-around.'

Sophie turned back to Polly Nelson. 'I think we'll call it a day and start to think about heading back home. We're all totally whacked. Can you let me know when the PM will be? One of us will try to get across, just as an observer. That's if you don't mind?'

'Of course not,' Polly replied. 'You've been hurtling around my patch all day. It's no wonder you've had enough.'

'There's still one person I need to visit before we head back. He's up at Weston. Listen, is there any chance you could come with me, then drop me at the train station afterwards? It means I can send Barry home so he can get a bit of time with his partner. The rest can wait till Monday. We all need a bit of family time, just to stop us going completely round the bend.'

'Sure.' Polly smiled.

'And I have another favour to ask. Most of the people involved in the commune still live and work in your area — Bristol, Bath and Weston. Can I send Barry up to work with you for a few days? He knows the background. We discussed it on the way here and it's the reason I want him to go home now.'

'Not a problem. You can stay over at my place tonight, if you want. We could have a girls' night out on the town. How does that sound?'

Sophie smiled broadly. 'I could be persuaded. Martin's away on a school trip this weekend so I'm free.'

* * *

'Tim Brotherton?' Sophie asked. The man who'd opened the door was of fairly average height and medium build. He had brown hair and no obvious distinguishing features. Could he be the man Jade had spotted back in the woods? It was difficult to be sure. Jade's description could apply to any number of men. Pauline Stopley's description had been similar, so Sophie had to assume that the two observations had been of the same man. But maybe that wasn't the case. Maybe they'd been looking at different people.

'I'm Detective Superintendent Sophie Allen from Dorset police. This is Detective Chief Inspector Polly Nelson from Avon and Somerset police. I wonder if we could ask you a few questions. May we come in?'

The man said nothing. He continued to stare suspiciously at the two detectives until a woman appeared behind him. She'd obviously overheard what Sophie had said because she pushed the man aside, opened the door wide and gestured for them to enter.

'Sorry about him,' she said, showing them into a brightly decorated sitting room that had a very spring-like feel to it. 'He

110

goes like that sometimes, totally zoned out. I'm Judy Price, and this is my house. Tim's my partner. What is it you wanted?'

'It's Tim we want to see,' Sophie said. 'I think he's sort of lurking out there in the hallway. I can see a shadow through the open door.'

'Tim!' Judy called. 'It's you they want to see, not me. Can you come in?'

He came slowly into the room and sat down on the sofa next to Judy. Somehow he seemed to exude an air of nervousness and irritation at the same time. It took him an age to settle himself.

'How can I help you?' he finally said.

He's doing this deliberately to give himself thinking time, Sophie thought. 'Are you the Tim Brotherton who set up and ran a commune on a farm in the Quantocks about twelve years ago?' she asked.

'Yes,' he replied warily.

Judy stared at him. 'A commune? Really? You never told me about that!'

'Do I have to tell you everything about my past?' he said. 'I'm sure you haven't told me every little thing that you've done.'

'That's not little,' Judy replied. 'Setting up and running a commune on a farm? That's pretty major in my book.'

Brotherton merely shrugged. He turned back to face the detectives. 'So?'

'We've just come from the farm. According to the locals it's been empty since your group left and it's fallen into disrepair. We found a body this afternoon, buried in the woods just up from the top field. It's been there a long time. We haven't identified it yet. We think it might be a young woman.'

'Christ.' Tim Brotherton turned ashen. He put his head in his hands and ran his fingers through his sandy hair.

Judy looked horror-stricken. 'Tim? What is this?'

He turned his head slowly from side to side. 'I know nothing about a body. It can't be anyone from back then.

None of us would have done a thing like that.' He turned towards Sophie with a look of despair on his pale face.

'You haven't asked why I'm here,' Sophie said. 'Me, rather than just DCI Nelson here.'

'What's that?' he replied, sounding puzzled.

Judy said, 'Why is a senior detective from Dorset up here investigating a death in Somerset?'

'Exactly,' Sophie said. 'I'm here because a tramp was murdered in my area about two weeks ago. We think he spent some time in your commune all those years ago, Mr Brotherton. His name was Paul Prentice. Ring any bells?'

Brotherton put his head in his hands again.

'Where were you the weekend before last?' Sophie asked.

He raised his head. 'I was on a work-related trip to Portsmouth. I'm a freelance graphic artist and I've been doing work for a Portsmouth-based publishing company. I had a planning meeting with two of their in-house copywriters.'

'Which way did you drive?'

'I didn't. I went by train. There's a reasonable service from Bristol to Portsmouth. I went on Friday and came back Sunday.'

'Did you visit the Wareham area at any time during that weekend?' Sophie asked.

He shook his head. 'No.'

'I also need to know if there was a woman in the commune called Katie Templar. Not to be confused with Catherine Templeton, who I already know was there. Well?'

He sat up, rigid. Finally, he spoke. 'Yes.'

'So you knew both of them? Paul Prentice and Katie Templar? Can you confirm that for me, please?'

He looked up, tiny beads of perspiration on his face. 'Yes, they were both there. They left. I don't know what happened to them after that.'

'Did they leave together?' Sophie asked.

He didn't answer immediately but sat breathing slowly for several moments. 'Paul went first. We had a row and he walked out. Katie stayed on for a while longer, then she left as well. I assumed she'd gone to join him. We all did.'

'What was the nature of your relationship with Katie Templar, Mr Brotherton?'

'She was with me when I set the place up. She was one of the originals. They both were.'

'Did it turn into some kind of love tussle?' Sophie said. 'Is that what you're carefully trying to avoid telling me?'

'Look, I had feelings for Katie — I'll admit that. We were very close. But she fell for Paul in a big way. When he walked out, I guessed it wouldn't be long before she followed. I didn't try to stop her, if that's what you're driving at.' He ran his fingers through his hair, which was beginning to look damp. 'I wouldn't do that — force someone to stay against their will.'

'Were you lovers in the early days? You and Katie?' Sophie asked.

Brotherton fidgeted awkwardly on his seat. 'Look, we were young. Everyone fell in and out of love all the time. The atmosphere was very free, very happy.'

'You haven't answered my question.'

He sighed loudly. 'Yes, Katie and I had a fling at the start. But if you're suggesting that the body you found is her and that I killed her you're very wrong on both counts. She left. I know she did. Someone saw her go, trailing her bag and heading down to the bus stop. I guessed she was going to join Paul, wherever he was.'

'So she had a bag with her when she left? What, a suitcase?'

'Yes. It had a handle and wheels. It was red.'

'Did you ever try to contact her again? Maybe after the commune folded?'

He shook his head. 'No.'

'There's no trace of her after the commune, Mr Brotherton. Nothing. Thin air. So I'd really like to know how you can be so sure that the body we found today isn't her.'

There was no reply.

'Tell me about Trent Baker.'

Brotherton sighed. 'He joined us about halfway through. Some of the group thought that was when things started to get worse. That he started it.'

'Is that what you think?' Sophie asked.

He shrugged. 'I don't know. I don't know what to think any more. It all got . . . a bit nasty. Maybe it was him . . .' His voice trailed off.

'You're aware that he spent ten years in prison for attempting to kill Catherine Templeton, one of your other commune members?'

Brotherton nodded wearily. 'But that happened way after we closed the commune. It had nothing to do with us. Look, I've spent the last twelve years trying to forget all this. I'm not that person anymore.'

'What person, Mr Brotherton? Tim Brotherton the charismatic leader who set the commune up? Tim Brotherton the zealot who used every means at his disposal to get his way with the group? Tim Brotherton the manipulative individual who made sure women were kept in the roles allotted to them? And how many other Tim Brothertons are there that we haven't found out about yet?'

* * *

'I love your sledgehammer technique, Sophie. You fire these bits of information at some poor unsuspecting sod — wham, wham, wham. It nearly left me reeling. No wonder he was a nervous wreck by the time we left.'

The two women were in an upmarket Chinese restaurant in Bristol city centre. Sophie finished her mouthful of peppered chicken wings and licked her fingers.

'No point mucking about, that's what I think. I can be subtle when it's needed, but that guy didn't deserve gentle handling. He's an arsehole. I knew it before we met him. Rae managed to get a copy of a leaflet he wrote about the commune when it was still a going concern. What made us all

114

furious, and that includes Barry, was the dismissive way he wrote about the women there. In his eyes, they didn't count. It was all self-important, fatuous stuff about the need for men to find their real selves. The women's role was to cook for them, mend their socks and bring up the children. What he really needs is a punch in the face, but sadly we're not allowed to do that. Not in Dorset, anyway. If things are different in Bristol, do tell me and I'll join you like a shot.'

'You grew up in Bristol, didn't you?' Polly said.

Sophie nodded. 'My mum still lives here. In Clifton.'

'Ooh! The upper-crust part. Get you, posh bitch.'

Sophie laughed. 'As if. She's only lived there for the last ten years. It was always her dream, to live somewhere better than her parents did. She hated them for throwing her out when she was sixteen and pregnant with me. I thought she'd broken off all contact with them but, apparently, she visited twelve years ago when her father was on his deathbed. She'd discovered that she and I hadn't been left anything in their wills. She stayed only long enough to tell them that she was the practice manager at a big medical centre, that she owned a flat in Clifton and that I had an Oxford law degree and was a DI in the West Midlands task force. Then she said, "*so fuck the both of you,*" and walked out. A bit cruel, I thought, but there were thirty-three years of pent-up hatred in those words. She never expected them to leave her anything, but she did think they'd leave something for me.'

'Families are great when they work, but when they go wrong, boy, they can go wrong big time. Was he one of those harsh, preachy types?'

'Not really. It was my gran who was the fire and brimstone one. He was just weak and never lifted a finger to protect my mum from her vicious moralising. They were members of one of those brethren-type sects, full of spite for anyone who dares question them. His wife only outlived him by a year or so. I suppose I should think of them as my grandparents, but I can't. My Great-Aunt Olive and Uncle Reggie took on those roles when I was small. I loved them both. Great-Uncle Reggie was a rascal. His aim in life seemed to be to reduce me to fits of giggles.' Sophie gave a faint smile. 'Anyway, back to the case. What did you make of Tim Brotherton?'

'Maybe he's changed his tune since he wrote that pamphlet. His partner, Judy, didn't look as though she'd put up with that kind of rubbish. What did she say she did? A nurse?'

'She's a senior sister at Weston hospital, running an intensive care ward, so she'll probably have loads more responsibility than him, and my guess is that she'd let him know it. He's maybe seen a bit more sense now he's older.' Sophie paused. 'What did you make of his account of things? Did you believe him?'

Polly frowned. 'He's hiding something, but it's difficult to know what. If he was the leader of that commune, he'd have known everything that was going on, all the intrigues. They all do. The first thing they do is set up an inner circle of people to keep them informed, people who will be listening in on the gossip and chat. All secret groups, societies and the like work that way. They always have.'

'And Judy knows something, Polly. She was looking at me when I first told them of the tramp's death. Then she stared at Tim for a few seconds and dropped her eyes for the rest of the time we were there. I'm half expecting her to phone me sometime soon, once she's thought things through. Something was worrying her.'

'Well, time will tell. I can't say that he impressed me much. Don't commune leaders usually have a bit of charisma? Aren't they visionaries, always whipping their followers into a frenzy with their stirring talk of a second coming or the day of judgement?' Polly said.

Sophie nodded. 'And often getting loads of sex in the process. They earmark the most gorgeous women and talk them into bed with a load of hogwash about serving the lord's will. You can guess the kind of thing. "Give me a blow-job every morning and I'll promote you to archangel status."'

'You're joking.' Polly gaped at her.

'Absolutely not. It's well documented. There was even a quasi-religious cult in the Quantocks in the 1850s, where the women queued up for a chance to have sex with the leader, convinced he was God's representative on earth. A load of complete tosh, but they fell for his talk big time. That guy must have been in seventh heaven. The place was called the *Agapemone*, the Abode of Love.'

Polly shook her head. 'Beats me.'

Sophie laughed. 'Maybe that too. A lot of cults included a bit of flagellation just to get everyone in the mood.'

'Oh, my God. Can we change the subject?' Polly said weakly. 'This is putting me off my food.'

CHAPTER 18: WHAT A PEACH

Sunday morning

Trent Baker hadn't slept well. Anger and resentment were still swirling around in his head like thunderclouds. He was struggling to think of a way round the barriers that had suddenly been slammed into place during the police visit. He wasn't to contact Catherine. He wasn't to go near her. He wasn't to watch her. He wasn't to monitor her activities in any way. What a piss-pot situation to be in. Nosey farts, laying down the law and telling him what to do with his life. There had to be a way round their Gestapo-like restrictions, if only he could spot what it was. Unless of course he ignored Catherine for a few months and switched his attention to Brotherly Tim. The dick with the chick. Ah, now there was a thought. What about the chick? Judy something or other, a nurse. Sweet Judy blue-eyes. Punch that Judy. Yes. Maybe she needed a bit of close attention. And it wouldn't be all that difficult. She lived in Weston-Super-Mare, where CleanStyle's office was based.

He looked in the mirror. *You are brilliant, Trent Baker.* You are such a talented and good-looking individual. In fact, if there were such things as gods, you'd be one for sure. He rose from his chair and poured himself a celebratory glass of Scotch. Blast. That bottle he'd nicked was nearly empty. Time to pinch another? But off to Weston first.

Forty-five minutes later Trent's car drew into an empty parking slot close to Judy Price's house. That money he'd managed to secrete away before his trial and prison sentence had proved to be very useful. Not for him the penny-pinching life of a typical ex-con. No, he had brains and the sense to think ahead. He could afford a semi-decent car, unlike some of the plonkers he'd mixed with inside.

He looked across at the neat dwelling on the other side of the road. He'd been here before, of course, although it had been after midnight on that occasion. He'd scared a cat while sneaking through the shrubbery. Would she be here, or would she be working on a Sunday morning? Bloody Tim would probably be around somewhere. Or down at the pub? The trouble was, he, Trent, didn't have a plan. He'd hoped one would occur to him on the drive down here, but his brain had remained blank. He was looking for something to upset the smooth running of Judy's life, something that would stick a crowbar into the gently moving cogs of her daily routine. Her car. Yes, that could be it. A flat tyre. Or was that too tame? It would be nice to sneak a cowpat or some dog poo in through an open window to land on the driving seat, with enough time for it to fill the interior with its stink before she found it. How likely was that though? People didn't leave their car windows open nowadays, not even on summer days like today. And, let's face it, he would get too messy trying to handle the stuff. No good. And which car was hers anyway? It was difficult to tell. What about the hospital where she worked? Might that be a better bet? Maybe a visit was in order to check the lie of the land. Trent started the engine and slowly drove off.

The hospital looked modern and clean. It probably gave really good healthcare. Not like the service he'd had to endure in prison that time when he'd developed a chest infection. A crappy place with a crappy approach to sorting out his health problem. Bastards. They'd treated him as if he was a lump of dirt.

He strode in through the main entrance, clutching a clipboard and pen, not that he really needed them. Late morning was still visiting hours, so he managed to mingle with a group of people who'd just stepped off a bus and were making their way through reception. He stopped at the staff chart and spotted the name Judy Price. She was listed as senior ward sister in intensive care. My, didn't that sound impressive. Such a responsible job. How come bloody Tim Brotherton had managed to snare such a woman? Tim was all hot air and no trousers. What could she see in him? Maybe he'd come into some money from somewhere and that was the attraction. Maybe he'd painted his prick fluorescent yellow, coated it in honey and waved it at her one night when she was too drunk to notice what a complete waste of space he really was.

Trent pulled up short at the double doors that guarded the entrance to the unit. Beside the notice asking him to squeeze anti-bacterial cleaning gel over his hands was the duty staff list. Fuck. The nurse on duty this morning was a bloke. A bloke, for God's sake. What was the world coming to? He pushed the doors open and went in, stopping at the staff photo-board. Judy Price. What a peach. He looked around to check that no one was watching, then took out his phone and surreptitiously snapped her image.

'We don't allow mobile phones in here, sir,' someone behind him said. 'It's an ICU.'

Trent turned to face the person who'd spoken, a porter pushing a patient in a wheelchair.

'Sorry, I didn't realise.' Trent smiled innocently. 'Why not, just out of interest?'

'Interference with some of the equipment. Most of the rest of the hospital's okay, but not here.'

Trent nodded. 'I'll switch it off.'

'Are you looking for someone?'

'Umm, not really. I thought my brother was in here, but I just got a message that he's in a different ward. I'll head off.'

He walked back down the corridor and followed the exit signs to the car park. Maybe that had been pushing things a bit, considering the cop warning he'd got yesterday. Maybe he ought to play it sensible and toe the line for a while, just in case. He sighed. Too fucking boring. Why not have another look at the Brotherton house? Maybe the lovebirds would be out in the garden in weather like this, enjoying a cold beer. Snoozing on sunbeds. Maybe she'd be in a skimpy bikini, catching a tan. Then again, maybe he should just go home and think things through a bit more. Let's face it, if he did something stupid and got caught, he'd be back inside, pronto. And that would be the worst fucking thing in the world.

Trent started his car, drove out to the motorway and headed back towards Bristol. Maybe he should get drunk. Maybe he should visit that exotic massage salon round the corner from his place, the one that showed super-pneumatic chicks in its publicity photos. Did he have enough ready cash, though?

* * *

In fact, Judy Price wasn't spread out on a sunbed in a bikini, although she was outside, sitting in a chair on the small patio at the rear of her house, dressed in shorts and a T-shirt, sipping at a glass of iced orange drink. She was alone. She hadn't spoken to Tim since the row the previous evening, after she'd asked him to explain his involvement with the cult or commune that those two detectives had talked about. He was still in the house somewhere, sulking. She was still trying to make sense of what she'd learned. What had been the extent of his involvement? What kind of commune had it been? It sounded pretty violent, particularly if the death of the tramp was linked to it somehow. Only a seriously deranged individual would let their feelings fester for more than a decade before seeking someone out and killing them. Was there a chance it could be Tim? After all, he'd been very reticent about that holiday in Dorset. Even more worrying was the fact that he'd possibly been there at about the time the tramp had been killed, something he hadn't told the police. But he'd never shown the remotest tendency towards violence in the time they'd been together. She sighed out loud. People were just so bloody complicated. And some were far too adept at hiding their true selves below layers of carefully constructed, alternative personae.

Tim appeared, a jug in one hand and a bottle in the other. 'Thought you might want a top-up,' he said. 'And I've found some gin. Do you want a slug?'

She looked up at him from under her wide-brimmed sun-hat. 'That'd be nice. Not too much, mind. I'm already feeling a bit woozy.'

He looked tense. She could sense him biting his lip, having to exercise all his self-control in order not to start the plead-ing and self-justification again. She'd told him late the previous night that if he brought the matter up once more, she'd throw him out. Even if he didn't have anywhere else to go. Even if he was innocent of any wrongdoing. Even if he grovelled like a dog. She'd had enough of it and was within a whisker of ending their relationship. They'd spent the night in separate rooms.

* * *

Catherine Templeton stood hesitating at the entrance to the pub in Bath city centre. She soon spotted Russell sitting at a nearby table, eagerly waving at her. She wondered if he'd been there for a while in order to ensure that this date didn't go tits up like the last one.

She took a seat opposite him, smiling. 'Hi. A second chance, eh?'

'Thanks so much for agreeing. I hope you won't regret it.'

'Well, let's see how it goes,' she said. 'I realise now that it probably wasn't your fault. Have the police been in touch?'

He nodded enthusiastically. 'Yes, but only by phone and they wouldn't give me all the details. I think they must be a bit busy. It was a woman called Polly Nelson, a DCI. She said someone would be interviewing me in a day or two to take a statement. It's left me a bit puzzled. I mean, to be the victim of a crime without realising it. And it was all to get at you, is that right?'

She grimaced. 'That's what it looks like, although there's no proof. Intimidation and stalking by this creep I knew ages ago. He's been in prison for ten years for attempted murder. Of me.'

Russell looked shocked. 'My God. That serious? Do you want to talk about it?'

She shook her head. 'Not really. He's a warped little toad and I really don't want him in my head again. Let's look at the food on offer and talk about anything but him.' She studied the menu then caught the attention of a passing waitress. They made their selection, chose drinks and settled back in their seats.

Russell looked again at the attractive woman opposite him. 'I felt so down after that fiasco on Tuesday evening. I'm really glad you're giving me another chance. I'm on a bit of a high, to be honest.'

Catherine frowned. 'You mustn't think there's more to it than a friendly meal out, you know. We still have to see how we get on together.' She paused. 'To be honest, this whole business has shaken me. You say you're on a high. Well, I'm feeling tense and anxious. I hardly slept last night. That evil bastard has wormed his way back into my brain.'

'You said you didn't want to talk about him.'

'I know. But I suppose that's wishful thinking. If they do find hard evidence, he'll have a restraining order put on him. He might even end up back in prison. That would be a relief, I can tell you. It depends on the parole board. They'll be meeting over the next few days. Until that happens, the police want to keep him in his job. They said that it would help to keep him off the streets for a few days. What did they say to you?'

Russell shrugged. 'Not a lot. They told me that someone might have got hold of my phone and that's about it.' He paused. 'Does he really hate you that much?'

'Unfortunately for me, yes. But it's not just me. He hates everyone. There's only one person in the world of any importance to Trent Baker, and that's Trent Baker. Everyone else is just here for his convenience.'

CHAPTER 19: THE PACKAGE

Monday morning

Barry arrived at the incident room in Taunton police station earlier than expected. He had with him the package Rae had discovered in the derelict farmhouse's hidden cupboard, already forensically examined back in Dorset. It had yielded a set of fingerprints that failed to match any that were on file. He spread the items out on the desk that had been allocated to him, and was looking at them when Polly Nelson appeared.

'Good morning, Barry. Great to have you with us, even if it is only for a couple of days. Have you got somewhere to stay?'

'I've gone for a local pub that the boss recommended. The Golden Hind? You know what she's like. I'm not checking in until later, though.'

Polly laughed. 'It is a good choice if you like old inns. Low beams, log fires and the like. The food's meant to be good. I suppose I ought to look for a place to stay too. The motorway from Bristol was bedlam this morning.' She looked at the items spread out on the desktop. 'Is that what I think it is?'

Barry nodded. 'It's all been through forensics at our end, so we're safe to have a closer look.'

Polly looked across the room at one of the junior officers who didn't seem to be doing much. 'Get us a couple of coffees, will you? We'll put some money in the kitty later.'

They slipped on latex gloves and started examining the first item, a notebook written in a thin, spidery hand.

'I've seen this writing before,' Barry said. 'It's the same as the letter we found at the site where the tramp was killed. We're pretty certain it was the young woman, Katie Templar, who wrote it.'

'Possibly the body we dug up on Saturday?'

Barry nodded again, his ginger hair catching a ray of sunlight streaming in through the window. He turned the page over. This was fascinating stuff. The initial part of the notebook detailed the commune's early days and was full of enthusiasm. It was clear that the writer had an important position in the commune and was consulted on many of the decisions. Within a couple of months, the initial eagerness seemed to dissipate. Irritation began to creep into her entries. The two detectives flipped through to the final pages. There, the notes were bleaker and much briefer.

'We'll need to read it more carefully,' Polly said. 'There are names, dates and places mentioned. It looks quite personal, doesn't it?'

Barry agreed. 'It looks as though it links into the stuff we already have.'

The next set of documents were the title deeds to the farm, showing that Katie Templar was the original owner. It had been left to her by her uncle and aunt after their deaths. It was apparent that several years later, when the commune started, she transferred the ownership to a trust, the Heathfield Commune, the trustees of which seemed to be Katie herself, Timothy Brotherton, Paul Prentice and an Andrew Atkins.

Barry looked up, frowning. Atkins? Where had he come across that name before? He'd seen it somewhere very recently, maybe in connection with this case. He shook his head slightly, as if the movement would dislodge the information he wanted and bring it to the fore. It didn't.

'Something occurred to you?' Polly asked.

'It's the name Atkins. It rings a bell. It's no good me puzzling over it, though. It'll come to me in its own sweet time.'

'This tends to reinforce what we gathered when we interviewed Brotherton on Saturday. He finally admitted that when the group started, he and Katie Templar were an item, but they fell out later.'

Barry absentmindedly tugged at his ear. 'And Paul Prentice, our dead tramp, was one of the other two trustees. So what do we have? Four trustees. Two of them dead, probably both murdered. One still around, who happened to be the group leader, and this fourth one, Andrew Atkins. I'm going to phone Rae. I'm sure that last name was linked to something she was talking about. If so, we could find it in her notes somewhere, but it'll be quicker to ask her in person.'

He made the phone call, wandering towards the window and listening. He hurried back to Polly with a triumphant look on his face.

'One of the locals Rae spoke to last week was a Babs Atkins. She lives in one of the tiny villages along from Nether Stowey. Do you think a visit might be in order? This Andrew Atkins might be related to her.'

Polly nodded. 'You do it. It'll give me time to read that diary in detail. But let's look at the rest of the stuff before you head off. You know what I don't understand? When the commune failed, three of the trustees were still alive, assuming Katie Templar was dead by then. So why has it been left to become so derelict? Why didn't they sell it?'

'Maybe they didn't know Katie was dead — if that body does turn out to be her,' Barry said. 'And by then, Prentice had done his vanishing act. Maybe that's why he disappeared from official records and started living as a tramp. Without him there to sign the transfer, the place couldn't be sold so easily.'

Polly frowned. 'You mean he knew that sooner or later the truth was bound to come out? By staying hidden, he made sure the place remained as it was. Clever, in a way.'

'I wonder if he guessed that she was dead. If so, it was vital that he stay hidden. With two of the trustees gone, the other two couldn't act on their own,' Barry said.

'Unless he was involved in her death.'

Barry hesitated. 'We're not convinced of that. All the evidence is circumstantial, but it seems to show that Prentice was a decent guy who cared for Katie. Did you know it was the boss's daughter that found his body?'

'No. She didn't tell me that.' Polly looked surprised.

'It was Jade, her eighteen-year-old,' Barry said. 'But she didn't just find him, she knew him too. She used to take him food and make sure he was alright. For all we know, it was Jade who was closest to him in recent years. She's even looking after his dog. Anyway, she's adamant that he was one of the nicest blokes she's ever come across. We can't dismiss that. And I trust her judgement, to be honest — at least until we discover hard evidence to the contrary.'

The next notebook was a farming record. It showed what crop had been sown in each field, the annual yields, along with the costs and health records of the farm livestock. Whoever kept the record had even listed the number of eggs collected each day. The writing wasn't Katie Templar's. The initials *A. A.* appeared at the end of each entry.

The final folder contained a collection of bank statements and financial records, all related to the Heathfield Commune. They affirmed that Katie Templar was the original owner and the person responsible for the finances. And that wasn't all. Closer examination of the documents showed that she'd loaned the commune twenty thousand pounds of her own money when the cash-flow problems began to get serious. That money never appeared to have been repaid. It was possible that the friction and subsequent possible murder hadn't been about fractured relationships at all. Instead, money might have been the catalyst for the break-up.

Barry decided to set out immediately to interview Babs Atkins, leaving Polly to study the material more closely. Before either of them could make a start they received a phone call from the local forensic unit. The few shreds of clothing that had been found with the body had been partly identified as coming from a nightdress.

'That's odd,' Polly said. 'Didn't Brotherton say that when he last saw Katie Templar she'd been in outdoor clothes and pulling a suitcase?'

'A red one. Either he's lying or the body isn't her.' He looked at his watch. 'I'll head off now. It'll take me, what, half an hour or so to get to the Nether Stowey area?'

He glanced again at the folder containing the financial records. 'We've got the very person to wade through this stuff. Lydia Pillay is with Bournemouth CID but had a two-year spell in the regional fraud squad in Bath. She's just back at work from a long absence recovering after a thug half-killed her. She can only do office-based stuff for a couple of months. She'd enjoy going through this. Okay with you?'

'Of course. I met her a couple of times when she was in Bath. Not a problem.'

CHAPTER 20: MEMORIES

Monday morning

In the morning sunshine, Holly Cottage looked just as enchanting as Rae had said. Barry rang the doorbell and waited. He'd decided not to let Babs Atkins know he was coming. The reason for this was the usual one: forewarned, the interviewee had time to rehearse their story, which made it more difficult to get to the truth. Much better to catch them off guard.

The door opened and a neatly dressed, grey-haired woman looked out at him, a look of polite enquiry on her face.

He smiled. 'Mrs Atkins? I'm Detective Inspector Barry Marsh from Dorset police. My colleague Rae Gregson interviewed you a couple of days ago. Would you have a few minutes to spare? I need to check up on a couple of points.'

A flicker of anxiety, and then she forced a smile. 'Of course. Come on in. I've just made myself a coffee. Would you like one?'

'That's kind of you.' He followed her through to a large kitchen at the rear of the cottage.

'This is lovely,' he said. 'Rae told me what a great view you have. She wasn't exaggerating.' He accepted the proffered mug and took a sip.

'So what did you want to know?' She sat down opposite him at the large kitchen table.

'Andrew Atkins. Is he a relation of yours?'

Babs turned pale and put a hand to her face. 'He's my son.'

'He was a member of the commune that Rae asked you about?'

'Yes,' Babs whispered.

'Why didn't you tell Rae?'

Babs hesitated. 'I didn't think it was relevant.'

'But he was one of the four trustees that owned the farm. Didn't you know that?'

She shook her head. 'I knew he was one of the leaders, but not that he had an official position. He never told me that.'

'So what did he tell you?' Barry asked.

She paused, seeming to muster her thoughts. 'He knew the man who originally owned Heathfield Farm because he did some conservation work there when he was in the local scout troop. He worked there for a few years after he left school. That was before the old chap died and the commune moved in. He got to know the leader, someone called Tim. When the group arrived and settled at the farm, he stayed on. We hardly saw him after that.'

'Where is he now?' Barry could see she was upset and spoke gently.

She shook her head, her voice trembled. 'I don't know. I haven't seen him for years. We got Christmas cards from him until a few years ago and they always had a short letter inside, but they stopped coming soon after Harry — that's my husband — died. I tried to find out where he was, but I never got anywhere.'

'Do you remember the postmark on the envelopes? That might help trace where he is.'

'Bournemouth and Poole. I tried to find him when Harry became ill, but it was impossible. My other two children told me to forget him. They said he obviously didn't want to be found.'

Barry groaned inwardly. Now what? The team had assumed the tramp was being honest about his identity — Paul Prentice, the name he gave to Jade Allen. She'd told them that the tramp she knew as Paul spent each winter in a hostel in Poole. What if he wasn't Prentice at all? What if he was really the other missing trustee, Andrew Atkins, and had taken on the identity of Prentice for reasons of his own? This whole case was becoming ridiculously complex, particularly with three of the four farm trustees now apparently dead or missing.

Babs stared at him. 'Of course. You're from Dorset, aren't you? Investigating the death of a tramp.' She gave a slight smile but then, as the realisation hit her, put a hand to her mouth. 'Oh no. Surely it's not him? It can't be. Didn't your colleague say you knew who he was?'

'We had fairly strong reasons for thinking he was someone called Paul Prentice but there's been no formal identification as yet. We should know tomorrow one way or the other, once we see some dental records that have finally turned up. Please don't worry unnecessarily, Mrs Atkins.'

'I just couldn't bear it. It's breaking my heart to think that Andrew's been living as a tramp all these years.'

'The chances are it is Paul Prentice because of the things of his we found. Do you have a photo of Andrew, maybe one taken just before he vanished? And I'll need a description, particularly of any distinguishing features.'

Babs seemed to calm down a little. 'He's of average height and about eleven stone — at least he was. He's got mid-brown hair, slightly curly. There's a scar on his lower stomach from an appendicitis operation he had when he was in his late teens, and another small one on the little finger of his right hand from where he gashed himself badly on a bit of broken glass when he was small. That's all I can think of right now.'

'From what you've said, it doesn't sound like our tramp. He was taller for a start. Can you tell me what Andrew was like as a person, and what he did for a living?'

Babs looked into the distance. 'He was our youngest. I suppose we spoiled him a bit, but he was a nice little lad when he was small. He used to amuse the older two by chuckling at them. This was before he could speak. He was amiable enough as he grew up, but he wasn't as hard-working as the other two at school, so didn't cover himself in glory where academia was concerned. He was always interested in the outdoors and worked for a few of the farms around here until the commune opened and he joined. I think he probably got sucked in — you know, to that lifestyle. He was a bit weak-willed and easily led.'

'Is there any reason why he would have chosen Poole or Bournemouth when he upped and left? Does he have family or friends there?' Barry asked.

She shook her head. 'No. But I did hear he liked surfing and beach life. Maybe it was that.'

Barry looked doubtful. 'Really keen surfers go to Cornwall. It's a bit tame down our way, none of those big Atlantic rollers.'

She shrugged. 'He probably fell in with a group of people and left with them, you know, after the farm closed up. Maybe that's where they went, and he stayed with them.' She paused. 'I heard that a woman's body was found at the farm at the weekend. Had it been there long?'

'I can't say much, Mrs Atkins, but it had certainly been there a while. Obviously, our investigations are ongoing and urgent.'

'Andrew wouldn't have been involved in that, honestly. He wasn't that type of person.'

Barry changed the subject. 'Did he leave anything here? Personal belongings, papers, diaries or anything like that?'

Babs hesitated. Barry watched her closely. He guessed she was wondering whether she'd be doing her son a favour by cooperating with the police. Did this mean she had some doubts about him after all? Finally, she said, 'I think he left a few things, but I haven't looked at them for years. Our two older children did a clear-out after Harry died, so they might have been binned. Let me look.' She rose from her seat.

'Can I come with you?'

'If you must,' she said reluctantly.

Her son's bedroom was now a tiny guest room, tucked under the sloping roof and decorated in pale green.

'I know there's nothing in the wardrobe or drawers because I keep them clear for when my nephews or nieces come to stay. But there's a hatch to a small storage area under the eaves. Harry put Andrew's stuff in a box and shoved it up there when he decorated this room last.'

She pulled a chair beneath the hatch and opened it up. Standing behind her, Barry could see a small cardboard box, perched on a couple of boards. The rest of the loft area was empty. Babs pulled the box down and began to sort through the contents, which consisted of school reports, a scout uniform complete with badges, an old teddy bear, a couple of boys' adventure comics and a fishing reel.

'The rod broke when Harry was packing the stuff up, so we threw it out,' Babs said.

A poor record of a life, and none of it gave any insight into the adult Andrew Atkins. Babs replaced the box and they started to make their way down the stairs.

'Did he ever bring anyone from the farm here, Mrs Atkins? A girlfriend perhaps?'

With a foot on the top step, Babs paused. 'Well, yes, he did once. Let me think. He hadn't planned to visit. I seem to remember that he was on his way to Taunton with this young woman and stopped off on the way.' She continued on down the stairs, back into the kitchen. 'It was so long ago. Oh, I remember. She played the trumpet and had ordered a new one. There's a famous wind instrument shop in Taunton and they were going to collect it. They called in to borrow a street map of Taunton. I gave them a cup of coffee and a slice of cake. They were both so thin and hungry-looking.'

'Can you remember her name?' Barry asked.

'Yes. Linda Brooker. She came from Bridgwater and I knew her mum once. She used to help out in a café in the town that Harry and I went to for coffee when we were shopping there.'

'Linda? Or her mother?'

'Oh, her mother. I've no idea what Linda did, apart from playing the trumpet and living on the farm.'

'Have you seen her since?' Barry asked.

Babs shook her head. 'Nor her mum. I don't go to Bridgwater anymore since Harry died. I just use the local shops in Nether Stowey.'

'Can you remember what this Linda Brooker looked like?'

'Well, she didn't look much like her mum, that's one thing I can tell you. I remember saying that to her and she laughed. She had short cropped hair that was almost black, but it could have been dyed. She was tall, about the same height as Andrew, and she had a gap between her two front teeth. I can remember thinking that if she got that fixed, she'd be really pretty. I think she lives in Taunton now.'

Barry reckoned he'd got as much information out of Babs as he was likely to get. He handed her his contact card. 'If you remember anything else, however unimportant it seems, phone me on that number. And thanks. You've been really helpful.'

CHAPTER 21: SOME CARDS AND A FEW QUID

Monday afternoon

Barry emailed Sophie to give her a quick rundown on what he'd discovered. Then he set to work in the Taunton incident room, trying to trace the two new names, Andrew Atkins and Linda Brooker. Babs had said she thought Linda was living in Taunton. Were she and Andrew still together? Why hadn't Andrew stayed in contact with his mother, particularly after the death of his father? This whole investigation was populated with people who behaved in unpredictable ways. Maybe that was only to be expected with people who had once lived in a commune. Wasn't the rejection of an orthodox lifestyle one of the core characteristics of such a group?

Atkins was proving to be very elusive. Just like Paul Prentice, he didn't appear in any local records. Either, like the dead tramp, he'd dropped off the radar completely or he'd moved away from Somerset and was keeping a deliberately low profile. Linda Brooker did turn up, however — at least Barry hoped it was her. A Linda Brooker of the right kind of age did indeed live in Taunton. Barry headed off to find her.

Montgomery Flats was a small block situated in a former council estate. Barry locked his car and strolled over to the main entrance, where he found the front door wedged open with a brick, despite a notice warning the occupants to keep it locked for security reasons. He went in and made his way up to flat twenty-two on the third floor of the four-storey block. The door was opened by a dark-haired woman wearing patterned leggings and a T-shirt. She was barefoot, flushed and out of breath.

'Sorry,' she gasped. 'I've just come in from a run. It's my day off today.' Barry spotted the slight gap between her two front teeth.

'I'm impressed,' he replied, showing his warrant card. 'It's good to see someone doing their best to keep fit. I'm DI Barry Marsh from Dorset police. I'm looking for a Linda Brooker who lived on the Quantocks for a short while some years ago. Is that you?'

She gave a cautious nod.

'It's possible that you may be able to help us with an investigation. Can I come in for a couple of minutes?'

'I suppose so. I was about to have a quick shower and a cup of tea, but that can wait, I guess. I'll need to go out in about an hour, to pick up my son from school. What did you want exactly?'

Barry followed her into a neat living room whose windows looked out towards the town centre.

'I understand you lived at Heathfield Farm for a while about twelve years ago. Is that right?'

She turned away. 'I think I'll put the kettle on. Do you want a cup of tea?'

'Fine. Thanks.'

She went into the kitchen, leaving Barry to have a quick look around the lounge. He saw a couple of framed photos, both of a young boy. Barry guessed they were taken about a year apart. There were no other photos on display, so he went across for a closer look. The young lad bore a marked resemblance to Linda, but with a slightly turned-up nose, rather like Babs Atkins. Interesting. The same shelf bore several cards, closely crammed together, all wishing Logan a happy birthday. Barry wondered how long they'd been there. They had the slightly curled look of cards that had stood for several weeks.

Linda returned to the room with two steaming mugs.

'You didn't answer my question,' Barry said.

She sighed. 'Yes, I was there. For nearly two years. It was a long time ago, though.'

'Tell me about it.' He took a sip of tea.

'It was a sort of commune,' she said, 'run by a guy called Timothy. A bit religious but not one of the mainstream ones. He had a down on those, so he made up his own. He was a bit driven. Sort of obsessed. Why do you want to know?'

'Did you also know someone called Andrew Atkins?'

He watched her eyes flicker. 'Vaguely.'

'It's Andrew I'm trying to trace. Do you know where he is?'

'No.' The answer was too quick and too sharp.

'Is that your son in the photos on the shelf?'

'Yes. Logan. He's six.'

'Is Andrew the father?'

'What makes you think that?' Now she sounded really wary.

'The photos. He looks a bit like Babs Atkins, particularly his nose. And there's a card from her there. "From Granny Babs," it says.' He paused. 'I didn't notice one from Andrew, though.'

Linda stared into her tea. 'Haven't seen him in five years. He disappeared when Logan was a tot.' She took a sip and looked up at Barry. 'Not a great loss. Too fond of the old wacky-baccy. And booze. And anything else he could lay his hands on. He wouldn't consider remembering his own son's birthday important. The only thing of importance to Andy is Andy.'

'Did you stay together after the commune broke up?'

'Sort of. On and off. It went on like that for years. I knew I was being used. He only appeared when he felt like it. Then

I got pregnant. He stayed for a bit longer after that. Then he said the strain of having to look after a baby was doing his head in. I went back to work, see, soon after Logan was born. All Andy had to do was look after Logan, but he couldn't even do that properly. Waster. He stuck around for a year, then just fucked off without a word. Bastard.'

'I need to find him, Linda. If you know where he might be, please tell me.' Barry waited.

She remained silent for a while. 'We did get a couple of cards the first year. I think he was in Poole then, maybe working on a local farm. He mentioned something about it in one of the cards.'

'Linda, have you any idea why Babs didn't tell me about Logan? She's sent him a birthday card — it's there on the shelf — but she never said anything to me about him.'

Linda shrugged, as if dislodging Babs herself. 'She's an odd one. She lives a fantasy, a world of posh romance stories where everything's always perfect. Abandoned kids and partners don't exist for Babs. I don't think the rest of her family know about Logan. Her other grandchildren don't know they've got another cousin. It's sick, isn't it, the way some people cover up what they think's a skeleton in the cupboard or something? She's too churchy for me. I can't stomach her. She never lifted a finger to help when we needed it. Now she thinks she can get round me by sending a card and a few quid on his birthday. Well, fuck her.'

Barry left the flat feeling depressed. Why did so many relationships end up like Linda's, full of bitterness and resentment? He made his way to the car, still bemused, and headed to the motorway, where he turned his mind back to the investigation. Maybe some of the answers would be found back in Dorset after all, if Andrew was still working in the Poole area. It was a big if, though. Maybe he should pay another visit to Linda in a few days' time. With any luck, his questions might have brought long-forgotten memories to the surface.

* * *

Sophie had suggested that Barry should pay a visit to Judy Price, but not when Tim Brotherton was around. He checked that she was still on duty at the Weston-Super-Mare hospital and drove there. Would she open up to him? The boss thought there was a good chance. She'd have had two days to mull over the revelations about Tim's background. That was about the right amount of time. Leave it too long and there was a chance she'd come to terms with it.

He arrived just as Judy was returning to the ward office after dealing with an emergency.

'What now?' she said wearily

'When he spoke to my boss on Saturday, Mr Brotherton denied ever having been in the Wareham area and gave the impression he hadn't visited Dorset recently either. She wanted me to check if you knew anything about that. We're particularly interested in two weekends ago.'

She remained silent.

'I take it you have some doubts,' he said eventually.

'I wouldn't have known any different, except that he brought back some Dorset cheeses. I'm a cheese lover, you see.'

'And that was what caused you to wonder if he was telling the truth?'

'Yes. I had no other reason to disbelieve him. My first thought was that he could have bought them in any deli. Blue Vinny is available in a lot of places nowadays, but the paper bag it came in was from a deli in Wareham. A bit of a giveaway, wasn't it?'

'I'm grateful for your honesty.'

Judy shrugged. 'There's no future in our relationship. He lied to me. He's always been too secretive, and it was obvious on Saturday that he's kept major parts of his past hidden from me. I'm just finding it all a bit much. I still don't think he's capable of violence though. I'm sure he wouldn't kill or even assault anyone. He's harmless, I'm sure of it. A bit of a lost soul really.'

'You were right to tell me. We'd have found out in the end and it would have cast suspicion on you. Where is he now?' Barry asked.

140

'I don't know. He was out when I got up this morning. He's been sleeping in the spare room since Saturday, so I don't know what time he left.'

Barry didn't like the sound of this. 'Would you trust me with the keys to your house? I should go there right away.'

'I'll come with you. I'm on my lunch break now and it's only a couple of minutes in the car. I didn't look to see whether his stuff was still there before I left. If he's taken all his belongings, it puts a different complexion on things, doesn't it?'

Their worries were unfounded. Tim's clothes and possessions were still in her house. His clothes were in their usual places and his books still sat on the shelves.

'It looks as though he intends to come back,' Barry said.

'Yes, but when?'

'I'll have to find out. We need to know where he is.'

Barry called Tim's mobile number. It was finally answered with a grunt.

'Mr Brotherton? This is DI Marsh. Where are you?'

He listened. 'That's all very well, but I thought my colleagues made it clear a couple of days ago that we need to know your whereabouts. You can't just wander off without telling us. You need to return to Ms Price's house this evening or let us know if you're staying somewhere else. We're in the middle of a complex murder investigation here and can't have key witnesses wandering off. Judy had no idea where you were. Why didn't you leave her a note? Or get a message to us?'

Barry put his phone back in his pocket and turned to Judy. 'He says he's with a client. I'll need to go and check that he's where he says he is and make clear to him that he either stays put or I stick him in custody.'

'So he is a suspect, then?' Judy looked grim.

'Of course. Particularly in the light of what you told me. I can call in on him on my way to the hospital. By the way, does he have a lumberjack-style shirt?'

She raised her eyebrows. 'A couple. But don't most men? Don't you all like to imagine you're rugged outdoor types, able to live off the land? But I don't think he's worn one for ages. I do the ironing and I'd have noticed. Why?'

'Just a line of enquiry. What type of car does he own?'

'A blue Renault. It's falling apart, but he doesn't have the money to replace it yet.'

* * *

Barry hated post-mortems like this, where there was no body as such, just a collection of bones. He found it impossible to visualise them as a flesh-and-blood person, someone who'd lived and breathed, laughed and loved. They seemed so devoid of any humanity, just a specimen. He remained in the background and let Polly Nelson take charge. She was the SIO, after all. The examination didn't take long. After all, what was there to examine?

'Is it a woman?' Polly asked. 'You can confirm that?'

The pathologist looked up at her. 'A youngish woman, I'd say, probably between twenty and thirty. Possibly quite slim.' He poked around at the ribcage. 'Several nicks on the bones here, all clustered around the upper thorax region. That kind of mark is left when someone's been stabbed repeatedly.'

'Could there be any other cause?' Polly asked.

'I can't see how. It fits the pattern for this type of assault exactly.'

This was disconcerting. Barry's thoughts began to race. Hadn't Trent Baker inflicted those same injuries on Catherine Templeton?

142

CHAPTER 22: UNDER THE OAK TREE

Monday afternoon

Sergeant Rose Simons and her sidekick, PC George Warrander, pulled off the Arne road onto the grass verge and climbed out of their squad car.

'Why are we up at this end of the county again, boss?' George asked. 'You'd think it'd be better to call out the local crews.'

''Cause we're the cream, Georgie boy. Everyone knows it from the chief constable downwards. Something special needed? Call in the super-team. Oh, shit.'

Rose was still half-sitting in the car, with her legs and feet outside. She was examining the sole of her right shoe.

'Bloody dogs. Even bloodier dog owners. Why can't they clear their mess up like they're meant to? Is it too much to ask?' She wiped her foot on a nearby clump of grass and looked up at her partner. 'Don't you even think about laughing. Not even the slightest smirk. If you know what's good for you, you'll turn around and keep walking.'

'Yeah, but I don't know where I'm going.'

'Don't be a wimp, George. Of course you do. We're heading off on that footpath just ahead and then up the slope. They want us to look for that dog collar. Apparently, a kiddie out with the family found one last week and chucked it up into a tree. Can you believe it? What kind of kids are people breeding nowadays? Is there some kind of deviancy gene incorporating itself into human DNA to make the little buggers behave like that?' She stood wobbling on one foot and examined her shoe. 'Okay, I'm back in business — hold on a mo.'

She caught up with George as he reached a stile and followed him across, breathing heavily. 'Are these things getting higher? They are, aren't they?'

He decided not to answer. Any remark that cast aspersions on her fitness would be sure to set off a tantrum that could well last the rest of the day.

'The report said the family were about half a mile west of the crime scene on the shoreline. That would have put it just beyond the search zone by my reckoning. What kind of little toad kicks a piece of evidence nearly half a mile and then lobs it up into a tree? Needs a clip round the ear if you ask me. At least the father phoned when he heard we were looking for a lost dog collar, so someone in the family has a sense of social responsibility. Maybe there's hope for the kid yet.'

'How are we going to spot it if it's up a tree?' George asked.

'It's an oak, apparently. Standing by itself. And that's where you come in, young George. I'll give you a leg up and you can indulge in a spot of tree climbing, just like when you were a lad. Pity you didn't bring your shorts and your Spiderman T-shirt.'

The long-suffering George plodded on. He had never enjoyed climbing trees. They passed the clearing where the tramp had lived, then the spot where his body was found. Up the slope to the ridge top, then down towards the shoreline where they followed the estuary water inland towards Wareham.

George stopped and pointed. 'That could be it, a couple of hundred yards ahead.'

They approached the oak and stood looking up at it.

'This'll be like a needle in a haystack,' George said. 'It's huge. And look at all those leaves. It could be anywhere up there.'

Rose shook her head, looking smug. 'Only if it hasn't already come down. There was a bit of a strong wind a couple of nights ago. Fingers crossed.'

Their luck was in. After about ten minutes spent poking around in the undergrowth beneath the tree, Rose spotted something glinting in what little sunlight had managed to make its way through the foliage. There it was. A small, frayed collar, with a steel cylinder still attached.

'Ooh, look at you, you beauty,' Rose said. 'Time to break out the champagne, George. Let's have a toast.'

George dutifully extracted the bottle of water and two plastic cups from his rucksack, while Rose carefully slid the dog collar into an evidence bag. They sat on an exposed tree root.

'What could be better, eh?' Rose said. 'Sitting here in dappled shade, sipping a drink in the company of a young, luscious beauty like me. You are such a lucky guy, George. I hope you realise that.'

George wondered, not for the first time, whether it was time to put in for a transfer.

* * *

Dave Nash, the head of Dorset's forensic team, eyed the dog collar with distaste. It was badly frayed, grubby, and the small cylinder was hanging by a thread. A technician had already carried out a DNA swab and a fingerprint test.

'How do we know it's the right one?' he asked, poking at it with a pen.

'Oh, come on, Dave.' Rose was scornful. 'It was in the right place and matches the description. You can just see a bit of the original red colour through the dirt, which is how our illustrious witness described it. And I, for one, am not going to argue with *her*. It'd be more than my life's worth. Just get it checked over, will you? We haven't even opened it up to see what's inside, and you know what a nosey bugger I am.'

Without deigning to reply, Dave slid on latex gloves and attempted to unscrew the capsule. It refused to budge.

'It's jammed,' he said, rather unnecessarily. 'I don't know whether it's due to dirt and grime or if it's been overtightened.'

But with a vice and a small pair of pliers, he managed to unscrew the top. He hooked out a tiny slip of paper and examined it under a magnifying glass.

'Okay. We have something. Take a look.'

He handed the glass to Rose, who peered at the tiny scrap.

If I get lost and you find me, please contact Katie Templar. Or Kirkham House, St Ann Street, Salisbury.

Rose smiled. 'Aha! This is what those 'tec types call a clue. I wonder if the thug who killed the tramp tried to get the top loose but couldn't do it. That might be why he chucked it into the undergrowth. I think we'll head off and see her ladyship. I might get a medal. George might get a choccy bikkie and a pat on the head.'

* * *

With Barry still in Somerset, Sophie decided to send Rae to Salisbury. She knew the city well, having been based there some years earlier, pre-transition, when she'd been an unhappy, over-stressed and confused male rookie detective.

Rae arrived late in the afternoon. The city centre was thronged with schoolchildren waiting noisily at bus stops, mixed with small groups of tourists taking photos of the medieval buildings. Rae threaded her way through the crowds to St Ann Street in one of the oldest parts of the city, close to the immense body of the ancient cathedral. The house was in a narrow street of old, immaculately maintained buildings, all several hundred years old. The white walls of a Tudor-style pub on one corner gleamed in the sunlight. Kirkham House was one of the statelier residences. Rae guessed that it would have been built for a wealthy merchant several centuries ago. Who would live there now? A rich banker or financier? A senior surgeon?

Rae went up to the deep maroon double doors and rang the doorbell. The woman who answered was slim, grey-haired and looked to be in her sixties. She wore a cream blouse and matching linen skirt, and filigree gold jewellery around her throat and wrists. Her pale olive face wore a distant and slightly haughty expression. She said nothing, merely waiting, eyebrows raised slightly.

'I'm Detective Constable Rae Gregson from Dorset police. I'm looking for someone who may remember a Katie Templar from many years ago. Would you be related to her?'

Obviously annoyed at the intrusion, the woman shook her head. She took a step back, made to close the door and then stopped dead. A puzzled look appeared on her face.

'Did you say Katie Templar?' She spoke in clipped, modulated tones.

'Yes, that's right. Did you know her? Did she live here by any chance?'

The woman put out a hand to the wall as if to steady herself. 'She didn't live here, not as such. She was here for a short while, many years ago. She was my son's girlfriend. They came for a visit before they went away together.'

'Your son? What's his name, please?'

'Paul. Paul Prentice-Jones. But we haven't seen him since that visit. He left with that Katie girl and we haven't seen or heard from him since. He'd sometimes talked about going to Scotland.' She looked down and said softly, 'We argued and some awful things were said.'

Rae thought fast. 'Can I come in? I may have some news for you.'

CHAPTER 23: KIRKHAM HOUSE

Tuesday morning

Barry had managed to send the folder containing the commune's accounts to Dorset headquarters by overnight courier so, by late morning Rae was in the CID office in Bournemouth, discussing them with DS Lydia Pillay.

'I've got this money stuff that came from the farm. I'm not sure that it needs an expert like you to make sense of it, but the boss was insistent.'

'I guess she wants to make me feel useful. Basic psychology, Rae. Actually, I'm glad. Kevin is running out of things for me to do and what he does find is all pretty low-level stuff. It'll be a welcome change.'

'How are you getting on?' Rae asked.

Lydia shrugged. 'Okay. I do mornings here, then go for physio most afternoons. I've been told I can start running again next week, which'll give me a big boost — or else it'll finish me off. Let's have a look at this stuff and see what we've got.'

The two detectives spent the next hour working through the contents of the notebooks, bank statements, and other bits and pieces the folder contained. Financial pressures could have devastating consequences for personal relationships. Was that what had caused the commune to break up? Katie Templar seemed to have provided the initial cash that got the group up and running, as well as the farm itself. Was she being pressurised to cough up more money as difficulties surfaced? Or were the stresses created by the arrival of Trent Baker the cause of the group fracturing in the way it did?

Several things became apparent. For the first year, the farm seemed to pay its own way, though only just. Rae remembered that Babs Atkins had spoken of reasonably good crop yields. Katie had inherited the farm as a going concern, complete with animals and crops already in the fields, so it was no surprise that the first year was a success. But Babs had also surmised that once the group was forced to rely on its own efforts and experience, the situation deteriorated. This showed up in the figures. Katie had transferred several lump sums of her own money into the commune account, and this had continued, at intervals, for a further eighteen months. Much of it had been spent on essential supplies and vet bills but towards the end several sums had been transferred out again to a different account. Who by? Had it been authorised? It wasn't clear.

'I need to check the mandate details with the bank, if they've still got a record from that long ago,' Lydia said. 'It would have been sensible to have three or four signatories to the accounts, requiring two people to authorise a payment. But we can't clarify that from the chequebook stubs that we have. I'll have a go now.' She picked up her phone.

Rae took the stubs across to the window and examined each one carefully. For the first two years the handwriting looked consistent — thin and flowing. Was it like the writing on the letter by the mysterious Katie? Rae checked her copy. It certainly looked the same. But later on, the writing in the chequebook changed entirely, becoming thicker, bolder. And, finally, two cheque stubs that looked scruffy, dashed off, hard to decipher. Payments made out to almost indecipherable names that may have begun with the letter *B*. It was as if the names had been deliberately scrawled so as to make it well-nigh impossible to read them. Brotherton? Baker? The amounts were clear enough, though, and they were substantial. It meant that three different people had acted as treasurer during the lifetime of the commune, with Katie Templar being the first. Interesting. Did the last cheque she signed correspond to the date she disappeared? At least it provided a basis upon which to work.

She went over to the corner of the room where the tea things were kept and made two mugs of coffee. She set them down on Lydia's desk just as she finished her call to the bank.

'It'll take a day or two, but they think they'll still have the mandate history on record somewhere at head office,' Lydia said.

'What's your overall view of the finances? Can you tell from the stuff that's here?'

Lydia shrugged. 'Can't be absolutely sure, but I'd say they were struggling. They were bound to, even from the off. Too many people for a relatively unproductive farm to support. I did some work on farming fraud when I was in Bath and you get a feel for the financial viability of a farm. It's often related to the number of people relying on it for their livelihood. Looking at the crop-yield figures and the money coming in, this type of place could only just support a single family. How many people were at Heathfield? Do we know?'

'Somewhere in the twenties, we think, but we can't be sure.'

'In that case it was a disaster waiting to happen. There was no way it could support that many people without some other source of income. These sums transferred in by your suspected beneficiary . . . who was she by the way?'

'We're pretty sure her name was Katie Templar. She inherited the farm from an uncle. We're only just starting to find out a bit more about her,' Lydia said, taking a sip from her cup.

150

'Well, the amounts here are nowhere near what would have been needed to keep that many people fed, clothed and comfortable. Which begs the question, were they getting money from another source? If so, what was it and why doesn't it appear in these accounts?'

'The only way we can find out is by confronting Tim Brotherton. Apparently, he went walkabout for a while yesterday, but Barry's got him pinned down now.'

'Sign of a guilty conscience,' Lydia said. 'This Katie had already coughed up quite a lot of her own money. Maybe she drew a line at some point, refused to give more. Do we know anything else about her?'

'You mean her personal finances and stuff? That's my other task, trying to track down where she lived and what she did before she joined in with the commune lot. Maybe she was the only one of them with any money. I wonder if she came from a wealthy background,' Rae said.

'Do you think she might have been killed because of the commune's money issues?' Lydia asked.

Rae shrugged. 'It's a possibility, isn't it? Assuming the body is hers. We won't know until we get a match with dental records or DNA. My own guess is there was more to it than that. This guy Trent Baker seems to leave a trail of chaos and violence in his wake wherever he goes. And we don't really know about Brotherton himself. He was the messianic leader right from the start, according to the locals. And it comes through in that leaflet he wrote. The boss reckons he's trying to hide that part of his past. But he'd have taken it badly if his pet project was starting to unravel, wouldn't he? And we've only talked to a couple of other people who were there at the time. Could there have been someone else there who was capable of murder? Someone we don't know about? It's a real problem that it happened so far in the past and they're all so secretive. You'd think a new-age type commune would be more open, more free and easy. Unless they have something to hide.'

Lydia laughed. 'Sex and drugs and rock 'n' roll.'

'Don't get me started,' Rae said. 'The boss was talking about that. She reckons that's exactly what a lot of these communes were about. I had a good look round at the weekend when I was there, but there was no evidence of cannabis production, or any other type of drug. They might have been users but there's no evidence they were manufacturing the stuff.'

'Where is she by the way? She was supposed to call in this morning, but she phoned to cancel. She sounded as if she was in a rush.'

Rae pulled a face. 'She's always in a rush, ever since she got promoted. Too much to do and not enough time. I worry about her.' She paused. 'She's gone to Salisbury this morning to interview Paul Prentice's parents — at least, the people who might be his parents. I saw the mother yesterday. She clammed up completely. She was in shock, I suppose. They're a bit out of my league, to be honest. Apparently, he's a retired senior judge. And she seemed so detached and distant. It was really strange. With Barry still in Somerset, the boss decided to go herself. She asked me if I'd prefer to continue questioning her, but I chickened out. This is the top layer of the British establishment we're talking about here, and I'm not up to it. You might have coped okay.'

'I doubt it. What? A gay feminist with a Hindu upbringing? I think I trump you in the anti-establishment stakes. You're only trans.' Lydia laughed.

* * *

'Lady Prentice-Jones?' Sophie had done her homework and made sure she used the correct form of address. 'I'm Detective Superintendent Sophie Allen from Dorset police. You briefly met one of the junior members of my team yesterday. May we talk?'

'Of course. Come in.' The woman did not betray the slightest sign of emotion.

152

Sophie was shown through to a sitting room at the rear of the house, beautifully decorated and furnished — fine art on the walls, a collection of delicate porcelain adorning the surfaces and a grand piano occupying one corner. The French windows were open, giving a view out towards an immaculately tended lawn and garden. A grey-haired man rose from an armchair where he'd been reading a newspaper and came across, hand extended. He looked puzzled. 'Have we met? You look familiar.'

'Yes, several times when I've appeared in your court. But I think the most recent occasion was about four years ago when we both appeared as guest speakers at a seminar on law and justice at Exeter University. You were about to retire, if I remember rightly.'

'Oh yes. My life has changed quite dramatically since then. Less to do and far more time to do it in. I'm sure I keep getting under Marion's feet. Sit down, please. We have some tea or coffee ready. I must apologise. We usually have a housekeeper here during the day, but she's on holiday at the moment. The agency girl we booked to replace her doesn't seem to have turned up yet, but Marion is coping marvellously.'

Sophie smiled. Rae had been right. This was a different world, inhabited by people who had housekeepers, cooks, au-pairs, gardeners, chauffeurs, to take care of the day to day tasks. What would they know of the managed chaos of most people's lives?

'It's a lovely house,' she said.

'Yes, we do love it. We've been here for nigh on twenty years, haven't we, darling?' He looked across at his wife, who still seemed distracted. And no wonder. The news that Rae had delivered the previous day must have hit them like a bombshell.

'Take a seat.' Sir Roger waved vaguely at a chair set to one side of an ornate fireplace. He settled himself down opposite while his wife, Marion, perched nervously on the edge of a nearby couch.

'The news that DC Gregson brought yesterday must have come as a shock,' Sophie began.

'Yes. We thought Paul was somewhere near the Scottish Borders. He'd sometimes talked about settling there in the years before he vanished, maybe setting up a small, self-sufficient farm.'

'Rae would have told you that we're treating this as a murder enquiry and that Paul had been living rough in Dorset for many years. We need to get to the bottom of his disappearance. When was the last time you saw him?'

'As Marion told your officer yesterday, he came calling with a young woman in tow. They'd been to London for some reason and arrived here totally unexpectedly. We had a dinner party that evening with some important guests, so it was rather inconvenient. We'd never seen the girl before, and she looked rather dishevelled. Ill, almost. Paul looked strained. We made a dreadful blunder, I'm afraid, and offered to pay for them to stay in a local hotel instead of putting them up here. Paul was not pleased. I suppose we can see the error of that decision now, but neither of us realised that they were both under a good deal of strain. It must have seemed rather unfeeling to them.'

Sophie looked at Marion. 'And you're fairly certain that the young woman's name was Katie Templar?'

'Yes. It took me a few moments to remember it yesterday when your young constable came to call. But yes, that was her name. How did you trace her to us?'

'Paul's dog had a small owner's canister attached to its collar. It had a slip of paper inside with the name Katie Templar on it, and this address. Our problem is that the dog is only about five or six years old. We think Paul put that slip of paper inside to provide us with key information should anything happen to him. It's less obvious than having it engraved on a disk. We wonder if he suspected that someone was looking for him and meant him harm. What my colleague didn't say is that we found the body of a young woman at the weekend, buried on a farm in the Quantock Hills in Somerset. We think it has been there for at least a decade, and that it's Katie Templar, but we haven't yet managed to confirm that.'

Marion looked puzzled. 'Why would she be buried on a farm? How did she die?'

'It looks as though she was murdered.'

There was a shocked silence.

'It wouldn't have been Paul. It couldn't have been. He was clearly besotted with her,' Marion protested.

'We're still at an early stage of the investigation, so we can't rule anything out as yet. But from what we've learned so far, it seems that they were indeed strongly attracted to each other.'

The couple glanced at each other, and some unspoken agreement passed between them.

Prentice's father cleared his throat. 'You'll be wanting to know why there was so much ill-feeling when they left that he never contacted us again.' He was speaking to Sophie, but his eyes were on his wife.

'That would be helpful, yes,' Sophie said.

There was a pause before Marion spoke, even more quietly than before. 'They'd been to London so that she could have an abortion. We found out the next morning when they called again. I still cannot abide the thought of someone committing such an act. To me, abortion is murder. I told them so. I said they were murderers, and that they'd committed the ultimate sin and I could never forgive them. Paul must have known how I'd feel. It's a key part of my religious belief.'

Sophie looked closely at her. There was something else that had not been said, she was sure of it.

'Was Paul the father?'

Marion shook her head. 'No. It was someone else in the group they were living with in Somerset. But Paul was smitten with her. He'd helped her with all the arrangements and even gone with her to the clinic. Apparently, he'd planned for them to stay here for a few days while she recovered, but

155

they left when I told them what I thought. I can't compromise my moral beliefs, even where my own son is concerned.' Even now, all those years later, Marion's expression was determined, uncompromising.

Sophie looked at Paul's father. He looked miserable and defeated. Sophie guessed that he didn't feel the same way as his wife but had deferred to her out of loyalty. And had continued to do so for more than a decade.

'Did Paul go into a career after he left university?' Sophie asked.

'Yes,' Marion said. 'He was in an investment bank of some kind, but he didn't like to speak about it. He felt it was immoral in some way. He was talking about working in another field entirely when he was here that time. As I said, he mentioned farming.'

'We're having problems tracing any information about Katie Templar. Can you remember anything about her that might be useful to us?'

'She was a bright young woman, from what Paul told us,' the father said. 'She had a first in economics from Durham University. I think her family originally lived in Bath, but her parents died in a car crash when she was young. She was brought up on a farm by an uncle, if I remember rightly.'

Marion frowned at him. 'How did you know that? Paul never told me.'

'I tried to talk to him just as they were leaving. I wanted to say how sorry I was. Sadly, it didn't work.' He shook his head.

Marion glared at him. 'I refuse to apologise for my beliefs.'

'He was our son, and I loved him,' Paul's father said quietly.

'Do you know how they met?' Sophie asked.

'At university,' he said. 'Paul was there for a year, doing his master's. He already had a first degree in history.'

A charged silence ensued. Sophie cleared her throat. 'Can one or both of you come down to Dorchester to identify him? I can take you down now if you like and get a driver to bring you back.'

'That won't be necessary. I can drive. We have no other engagements today, do we, Marion?' He waited for his wife to speak. 'What made you think it was Paul? Was his name on file somewhere, or did someone know him?'

'The latter. In fact, it was my daughter. She'd been keeping an eye on him for several years apparently, without telling anybody, and she got to know him quite well. She's looking after his dog.'

Marion said quickly, 'I don't think we can keep a dog here, even if it was his. It would create too many difficulties. We're away so much, you see.'

Sophie chose not to say anything.

CHAPTER 24: OLD FRIENDS

Wednesday morning

Her morning shower over, Catherine Templeton went into her bedroom, threw on some clothes, drew back her curtains and gazed out onto a street glistening with rain. Just as forecast, the warm, sunny spell was over, to be replaced by the usual British weather of sunshine and showers.

She was still uneasy, even though the evening out with Russell Poulter had been a qualified success. She knew what the problem was — the thought of Trent Baker back on the streets and devising more malevolent schemes. How had she ever managed to become embroiled with that evil piece of lowlife? A combination of naivety and alcohol, paired with her usual inability to discriminate. She was a poor judge of character and managed to get herself into tricky situations far too easily.

Within days of her arrival at the farm they'd become lovers. The affair had continued on and off for some time, until it began to dawn on her what he was really like, this monster with the angel face. He was disruptive, manipulative and seemed to want to cause as much mischief as he could within the commune. She came to the conclusion that he'd never grown up.

At first she'd believed that he was Tim's official second-in-command and had been since the beginning. She soon discovered that he'd arrived six months after the commune had been set up and that many of the group members were very wary of him but daren't say so to the others. She had been shocked to discover that the man she'd been sleeping with every night was so devious. Still, he had his uses, and she succeeded in keeping him as an ally for a while longer. Then came the gradual realisation that the commune was falling apart, riven by small factions, each pursuing their own agenda as the whole enterprise languished. Tim, the supposed leader, kept himself aloof. When she saw what was happening, Catherine decided to act. It was right up her street, using her guile to influence a man into seeing things from a different perspective. She got to work on him.

In fact, there had been more to the group breaking up than mere cash-flow worries. She'd sensed genuine fear among some of the people who'd begun to make plans to leave. She exploited the situation a little, so as to worm her way into a position of influence. She knew that several of the original members had already left silently in the night. Was that the cause of the unease that she sensed? It needed someone strong to take charge, but not Trent Baker with his double-dealing. She tried to work her way into a more senior role but was just too late. Everyone was making preparations to leave and couldn't be persuaded to change their minds. Lean, hungry and suspicious, they slipped out of the farm and down the lane with their meagre possessions slung on their backs. And as she watched them go, one by one, Catherine began to realise that unless she also got out fast, she might be left alone with a handful of fanatics and mad Timothy, Andy and Trent Baker. So she too began to make secret plans. It was a time of shifting alliances. She realised now that she'd misread the situation and had left it too late.

So here she was, twelve years later, being forced against her will to think again about that time. She'd thought the farm had been forgotten years ago and that she was a new person with a normal future. Then the police had come calling, with a story about the body of a woman having been found in the woods near the farm. Catherine knew who this was. Now she had to work out if anyone else suspected that she knew. And if they did, was she in danger?

She took one last look out of her bedroom window before heading down to put the kettle on. A man was walking slowly along the opposite side of the street, scanning the houses on Catherine's side. She stepped back from the window and watched him progress. He arrived opposite her own house and stopped. He seemed to be looking directly at her. Catherine gasped and stood right back from the window. Her doorbell rang. As if drawn by some invisible force, she went downstairs and opened the door.

'Catherine? It's me, Tim Brotherton, from the farm all those years ago. I heard that you've been trying to contact me.'

'I know who you are,' she hissed. 'And I most certainly haven't been trying to contact you. Are you mad, coming here like this?'

'Can I come in for a moment? It's important.'

That bloody commune. It was beginning to dominate her life again and was driving her round the bend. She took another look at him. He'd aged, and not well. Gone was the look of arrogant self-confidence, gone the zeal. He looked tired and worn down, thinner than she remembered.

'What do you want?' she asked through the barely open door.

'Look, we can't talk properly with that chain across. Can't you let me in?'

'No. Say what you have to say. I'll listen and then decide. I ought to warn you that I'm in contact with the police. They're keeping a safety watch on me.'

'It's about Trent Baker. I think he might be stirring up trouble. I thought you needed to know.'

'Idiot. Why do you think the police are keeping an eye on me? For fuck's sake, Tim. It's me he assaulted and nearly killed, not you. That's the reason he's been locked up and out of everyone's hair for the past ten years. Did you come round offering me help then, when I really needed it? Fuck, no. Not a word. You can go take a running jump, the lot of you.'

'Look, I'm sorry. I thought it was best not to meddle, not at the time. Honestly, what could I have done? The court found him guilty and he was put away. If I'd have been around, I'd have been called in and that could have made the whole case against him more complicated. The press would have had a field day. You know how they love cult scandals. Trent might even have got off.'

Enraged, Catherine took the chain off and flung the door back. 'What do you mean, got off? He attacked me with a knife, stabbed me three times and nearly killed me. How could he have got off? Are you saying that attack could somehow have been justified, you twisted bit of shit? For God's sake!'

Brotherton held his hands up in mock surrender. 'That's not what I meant, and you know it.' He glanced around. 'For Christ's sake, Catherine, all your neighbours are watching. And if you must know, the police have been round to see me too. I don't bloody know what's been going on and I need to talk it all over with someone. You're the obvious person. Please. Can we talk? Sensibly?'

She stepped back to let him come in. 'But don't try anything. Life changed for me after that assault and I learned that I had to defend myself. No other bastard would hurt me again. I'll make mincemeat of you if you as much as come too close.'

She pointed to the kitchen, taking a quick look out of the door as she closed it. He'd been right. Several neighbours were at their windows. She gave them a cheery wave. She took a shoulder bag off a nearby coat hook, went through to the kitchen, told Tim where to sit, and perched opposite him.

'I've got pepper spray in here, so you'd better keep your distance. What do you want?'

'I'm not going to harm you, Catherine,' he said. 'Why on earth would I? I never hurt anyone back at the farm, and I'm not going to start now. Can't we just talk like old friends?'

'You do know the police have found a body up there? Any idea who it is?'

Tim shook his head. 'The police haven't said.'

Catherine almost shouted. 'For God's sake, Tim. I'm not stupid. You knew everything that went on in that place. I picked up on some odd vibes before I left and I knew there was some kind of shadow lurking over the place. Did something happen that you covered up?'

He shook his head. 'I said I don't know who it is or how they got there. Was it even anything to do with us? Maybe it predates our time there.'

'Okay, let me rephrase that. Have you *guessed* who it is?' She watched him carefully.

'No, but I'm sure they think it's Katie Templar. Do you know anything?'

She snorted. 'Of course not. Have you had a formal interview with the cops?'

He nodded. 'They've been all over my place. I've even had to hand in my passport to stop me doing a runner. It's all too much. First Prentice being killed and now this. I can't believe it.'

'Haven't the police warned you off trying to contact anyone from those days? Doesn't it look suspicious, you coming here?'

'What do you mean?' he said.

She laughed. 'You're just the same, aren't you? So bound up in yourself and your own beliefs that you can't see anything from another person's point of view. The police will be watching you, idiot, and then the first thing you do is come calling on me, someone from the old days who you haven't seen for more than a decade. I mean, how's it going to look to them?'

'Yeah, but you're in the clear. You wouldn't have been involved in any of the other conflicts, not with the fights you were having with Trent. That was enough to wear anybody out.'

She folded her arms. 'Look, this is all very nice, but I have to get to work.'

'What do you do?' he asked.

'I'm an assistant pharmacist. Don't you even remember that? You said I'd be useful on the farm. I could help treat the sick. If you ask me, the sickest person there was you know who, and he was sick in the head. And I'm not sure you were much better.' She stood up. 'I don't know what you've come here for. Do you even know?'

'Not really. I'm feeling desperate, that's all. I just wanted to talk to someone.' His voice shook.

Serves you bloody right, she thought as she almost shoved him out of the door. He stopped on the threshold.

'Um, I don't suppose Andy has been in touch, has he?'

'Who?'

'Andy Atkins. You remember, he came from round there, more or less ran the farming part of the operation. Medium height, mousey hair with a turned-up nose.'

She shook her head. Was he really so lacking in insight? 'Why would he want to get in touch? Haven't seen him in years.'

Tim shrugged. 'I just wondered.'

Should she tell him the latest news or let him stew in ignorance? He was clearly anxious. He looked almost ill with it. Maybe she should give him one less thing to worry about. 'You don't have to worry about Trent Baker, not for a while at least. He's back in custody. The police phoned me with the news yesterday. He breached his parole conditions by trying to stir up trouble for me and was stupid enough to make it obvious. With his history of violence, they couldn't just leave him running around free.'

Catherine waited until she'd shut the door behind him and then leant back against the wall. Tim was one worried man. Were the police fingering him for the deaths? She breathed a sigh of relief.

* * *

Trent Baker was seething with impotent rage. To find himself back in custody only a few short months after his release from prison was just outrageous. It wasn't as if he'd broken any laws. All he'd done was wind a couple of people up a bit. Where was the harm in that, for Christ's sake? People were just too fucking touchy. Didn't anyone get a joke anymore? Did they even have a sense of humour?

He sat on the narrow bed in his cell, his back against the wall, trying to think of a way out. Was he sorry for his actions? No. Should he lie and tell them he was sorry? You bet. But how to go about creating a convincing story? That was the key. What line should he take? Maybe the years in prison had caused him to lose his sense of judgement, such that he'd made a gross miscalculation. He really and truly hadn't meant any harm. How would that sound? He could always switch on his wide-eyed, innocent look. That might help. The problem would come if they started to ask him questions, like why he'd decided to spike Catherine's date. Would they try to find out where he'd got his information from? How would he deal with that? If they ever got a whiff of the fact he'd been inside her house, poking around in her possessions, he'd be back inside faster than shit sliding down a sewer. He needed to do a lot more hard thinking, which wasn't something that came easy to him. Trent Baker was instinctive, someone who lived for the moment. Why couldn't other people see that? He sighed, scowled and tried hard to switch his brain into supercharged mode, a mental state that Catherine herself had told him about all those years ago. He didn't know what she'd been talking about then and he didn't now. Maybe it was down to all the junk he'd consumed at the time. Did that mean his brain was permanently screwed?

CHAPTER 25: NICE GUY

Wednesday morning

Barry Marsh looked at the clock. Trent Baker was due to meet his supervising officer about now for an emergency review meeting to discuss the extent to which he'd broken the terms of his parole. The outcome would be important for the police here in Taunton. Polly Nelson hadn't been sure what the decision would be. Had Baker clearly broken enough regulations to justify a return to prison? She'd thought the evidence was debatable. It would all depend on his performance in the interview, and that was an unknown factor. Baker's assigned SO had retired the week before and the new SO would be meeting him for the first time. Polly herself, as a senior detective in the local police force, had some input into the process but the final decision wouldn't be hers. Barry thought it likely that Baker would be given the benefit of the doubt, along with another chance to stick to his parole, but it was no good speculating. If Baker was deemed fit to continue his parole they'd just have to adapt and put improved protection measures in place for Catherine Templeton. As a visiting detective from Dorset, it really wasn't his problem. He needed to turn his attention to other aspects of the case and wait until Polly returned with news of the review.

He finished his coffee and considered the remaining problem, finding Andrew Atkins. What was the man doing now and, more importantly, where? Would he have stayed in farm work or would he have left agriculture like so many others? Barry wasn't making any progress in tracing the elusive Atkins in Somerset and was wondering where else he could be. It was always possible that his disappearance was down to rather more than a change of location. Could he be dead — one more to add to the list of commune victims? First, a tramp killed a couple of weeks ago, then a young woman twelve years earlier. Were there other bodies waiting to be discovered, each linked to the commune on the farm? Unless, of course, Atkins was in Dorset. He could be the tramp's killer, the man Pauline Stopley saw clambering over a fence near Prentice's place on the day of his death and possibly glimpsed by Jade Allen during her early morning visit there more than a week later. Barry decided to call Rae Gregson, who was still in Dorset, to see if she'd had any success with the search for Atkins. However, the news she gave him concerned a separate line of enquiry.

'I've found a pharmacy where a member of staff sold some antiseptic ointment to a man who'd been quite badly scratched by a dog,' she said. 'He had marks on his face and arms. She told him that he should see a doctor about it, but he seemed reluctant and wouldn't say much about how it had happened. The dates match. It was on the Sunday, the day after we think Prentice was killed.'

'Whereabouts?'

'Blandford.'

Barry thought for a few moments. Blandford was only half an hour's drive from the murder scene. Could there be something in it?

'Does the description match?'

'I think so. Medium height, jeans and a lumberjack shirt.'

'It fits what I've found out about this Andrew Atkins. It doesn't prove anything, of course. It could also describe Tim

166

Brotherton. But we need to trace Atkins. I wonder if he's settled on our patch, in Dorset. Maybe that's why he went there, to trace Prentice, and it's taken this long to find him.'

'Does he have a motive, though?' Rae asked.

Barry ran his fingers through his hair. 'I'm not aware of one yet. But we still don't know exactly what all the friction was about in that commune. All we know is that there was plenty of it. Can you tell the boss when she gets back from her conference and get her opinion? Meanwhile, do what you can to trace this Andrew Atkins character. He might hold the key to everything. I have a couple more leads to follow up here, but I should be back in a day or two. By the way, is there any chance of getting any DNA from that dog collar? Did Dave Nash say?'

'He's hopeful. There were a few specks of blood on it, but they could be from the dog. The results should be back soon.'

The call ended just as Polly Nelson came into the room. Her expression said it all. Baker had been released on parole again.

'It's a bloody mess,' Polly said, switching the kettle on. 'How he wangled his way through that, I don't know.'

'We both know the prisons are bursting at the seams. Putting him back inside uses up one more place. I wonder if the remand officers have been encouraged to keep the re-admittance figures down just to give prisons a bit of elbow room. Maybe they have to be a hundred percent certain before they can send someone back inside. And, let's face it, there was no real proof.'

'Yeah, so instead I've got to find the resources to keep an eye on the Templeton woman so she stays safe while that creep is still out on the streets. What about us and our lack of resources? What do they think we are? Bloody superheroes?'

Barry laughed. 'Aren't we? Oh, I thought we were. Anyway, I need to be off. I'm going to have another chat with Linda Brooker to see if she's remembered any more about life in that commune.'

* * *

Linda worked in a company that made specialist control units for various kinds of machinery. She was an assembly technician in the printed circuit board department and was clearly valued by her employers, judging from the attitude of the manager who greeted Barry. Either that or he was keen to find out why the police were visiting her. If so, his hopes were destined to be dashed. Barry kept quiet.

Linda showed him into a small office.

'I was hoping you might have remembered more about life in the commune since we last chatted,' Barry said. 'Names, relationships, whether people got on with each other, who fell out with who, arguments and so on. But maybe focus on the people who were most influential. Is that okay?'

'Well, I can try,' Linda said rather doubtfully. 'Timothy Brotherton was the leader. We had to call him Timothy, never Tim. He used to get angry with anyone who shortened his name. As if it was that important. Looking back, his whole attitude was a bit patronising, as if he was in on a big secret that no one else knew about. He used to lecture us all on the path to enlightenment.'

'So, who else helped to run things? Do you remember more now?'

She nodded. 'Andy acted as farm manager. He was fine at the start. He'd worked on the farm before the group took over, but just as an ordinary worker. The problem was, he was hopeless at making decisions which wasn't helped by the amount of booze he drank. I hooked up with him pretty early on, but he had other women as well. The commune prided itself on its open relationships. Tim used to say that petty jealousies and possessive thoughts had to be left outside the group. That approach just created chaos. I can see that now.'

'What about Katie Templar? Did you know her?'

'Yeah, she was one of the originals. I think she had something to do with the ownership of the place, but I never found out exactly what. She was with Tim at first, but that went sour for some reason. She hooked up with another guy, but I think there was a big row with Timothy and the other bloke walked out. Katie was like a lost soul for a few months till she left.'

'Do you remember when? When she left, I mean.'

'Not really. I know she always seemed sad. It didn't surprise me that she went.'

Barry took the photo out and showed her. 'Was this her?'

She peered closely at the picture. 'Yeah. And the guy's the one she was with after Timothy. I think his name was Paul. I was trying to remember all this when you called a couple of days ago, but I'm no good at remembering things from that long ago unless I've had time to think things over.'

'What was she like, this Katie Templar?'

Linda said nothing for a few moments. 'A bit posher than the rest of us. Quiet. She was slim and quite tiny, maybe about five two or three? The thing is, she was really nice and very trusting. And that was a mistake, 'cause not all the people there were in it for the common good, if you know what I mean. She got manipulated and sidelined, particularly once she fell out with the great leader.'

'What about her later boyfriend, Paul. Prentice, wasn't it?'

'Yeah, I remember now you've mentioned it. He left after a year or so, just vanished one night. That's when your Katie got really edged out. She was a bit of a lost soul. Paul was okay. He was a decent guy from what I remember. Maybe he could see the writing on the wall before the rest of us. There was a rumour that he was coming back for Katie and they were going to set up somewhere else. I thought he'd managed it because she vanished after another couple of months.'

'And Trent Baker? What was he like?'

Linda laughed. 'The hood with the halo. A devious thug, basically. But you wouldn't think so to look at him. He looked like a choirboy. He had dimples and pure white teeth. He could have been a model if he'd been taller, but he was only about five four.'

'Were you there when Catherine Templeton arrived?'

'I'm a bit fuzzy about the final year. Everything started going wrong and I was boozing more than I should have been. Like most of the others, I guess. There was a tall woman with long, dark hair. Sort of like a gypsy. Was that her?'

'Possibly,' Barry said. 'You can't remember anything else about her?'

'No. Anyway, you seem to know more than me. What is this all about?'

'Haven't you seen the news? Don't you know that we found a body buried on the farm? It's probably been there since the commune days.'

Linda put a hand to her mouth. 'No. Who was it?'

'A woman, probably quite young. About five foot three. Maybe slightly built.'

'Katie?' Linda gasped. 'Oh no. What are you saying? That she didn't leave but died there?'

Barry nodded slowly. 'She was murdered. That's why we need to trace these people, and why I need to find Andy Atkins.'

'I think he may have gone to Dorset to work for the Forestry Commission. About six months ago that was.' She stared at Barry. 'It wouldn't have been him that killed your tramp. He might be a lazy sod, but he'd never hurt anyone, not in that way.'

Barry thanked her for the information. He'd heard it all too many times before, people stating adamantly that someone they knew wouldn't hurt a fly. Yet too often that very same person was subsequently locked up for committing vicious murders. You just couldn't ever tell.

* * *

The warden at the homeless centre proved to be very helpful. He remembered Paul Prentice at once.

'He was here for a couple of days in late March,' he said. 'Nice guy, very polite. He was very self-contained, very controlled. He asked about the bus route west, to Bridgwater. I gave him a timetable.'

'Did he say what he was going there for?' Barry asked.

The man shrugged. 'Not directly, but I got the impression he was still looking for someone, same as before.'

Barry looked surprised. 'He'd been before? Looking for someone, you say?'

'Oh, yes. Every couple of years. It was good to see him again. He always made a contribution to our funds, as well as paying for his room.'

'Are we talking about the same man?' Barry fished out his photo of Prentice and handed it over. This was getting more bizarre by the minute.

'Yes, that's him. I know he slept rough a lot, he told me about it. But he wasn't short of cash. I know this is a homeless hostel, but he always booked a few days in advance and paid us the going rate for a cheap hotel room. And he always put a couple of hundred quid into the kitty.'

'How long did he stay for?' Barry asked.

'Usually it was about a week, maybe a bit less. Not that I saw a lot of him. He'd be out most of the day, off on the bus somewhere — searching, I suppose. But this last time something upset him, though he wouldn't tell me what. He left early. He still insisted on paying the two hundred, though. I went to the bank with him while he got it, 'cause he was in such a hurry to get away.'

'He had a bank account? Can you tell me which bank?'

'Down on North Street in the town centre, the one on the corner. He gave me the money, then went to get a bus back to Dorset. He kept glancing around all the time, as if he was worried that someone was watching him.'

'Did he tell you why?' Barry asked.

'Nope. He clammed up completely. He always had this look, sort of furtive, as if he was haunted by the past. It's common in people who've chosen to turn their backs on society and live rough. There's always a reason, isn't there? But that last time he looked as if something had finally happened. Or someone had turned up. That's more likely, isn't it? But if it was someone, it wasn't the person he was looking for. That much was obvious. He went up to the Borders a few times as well. He didn't talk very much, but he did let that slip in one conversation we had. Berwick, I think. Berwick-Upon-Tweed.'

CHAPTER 26: WHERE DO YOUR LOYALTIES LIE?

Wednesday morning

Sophie drove to the Bournemouth police station as fast as the heavy traffic would permit. She hurried up the stairs to the CID office where Lydia was waiting. Rae had arrived a few minutes earlier.

'I hope this is worth it,' Sophie said. 'Here I was, all ready for a quiet morning in the office, drinking coffee and eating biscuits with my feet up. Now this.'

'We do have coffee here, ma'am,' Lydia replied.

'That stuff? No comment. Now, what's all this about?'

'The records have all arrived from the bank,' Lydia said, 'and I think they open things up. The reason I suggested you come over is because I've been decoding all the papers that Rae found at the farm. We need to cross-check. It's all set out here on my desk for you to see.'

The bank had sent several documents that listed the historic mandate details for the farm's accounts, which were associated with the group, the Heathfield Commune, and the trust that owned the property. The details confirmed the information they already had: that the original four trustees were Timothy

Brotherton, Andrew Atkins, Katie Templar and Paul Prentice. These were also the four signatories for the accounts, with any two of them needed to authorise transactions. Two accounts had been opened in the spring of 2003. One was a current account for routine expenditure, the other a savings account.

The bank details also reflected what they already knew about the commune having had a period of stability when it was first established. Then, some eighteen months later, Paul Prentice's name was removed, leaving just three authorising signatories. Katie Templar's name remained on the list for another year, but it was then also removed, to be replaced by that of Trent Baker. The final set of records showed that a request had arrived at the bank to determine whether it was possible to change to a single signature authorisation, but no steps had been taken to put this into effect. That request had been lodged by Trent Baker.

'Why do you think he gave up on that?' Rae asked.

'There could be several reasons,' Lydia said. 'He'd need a second signature to agree to that change, so maybe neither of the other two would authorise it. Or the bank convinced them that such a change would be a bad idea. The farm was owned by a trust, after all. Most banks wouldn't be comfort-able opening up avenues for exploitation. Then there's the more obvious reason — the commune fell apart at that point, so there was no opportunity to go ahead with it.'

Sophie thought for a moment. 'These mandate changes could mirror the dates when events we already know about happened. Paul Prentice left, so he was removed from the list by two of the others — see? That change was put into effect by Brotherton, with Atkins as second signatory. Maybe Katie Templar was never told of the mandate change and only found out later, by accident. Could that have triggered a seri-ous row? She vanished, then our remaining two decided, for whatever reason, to add Trent Baker. Any two of them could have started to squirrel away money in the final few months before the place folded. What about the trustee list, Lydia?'

'That's also interesting. Someone tried to get that altered and bring in new trustees at about the same time as Baker was added to the bank's signatories. But it didn't work. It looks as though Katie Templar set up the trust so that while she was alive, she always had the final say on who should be a trustee. So Prentice remained on the list even though he'd walked out, and she remained on it too, even after she vanished. As far as I can tell, the original list is still in place, as you thought when you were looking at the deeds a couple of days ago. Everyone would assume she was still alive somewhere, at least up until you found her body at the weekend. Two of them are dead, two still alive, but it would need a good lawyer to get the ownership sorted.'

'I may be able to help here,' Rae said. 'I managed to trace Katie's possible next of kin, an aunt of hers who lives in Berwick-Upon-Tweed. I haven't made contact yet, but she may well inherit Katie's estate, and that means her share of the farm.'

'I think we need to contact her right now, Rae,' Sophie said. 'We could try for a visit this week if she's okay with it.'

'Maybe try not to be too specific when you visit, ma'am?' Lydia added. 'Until we trace the actual trust document, we don't really know the full details. Rae's right that the ownership may revert to Katie Templar's family on her death, but we can't be sure until we've had time to check it all in detail. We may even need some legal advice. If it does return to her next of kin, it would explain why the others abandoned the place when she died. Her death would have caused the trust to fold, so they weren't the legal owners anymore. Technically, they were squatting. Which begs the question, why kill her? Doing so put a stop to everything.'

Rae shook her head. 'You're assuming the others knew about that clause. What if they didn't? True, Brotherton and Atkins were original co-trustees, so maybe they ought to have been aware, but there's another person who was a final bank account signatory but not a trustee. Our friend, Trent Baker. Why would he have known of the existence of that clause?

Even Atkins may not have been totally aware, from what Barry has found out about him. Didn't his ex say he was routinely drunk or high, or both? That crucial bit of information may have passed him by.'

Sophie frowned. 'Yes. Barry said she implied that Atkins wasn't the brightest lightbulb in the box. As for Baker, why does everything always seem to come back to him? Maybe we need to see him as well, while we're in the area. On second thoughts, we'll give him a miss at the moment. We need to find this Atkins guy first and get the facts straight. Any luck, Rae?'

'He's working in Wareham Forest, if it's the same man. He's been with the Forestry Commission for about three months.'

Sophie smiled. 'Wareham Forest again. That's a stroke of luck. I'll give Alice Llewellyn a quick call, though I doubt she'll be pleased to hear from me. She associates me with dead bodies.'

Don't we all, Lydia said to herself.

* * *

Sophie looked up at the trees looming above her and shivered. She could imagine the forest looking pretty in the sunshine, but on heavily overcast days like today the woodland felt gloomy and menacing. She and Rae waited in Alice's office while the ranger went to collect Atkins, currently with a team planting saplings in a cleared area. They watched out of the window and saw Alice return accompanied by a nondescript, mousey-haired man of medium height, dressed for outdoor work. He was wearing a lumberjack shirt, but then so were most of the other staff. He might have fit Jade's photofit image, but equally well he might not. He entered the office warily, looking around him as if he was expecting a trap of some kind. He looked older than in the photo that his mother, Babs, had supplied, but the slightly turned up nose

176

was a giveaway. Wouldn't Jade have noticed that if it had been Atkins poking around at Arne?

'Good morning, Mr Atkins,' Sophie said. 'Let's get our facts straight first. Are you the Andrew Atkins who lived on Heathfield Farm in the Quantocks a decade or so ago?'

He narrowed his eyes. 'Yes.'

'My understanding is that you were there for the entire period during which a commune tried to make a go of the farm, starting in about 2003 and finally leaving about three years later. Is that right?'

He nodded warily. 'I'd worked on the farm before that. I just kept on with what I'd been doing before.'

'Let's sit down, shall we? Alice, could we get some tea or something, please? Then make sure we're not disturbed for a while?' She returned her attention to Atkins. 'I'm Detective Superintendent Sophie Allen, and this is my colleague, DC Rae Gregson. We're from Dorset police, but we've recently spent some time in Somerset, in the area around the Quantocks. There's a lot we don't know about the farm and the commune, but we have to get to the bottom of it all because of a case we're investigating.'

'I'm not the person to ask. I only worked there. The stuff that went on in the commune had nothing to do with me.'

There was a pause as Alice returned with a tray of mugs.

'That isn't strictly true, Mr Atkins, is it? You were one of the four trustees that administered the farm and shared responsibility for it. And you lived there for just over three years. You were one of the signatories for the commune's bank accounts. Do you know why we're here?'

He shook his head.

'A tramp was murdered over at Arne a couple of weeks ago. His name was Paul Prentice. Twelve years ago, he was one of the other trustees of the farm. Of course, he wasn't a tramp then. We've already interviewed Timothy Brotherton who, we understand, was the group leader. Can you understand why we need to speak to you? There's a good chance that

Prentice was murdered because of something that occurred on that farm. We need to know whether anything happened that could lead to animosity strong enough for someone to act on it all these years later.'

'Don't know anything about that.'

'Where were you on the weekend of June the eighteenth, three weeks ago?'

He shook his head again. 'Just around, I s'pose. Prob'ly in Bournemouth with some mates.'

'You need to think back, Mr Atkins. We need exact information here. Where you were, who you were with, who can vouch for you. DC Gregson will get the details from you later. Meanwhile, we need to find out much more about that commune and the people there. So, have some tea and we'll get started.'

Sophie waited until Atkins had taken several mouthfuls. 'Tell me about Timothy Brotherton.'

Atkins set down his mug. 'He was the leader, sort of. He had the ideas and liked to give rousing speeches about the way people ought to live, free from the repressions of modern society. Said we ought to be set free and allowed to explore our own inner selves. It was a load of shit looking back on it, but it seemed okay at the time. We had a shedload of fun.'

'Were you with anyone in particular then?'

'Yeah, on and off. A chick called Linda. She was a good laugh and we thought we'd make a go of it as a couple, but you know how things are. It didn't work out for us.'

'Was Tim with anyone? At the start, I mean.'

'Yeah. But he didn't talk about it, and neither did his chick. It was a bit weird. He preached about sharing everything and everyone, but he kept her to himself. We didn't notice till later. And he didn't like people shortening his name to Tim. He used to hit the roof.'

'What was her name?'

'Katie, I think. She was kinda posh.' He took another gulp of tea and scratched his nose.

'Did you know her before?'

Atkins stared hard at Sophie for several moments. 'What? Did I know her before the commune?'

'Exactly. Did you know Katie Templar before the trust took over ownership of the farm? It's not a hard question, is it? Either you did or you didn't. We know she was one of the other three trustees, by the way.'

There was another long pause. 'Yeah. I worked on that farm after I left school. Her uncle owned it and she spent some of her holidays there. When he died, he left it to her.'

'What was she like?'

'What's a polite way of putting it? Petite? Kinda thin, but very pretty. She hooked up with Timothy when they were at university together, and they hatched up this plan to start a commune. But he always had an agenda. She just didn't realise it.'

'What do you mean, agenda?'

'To take over and run things his way. She got sidelined. He made all the running in that place and she didn't get a look in. He claimed he was in touch with God or something and a lot of the others believed him. She couldn't compete with that. Anyway, she was quiet and kinda shy. So they split up. He had his pick of the women and she hooked up with someone else.'

There was another lengthy pause. Sophie was growing irritated. 'Look, Mr Atkins, this is how it works. I know quite a lot about the place and the people there but I'm not going to tell you what. If you force me to keep dropping clues about what I know it'll annoy me and make me think you've got something to hide. Just tell me everything, all right? Names, relationships, personalities, weaknesses. Just get it all off your chest. Think of it as therapy.'

He stared back at her. 'She hooked up with Paul Prentice. Well, that's what we all thought. And what was wrong with that? Timothy was getting off with any chick he fancied but when he found out, he kinda exploded. There was a row and Prentice left. We always wondered why she didn't go too, but she hung around for a while longer, then she went. Don't know where.'

'How bad was this argument between Brotherton and Prentice?'

'Pretty rip-roaring. But it was behind closed doors. No idea what was said, but it was loud.'

'Did you see her leave? Katie Templar? Did anyone actually witness her setting out from the farm with her possessions?'

He looked puzzled. 'She slipped out during the night. No one actually saw her go.'

'Now we come to someone else who was there. Trent Baker.'

'Oh, him. Yeah, he was there. Could be a bit devious, Trent.'

'He became a signatory for the bank account. He must have got the agreement of the trustees and the remaining signatories. How did that happen? It doesn't really make sense if he was devious, as you put it.'

'Listen, nothing made much sense in that place, not near the end. I didn't have a clue what was going on. But somehow Trent managed to get into a position of power. It might have gone to his head a bit. It led to some God-almighty rows. He was one for the women, was our Trent Baker. He wouldn't take no for an answer. But by then Timothy, our great leader, had lost interest. It was everyone for himself and most people made a run for it with whatever they could find. God knows what happened to the money.'

'Was there any?' Sophie asked.

Atkins spread his hands. 'There should have been. I know we were making a loss, but Katie had been bailing us out till she left. There should still have been cash in the account.'

'So you didn't authorise any large transfers out of the accounts? Not in your role of account signatory?'

He shook his head, beginning to look bored. 'No. It must have been Timothy and Trent. It only needed two to access the money. I always wondered what happened to it. I haven't seen those two for years.'

Was he telling the truth? Sophie couldn't decide. His flat voice gave little away, but there was definite tension in the way he held himself. 'Have you remembered yet where you were that weekend nearly three weeks ago? Particularly on the Saturday afternoon and evening?' she asked.

'I was in Bournemouth. A mate of mine had a stag do so we did a pub crawl. Don't remember much. I got drunk. We all did.'

'DS Gregson here will need some names.' She paused. 'Have you been in touch with anyone else from the commune recently? Or has anyone tried to contact you?'

He shook his head. 'Not since I split with Linda. We were together for a few years after we left the farm.'

Time to shake him up a bit. 'We found a body, Mr Atkins. Buried in the woods above the farm. In the beech copse. You were the farm manager and had been there longer than anyone else. You would have known the place inside out. All the paths, fields and paddocks. All the hedgerows, thickets and wooded areas. You would have known which spots were out of the direct line of sight from the farm buildings and even how deep the soil was.'

He sat up, back on alert. 'Who was it?'

'Katie Templar. She didn't leave at all. Someone killed her. Now why would they do that, Mr Atkins? Why would someone kill a young woman who you've described as quiet and shy? There can't be very many reasons, can there? Money? Jealousy? Revenge? Any ideas?'

He shook his head. 'I didn't know. It's . . . a huge shock. We all thought she'd left. Everyone did.'

'Clearly not everyone. Someone knew exactly where she was. Where she's been for the last twelve years. And I'll find that someone, Mr Atkins. No one deserves to be killed and slung down a hole like that, least of all a young woman who everyone describes as being the most pleasant, mild-mannered and generous person in that commune. So you think hard about it and where your loyalties lie. Because here you are, working in south Dorset, only a few miles away from where

Paul Prentice's body was found, having moved here only a couple of months ago. How do you think it all looks to me?'

Atkins looked at the floor.

'By the way, where did you get those scratches on your wrist and face?' she asked abruptly.

His reply was short and sharp. 'I work in forestry. We're always getting scratched. It goes with the job.'

CHAPTER 27: LIKE A NEST OF VIPERS

Wednesday afternoon

Barry Marsh looked across the interview room table. Opposite, Tim Brotherton fidgeted in his seat, looking tense and nervous.

'I don't fully understand why you're detaining Mr Brotherton,' his solicitor said. His demeanour wasn't very different from that of his client. 'What actual evidence do you have?'

'He was the group leader, Mr Clarke. He was in a relationship with Katie Templar, one of the murder victims, when the group first moved to the farm. In fact, they planned the commune together when they were both students at Durham. After she inherited the farm, the group moved in. We know she became pregnant within a year or so. I'm trying to clarify when and why the relationship ended. Your client was also far closer to the other murder victim, Paul Prentice, than he's led us to believe. We're also aware that he lied in our earlier interview.'

'But is any of it relevant?'

Barry looked at him. Was he serious or was he just playing a game? 'Of course it's relevant. Katie Templar became pregnant and had an abortion. I want to know if that abortion was the cause of the break-up of their relationship, or if it happened the other way round.' Barry turned to Brotherton. 'So, which came first, Mr Brotherton? The abortion or the split?'

'The split,' Brotherton said sullenly. 'I didn't know she was pregnant until they came back from London, after she'd had the abortion. I felt bad enough about us breaking up. To then find all that . . . well, it just seemed incomprehensible.'

'Was the baby yours?'

'How should I know? How do I know who else she was sleeping with?'

Barry leant back in his chair. 'Do you really believe that? More importantly, did you believe it at the time? You knew her better than almost anyone. Was she the kind of person that would have cheated on you? It doesn't fit in with what other people have told us about her.'

Brotherton shook his head. 'I s'pose not. No, she wasn't like that.'

'So how did you react when you found out?'

'I was bewildered. It seemed like everything was falling apart. All we'd dreamt about. It was the end. That's how it felt.'

'But you'd already split up, from what you've said. Why did you take it so badly?'

'She still meant a lot to me, even if we couldn't make a go of it. We'd been together for four years by then.'

'What caused the split?'

He stared down at the table. 'I think we'd known for some time that our personalities just didn't mesh. We argued about it. But it wasn't just that. She just couldn't see. She couldn't see the way the group needed to go. She wanted it to focus on the creative side — writing, art, crafts. I felt that stuff was all a bit twee. I wanted to concentrate on attaining enlightenment.'

'Religion?'

'You could say that, but not tied to any one religion, more to do with self-development through spirituality. And that was why we argued. And, finally, it got to us. Paul was on her side. He jumped in pretty quick.'

'Did you resent that? Katie and him getting together?'

Brotherton shrugged. 'I did at first, I suppose. But he could offer her what she obviously needed, some close emotional support. I was never any good at that. I'm still not. But I didn't harm either of them, Inspector. That would go against everything I believe in.'

Barry decided to change tack. 'What about drugs, Mr Brotherton? Our understanding is that they were freely available in the commune, judging by what people have told us.'

'That's an exaggeration. Some people smoked grass. I did, sometimes. But we weren't a drug cult. We tolerated it but we didn't promote it.'

'Wasn't it another cause of the split between you? The two of them were unhappy with the level of drug use, but you encouraged it? It's easy for you to deny it now, twelve years later, because it doesn't suit the picture you want to paint. But the reality is that you were happy for the group to go along that line. They weren't. And that caused another problem for you because Katie owned the farm.'

'The trust owned the farm. She transferred it at the start.'

'So you may have thought at the time. But wasn't the reality that she always had the final word on who became a trustee? Didn't that become a problem for you once the disagreements began to surface? You couldn't manipulate the decision makers as much as you'd have liked? By the way, what was your degree subject at university?'

'Ancient history.'

'Whereas Katie had a first-class degree in economics. And, as far as we can gather from the recollections of her fellow students, she did a short unit in law. Maybe she knew her stuff, Mr Brotherton. Maybe she always had her doubts about you and the long-term viability of your plans. And maybe that's why she died.'

'I didn't kill her. I didn't kill Prentice either. I keep telling you.'

'So why were you in Dorset that weekend a couple of weeks ago? Don't deny it. We know you were there. It really doesn't help your situation, Mr Brotherton, when you keep telling us something we know is a lie.'

Brotherton remained silent for almost a minute and Barry wondered whether he was digging his heels in. Would it be *no comment* from this point on?

'I went to try and warn him. That's if I could have found him. I never did though. I asked around the town centre in Wareham and got a rough idea of where he might be, but it was a wasted effort. I was only there for a few hours on my way back from Portsmouth.'

'You told my boss that you went by train.'

Brotherton shrugged. 'That wasn't true. I drove.'

'Why lie about it?'

Again, a shrug. 'I knew it would implicate me if I told the truth. I guessed you'd jump on the fact that I was in the area and use it to nail me unfairly.'

'So what did you want to warn Prentice about?'

'That Trent Baker was out of prison. He needed to know. I'd come to realise what a thug Baker was after his trial for attempted murder, when he tried to kill that woman. It all began to make sense at that point. I took him on trust before, when he first appeared. That's why Prentice left the farm. Trent Baker threatened to kill him. I thought he was joking.'

Barry frowned. 'I don't understand the reason for the conflict between them — Paul Prentice and Katie Templar, on the one hand, and Trent Baker on the other. Why was there so much hatred?'

Brotherton lowered his eyes. 'I don't know.'

'But I think you do, Mr Brotherton. Or even if you don't know for certain, you have a pretty good idea. Was there more than one reason? Maybe Baker fancied Katie Templar and was jealous of Prentice? Or was it his general attitude?' Barry stopped. An idea had just begun to form in his head. 'Or was it that he wanted the farm to go in a different direction entirely?

Was he pushing for the commune to start being producers of cannabis and other stuff, rather than just consumers?'

Barry saw Brotherton's eyes flicker. He looked up. 'I'm not saying any more.'

* * *

Polly Nelson had been watching the interview via a video link.

'What do you think?' she asked when Barry returned to the incident room.

He shook his head. 'I don't know what to think. He's still hiding something, but I can't say what it is. The problem is, we don't have any direct evidence. He's fingering Trent Baker for it all, without saying so directly. And, let's face it, Baker has a track record of extreme violence.'

'Your boss wasn't particularly impressed by the other one, Atkins, this morning. Could all three of them be implicated? But where's the motive? What was so bad that your tramp needed to be silenced, now after all these years? Had a new threat shown up? Had he discovered something that might have nailed them for the girl's murder?'

Barry shook his head. 'Remember, no one knew what had happened to her. Apart from the killers, no one knew she was dead until we found her body on Saturday. Maybe Prentice guessed. And that begs the question: if he guessed she was dead, why didn't he do anything about it until now?'

'Have you got any other lines of enquiry on the go?'

'Rae's following up on the Katie Templar back-story. At the moment she's the great unknown. The boss is working her way through the Trent Baker trial material from twelve years ago, trying to get to the bottom of what went on between him and Catherine Templeton. We're hoping she'll pick up some more people to talk to who were members of the commune. And we've got Lydia looking at this stuff I discovered about Prentice and his trips to Taunton. A lot of it is financial stuff, banking records and all that. She's still stuck at the

Bournemouth CID offices because of her injuries. I think she's frustrated and angry because it'll be a couple of weeks yet before she's able to get out and about, so anyone she phones had better watch out.' He laughed.

'What are your thoughts about it all, Barry?'

He shrugged. 'It's a real knotty one. You know, I wouldn't really trust any of them. The boss is convinced they're all hiding their own secrets, but each of them for different reasons. She described the whole lot of them as being like a nest of vipers, and she's right.'

'Maybe Katie Templar and Paul Prentice were the only normal people in the commune. Oh, we've got the results of the dental records. The body definitely is Katie Templar. She registered with a dentist in Bridgwater all those years ago. For some reason her records were still on file and matched perfectly. Probably broke some data privacy law, but useful for us.'

CHAPTER 28: LIAR

Wednesday afternoon

The trial records gave Sophie a fascinating insight into the characters of the two protagonists, Catherine Templeton and Trent Baker, although much of it came from reading between the lines. Sophie wondered how two people with such antagonistic personalities had ever got into a relationship in the first place. Baker came across as devious in the extreme, stirring up trouble whenever he could, coupled with a liking for violence. Catherine had a hot temper that she made little effort to control, and Sophie wondered if her sense of right and wrong was more than a little suspect. Or was she reading too much into the words of witnesses called by both sets of barristers? There was no doubt that the jury had come to the right verdict. It had been unanimous. Trent Baker had attempted to murder Catherine Templeton one spring evening, ten years earlier, on a footpath close to the White Unicorn pub in a village near Taunton. Catherine had been there with a group of work colleagues celebrating a birthday and Baker, along with a friend, had called in after they'd been fishing at a nearby river. After some heated exchanges, he'd followed her out and stabbed her with his fish-gutting knife. His fingerprints were on the handle, fish slime was still on the blade when it was recovered from the undergrowth nearby, the slime matching the gutted fish in the rucksack found in his car. Copious amounts of Catherine's blood had soaked into his clothes. It had been a straightforward case for the police and an easy decision for the Crown Prosecution Service to rule on.

The judge's summing up had been very clear: Baker was unquestionably wicked and prone to violence when his temper was roused. The victim was fortunate to have survived and Baker was similarly fortunate not to be facing a murder charge. Nevertheless, there was no doubt he was a danger to the public and needed to be taught a lesson. A long sentence was required because of the savage nature of the attack and his previous history of assaults. The judge gave him a minimum of ten years behind bars.

Sophie went back and studied the trial records more closely. The court had been told something of the on-off relationship between the two, although Catherine consistently maintained that the *on* part had only lasted three weeks, whereas the *off* part was rather longer, at three years. Sophie was rather surprised at the lack of any detail regarding their time together at the farm. Was it down to careless cross-examination by the respective counsels or had it not been considered important enough? Or had both of the main players chosen to be deliberately vague for reasons that were never made clear? She had hoped to learn more about the friction between these two jaggedly interacting personalities. It must have been observed by other commune members, so why had so few been called as witnesses? It was puzzling.

The argument in the pub had broken out when Baker had passed the table of partygoers on his way to the bar. He'd claimed not to have even spotted Catherine in the group until he'd overheard the phrase *slime-ball Baker*, spoken by Catherine to one of her friends. She denied this, stating that he'd made a vile comment to her first, calling her *wonder-whore* as he passed by. A slanging match had ensued, only brought to a halt when both parties were restrained by their respective friends. It flared up again when Baker returned to the bar for another drink and he was asked to leave by the landlady. He did so with bad grace and a great deal of seething anger. The conclusion of the prosecuting counsel was that he had dumped his gear into his car at the riverside, but then turned back and lingered in the shrubbery in the pub garden. Traces of his presence had been found on the foliage of several bushes and a set of footprints, identified as being from his shoes, were spotted on the surface of the soil.

Complaining that these altercations had ruined her evening, Catherine had decided to set off for home early. At the time she only lived a short walk away from the riverside pub, little more than a five-minute stroll along a footpath through a small area of woodland. Trent Baker had followed her, spun her round and stabbed her four times in the abdomen. He'd then hurried off, back to his car. One of Catherine's friends, concerned for her safety, had decided to go after her and had stumbled on her body, sprawled across the path and losing blood. She owed her life to the quick reactions of her friend and the speed with which an ambulance arrived.

The forensic evidence was clear, and the witness testimonies were conclusive. It had been an open and shut case. There was no doubt: Trent Baker's behaviour was intentional and ruthless. He was ruled by his own vicious temper and found it impossible to hold back once his blood was up. The important question for Sophie in the here and now was this: had the ten years he'd spent in prison altered him? Was he still that same hot-headed individual, governed by irrational rages? And, therefore, could Paul Prentice's death be due to a similar loss of control on Baker's part? Moreover, had he played a part in the death of Katie Templar while he was living on the farm?

It would be easy to ignore all the other bits of circumstantial evidence that they'd recently accumulated, assume it was down to the Baker temper, pull him in and charge him. But there were too many discrepancies. The man asking about Prentice around the time he'd vanished from Wareham town centre didn't fit Baker's description. Neither did the man seen by Jade poking around Prentice's campsite and by Pauline Stopley nearby on the foreshore. The small, white car, twice spotted on the Arne road, didn't match the description of his vehicle. There was also the fact that Prentice's dog had survived the attack. Sophie had the feeling that Baker would have been merciless towards the small mongrel, though she might be mistaken in that. Maybe he had a soft spot for dogs. Complicating it all were two major sticking points: Baker had been working during the weekend in question and there was no evidence from his employers that he'd skimped on any of his overnight shifts. His electronic tag had not registered him leaving Somerset or Bristol at any time in recent weeks. And, finally, Sophie couldn't dismiss the feeling she was having that the murder of Prentice had been thoroughly planned, leaving little evidence. It was, of course, possible that Baker had, for once, worked it all out carefully during his long spell in prison, but it didn't mesh with what they knew about him. Anyway, what would his motive have been?

As for Catherine, there were hints from witnesses called in her defence that she could show a prickly and slightly irritating side to her character at times. Maybe she should pay Catherine another visit. Sophie suspected that she'd been extremely economical in her accounts of both the time she'd spent at the commune and the relationships she'd had with the other members.

Sophie continued to scan through the trial documentation, not knowing quite what she was looking for. When she saw it, it hit her like a sledgehammer. Trent Baker's fishing companion on the evening of the assault on Catherine had been Andrew Atkins.

* * *

Rae was trying to build up a picture of the long-dead Katie Templar. She'd grown up in Bath and had been a hard-working and intelligent pupil at school. The death of her parents when she was ten had caused her to move some fifty miles south, where she'd lived with her uncle and aunt on the small farm in the Quantocks. She'd attended the local school where she'd continued to be her year's star pupil, winning prizes and awards. She'd also been involved in voluntary work as a teenager, looking after disabled members of the local community. She'd headed off to university on a high, but it wasn't long before another set of tragedies struck. First, her aunt died unexpectedly from an aggressive brain tumour, then her beloved uncle was killed in a motoring accident on the narrow lanes near the farm. Katie took a year out of her degree to deal with the will and to get herself back into the right frame of mind for academic work. It was when she returned to Durham that she met Timothy Brotherton.

This information gave Rae pause for thought. Had Brotherton manipulated Katie while she was still in a vulnerable state? Had he quickly spotted the opportunity she offered for realising his embryonic plans for a commune? Who might know? Maybe she needed to trace some of Katie's close school and university friends in an attempt to gain some sort of insight. It wouldn't be easy, though. Fifteen years had passed since Katie's university days, twenty since she'd been in her last few years at school. No time to lose.

* * *

Lydia couldn't quite believe what she'd discovered. It just didn't make sense. Paul Prentice still had more than fifty thousand pounds in his bank account. Where had it come from? Why had he spent most of the previous decade living rough as a tramp when he had that kind of money at his disposal? He'd only taken cash out on his visits to Taunton and the sums largely matched the contributions to the hostel, close to the amounts that the manager had described. Only a few card payments were recorded and these seemed to be for the purchase of rail tickets. It looked as though he'd made eight journeys in total, all at about the same price and all in the first five years after the failure of the commune. Could they be the visits to Berwick that Barry had mentioned?

Her first thought was that the money in the bank had its origins in some kind of fraud involving the commune's accounts, but this proved not to be the case. Clearly, Prentice had only been a part-time member of the farm community and seemed to have kept on working all through its existence. Lydia discovered that he'd worked as a senior economic adviser at a merchant bank, based in their Bristol offices. His money had come from several large bonuses that he'd earned from some far-sighted investments. Lydia checked through the information they already held about Prentice, gained from the boss's visit to Salisbury. It matched. The father had said that Paul worked in investments for a few years but that he was unhappy in his work. But it didn't answer the obvious question: what had happened to cause such a dramatic change in his lifestyle? It had to have been some traumatic event, surely? And why had he visited the north-east so often?

She knew that Prentice and Katie had paired up at the time of the abortion. The sketchy evidence in the police records tended to indicate that they'd formed a deep bond, although that only came from the letter Jade had discovered and the observations of Paul's parents. Lydia took another look at the contents of that letter. It pleaded with Prentice to come and rescue her, almost as if she were being held against her will. Was it possible that she'd been killed in the interim, before he could get there? How would he have reacted then? Of course, that would depend upon what the people at the commune told him. What would have been their most likely explanation? That Katie Templar had left and gone away somewhere, Lydia supposed. What would Prentice have done then? Probably made some efforts to trace her. So was that the reason behind the Berwick visits?

She decided to change tack and check the dates of his journeys. Would Barry have an idea from his conversation with the hostel warden in Taunton? She lifted the phone, but then put it back. Something in that emotional letter Katie had written all those years ago jarred. It didn't fit with what they knew. There it was. Katie had referred to a member of the commune who had taken on the role of medical expert. According to the letter, that person had previously worked in a pharmacy but was not a qualified pharmacist. Katie had also referred to that person as a *she*. Surely it was Catherine Templeton? But Catherine had insisted that she'd only joined the commune late, just before it collapsed. She'd claimed she'd never met or heard of Katie Templar. Was she lying? If so, why?

* * *

It took Rae most of the afternoon, but she finally managed to contact a woman who had been a close friend of Katie's at university. Sandra Bulmore had been on the same degree course and had shared a flat with her during their final year. She'd found a job locally after graduation and was still living in Durham. On the phone, Sandra said that she'd kept in touch with Katie for several years, but for some reason Katie had suddenly stopped contacting her, and she'd never heard from her erstwhile friend again. What she did remember, though, was that Katie had another aunt and uncle, other than her Somerset-based guardians. They were from her mother's side, whereas the Somerset couple had been related to Katie's father. They had attended Katie's graduation ceremony, travelling down from Berwick-Upon-Tweed especially for the occasion.

Rae and Lydia went to see Sophie in her office and told her what they'd found.

'There's a link here, surely,' Sophie said. 'Paul Prentice made several visits to the north-east in recent years and now we discover that Katie had family living there. Rae, can you organise yourself to make a visit? See this Sandra Bulmore in

Durham first, then head to Berwick. You can get a train there direct from Durham. Can you make a start tomorrow? You might have all these questions sorted and be back here by the weekend. Does that seem sensible to you, Lydia?'

Lydia pretended to scowl. 'Huh. I'm jealous. I'm stuck here on these bloody crutches and she's off gallivanting around the country.'

Sophie laughed. 'Rae, you'll need to bring back some local goodies, just so we stay on the right side of Lydia here.'

'A six-pack of Newcastle Brown?' Rae suggested, struggling to keep a straight face.

'That isn't remotely funny. Some local chocolate will be fine though.' Lydia's scowl softened into a smile.

'Given what you've discovered, Lydia, we need to have a rethink about Catherine Templeton. She's been lying to us and we have to find out why. Maybe she was more involved in the whole thing than she's been letting on. Maybe she's been pulling the wool over everyone's eyes about the nature of her relationship with Trent Baker. Maybe the picture she's painted of herself as the totally innocent victim of his evil manipulations is just a fiction. We need to know more about their back-story. Can you do that?'

'Of course. But there's something else you need to know. Catherine Templeton owns a car.'

'Yes, we know. It's a red Ford.'

Lydia smiled grimly. 'It is now. But she's only had that one since the end of last week. She traded in her old car in part exchange. It was a white VW Polo.'

CHAPTER 29: DURHAM AND BERWICK

Thursday

Rae loved travelling by train, so she had jumped at the chance of a rail journey to the north-east of England, particularly since she'd never been further north than York on that particular train route. She settled into her seat at Kings Cross station, thinking that she really ought to travel on across the border to Edinburgh sometime. Maybe a weekend break with Craig during the festival? He'd enjoy the fringe, especially its off-beat comedy shows. She waited until the train pulled out of the station and then took out her notes and spent much of the journey re-reading the somewhat sparse information they held on Katie Templar. It was her job to add some detail to the few facts they had. If all went well, she should be returning the next day with a much clearer picture of the young woman who seemed to have been universally liked and admired in the commune's heyday. But maybe that perception of her had been distorted by time, and the general unwillingness to speak ill of the dead. Had she really been the paragon of virtue that people now chose to remember?

The journey passed uneventfully, as had her early morning trip into London from Wareham, although that train ride had been more interesting in terms of the landscape. The East Coast Main Line was too flat and monotonous, until they approached York, and then both the countryside and the towns became more interesting. She descended onto the platform at Durham a minute or two earlier than scheduled, so she wandered around the station for a short while. The railway line was set fairly high above the city, partly on a viaduct, so she could look down on the old buildings and streets of the city centre, taking in the ancient cathedral and castle set on high ground above a tight bend in the River Wear. It was all very picturesque in the early afternoon sunshine. She decided to walk to the address she was visiting. She needed to stretch her legs after so much time cooped up in the train. It would probably take her about fifteen minutes to walk to her destination, a house in New Elvet. Apparently it was one of the old streets in the city centre, where the houses all looked expensive. Sandra Bulmore had also studied economics at university and maybe she had made a success of her subsequent career. She would be at home for the early part of the afternoon and, when they'd spoken on the phone, had offered to provide a lunch of sandwiches and other nibbles. Rae had gratefully accepted the offer. Anything was preferable to railway food.

It took her less time than she'd expected to get to the house, which was a beautiful white-painted building, probably dating back more than a century. Rae rang the doorbell and was surprised when it opened and she found herself looking down at an attractive middle-aged woman in a wheelchair. She was well-dressed, with short pale ginger hair and freckles.

She smiled cheerfully up at Rae. 'I'm Sandra, and you must be Rae Gregson, the detective. Come on in.'

The ground floor of the house had been adapted for wheelchair use, with open areas that Sandra sped through. Rae had trouble keeping up. They arrived in a sunny room to the rear and settled at a table set with plates of food.

'The tea's freshly made,' Sandra said. 'I phoned the station and they told me your train had just arrived. You made good time getting across here if you walked. If you took a taxi, then the driver took you for a bit of a ride. You know what some cab drivers can be like.' She grinned mischievously.

'No, I walked. I needed the exercise.'

'What, a young thing like you? And in the police too. Pah! I bet you're as fit as a fiddle.'

Rae laughed. Sandra's cheerfulness was infectious. 'I've spent much of the day so far sitting on trains. I just meant I needed to loosen up.' She looked around her. 'You have a lovely home.'

'It suits us. My husband runs a bookshop here in the town and our two sons are at the local secondary school. We all like it. I've been in Durham since I started university here. I've never really had the opportunity to move away, what with my disability, and I'm not sure I'd want to.'

'What's the problem, if you don't mind me asking?'

'I have a congenital defect in my joints. It first flared up badly when I was a student and it's rumbled on ever since. I have good days and bad days. On a good day I can manage to get around with sticks but on bad days like today, I need the chair. Funnily enough, it's why I became friendly with Katie back when we were both students here. We both took a year off, but for very different reasons. She to get the family finances sorted after the death of her guardians and me because I was getting experimental treatment that was in its infancy. When we started back on our course a year later, we recognised each other, became close friends and never looked back. Mind you, she was a lot cleverer than me. I really struggled to keep up with her.'

'That's useful to know. So she was a top student?'

Sandra smiled. 'Oh, yes. It wasn't obvious in her manner, though. She was very shy and never looked as though she'd say boo to a goose, but when it came to work, she really shone. Maybe that's why we became such good friends — we had totally different personalities. I've always had a bit of an in-your-face approach to life, whereas Katie could become socially isolated if she wasn't careful. She was a lovely person, though. I've really missed her all these years. How did it happen?'

Rae shrugged. 'We don't know. That's what we're trying to establish. It looks as though she was murdered, as I told you on the phone. But it was more than a decade ago, so any obvious clues have all but disappeared. But we're putting everything we can into it. My boss is committed to getting to the bottom of it all. Our involvement started with the murder of a tramp called Paul Prentice just a few weeks ago. It's all led on from there.'

Sandra frowned and took another sip of tea. 'I met Paul several times. He always seemed a genuinely nice guy. He came to visit, hoping for news about Katie, but I never had any. I kind of felt in my bones that something awful had happened to her. But why would anyone want to kill her? She had such a nice personality and he seemed a good guy. It seems wrong that two decent people should be murdered. The thought makes me shiver.' She pulled her cardigan closer around her thin shoulders. 'Look, help yourself to some food. You must be starving.'

The two women were quiet for a while, digging into the ham sandwiches and fruitcake. When talk resumed, Rae decided on a more specific line of questioning.

'Did you ever see Katie after she started living on the commune?'

'Yes. She came up for a visit soon after my twins were born. That was the last time I saw her. She seemed anxious, more so than usual. She said she was going to chuck that moron Tim Brotherton. She'd had enough of him. I said it was about time. I don't know what she ever saw in him or his madcap ideas. And he was cheating on her, that's what she said.'

'Was that before or after she found out she was pregnant?'

Sandra looked stunned. 'What? I never realised.'

'Yes. She became pregnant by him and had an abortion. That's when she became close to Paul Prentice. It looks as though he supported her through a difficult time.'

200

'He never told me, and he only visited five or six years ago. Maybe she'd sworn him to secrecy. My God, if only I'd known, I'd have tried harder to keep in touch with her.' Sandra looked crestfallen. 'Now I feel even more strongly that I let her down.'

'No, you didn't,' Rae said. 'You had two young sons and your disability to cope with. How could you have done more? I wonder if she mentioned any other names to you? I'll give some to you. I want you to think about each one and tell me if it rings a bell, no matter how distantly.'

'Okay, go ahead.' Sandra closed her eyes.

'Trent Baker.'

Her eyes flickered open. 'Yes. I remember she told me about him and that he was extremely manipulative.'

'Andrew or Andy Atkins.'

This time there was a longer pause before she spoke. 'It's possible, but I can't remember any context.'

'Catherine Templeton.'

The silence lasted for nearly a minute. 'I think there was a mention of another woman with a similar name to her own. Katie said she was a bit wary of her, but I don't think she said why.'

So, just as they had thought, Catherine had deliberately led the police team astray. Here was the confirmation. Rae decided against further questions about Catherine. She didn't want to give this woman any clues about the investigation, no matter how open and honest she appeared to be.

'Linda Brooker.'

Sandra thought for a while then shook her head. 'No, I don't think so.'

'Okay, that's good. I'd like to know if she mentioned anything else about life on the farm — you know, relations within the group and all that.'

Sandra scratched her chin. 'Only that it was getting her down a bit and she was thinking of taking the property back. Apparently there was an escape clause in the trusteeship, and she thought it might have been triggered. If so, she'd reclaim possession of the farm.'

Rae looked at her. 'What? She said that?'

'Well, words to that effect. This was twelve years ago, possibly more. But yes, that's more or less what she said.'

Rae exhaled slowly and told herself not to let her excitement show. This item of information was potential dynamite. They'd spent almost a week attempting to identify some motive for Katie Templar's murder, and here it was. They needed to trace a full copy of the trust document rather than trying to work on the bits and pieces of it that had come from the bank. Where could it be? Maybe they would have to contact every legal practice in the area around the Quantocks. Then an awful thought struck her. Katie had completed a law unit as part of her degree. What if she'd drawn up the document herself and not deposited a copy anywhere for safe keeping? There'd be no way for them to check on this supposed escape clause.

'Let's go back to Catherine Templeton. I want you to think about it for a while and see if anything else Katie said about her comes to the surface.'

'I can't see how. It was a long time ago and so much has happened since.' Sandra shook her head.

'There's a trick that my boss taught me to use. First, where were you when you had this conversation with Katie?'

Sandra looked puzzled. 'I think it was here, in this room. It was winter, though.'

'So where were you both sitting?'

'Across there.' She pointed to two chairs on either side of an ornate fireplace.

'Right. Let's go over there. Sit where you sat then.'

Sandra thought for a few seconds then hauled herself out of her wheelchair and settled in one of the chairs, indicating that Rae should take the other.

'Now close your eyes and try to imagine Katie here instead of me. You've been chatting for a while about the farm and the group of people living there. How did this other woman's name crop up?'

Sandra bit her lip. 'She was talking about her break-up with Tim Brotherton. How he'd started demanding that everyone call him Timothy rather than Tim. He'd said that Timothy was more biblical.' She stopped. 'And then she said she'd discovered he'd been sleeping with another woman. She said that she didn't care as much as she'd thought she would because she was getting sick of him anyway.'

'Go on.'

'That was when she said that the woman had a name similar to hers. She made a joke about it. Maybe Tim had been so full of his own self-importance that he'd confused another Katie with her. Either that or the drink and cannabis had addled his brain. I can remember saying that she was probably better off out of it and she agreed. I said that I'd always thought he was a poser, even when he was at university with us. She'd just been swept along by his good looks and his supposed access to plenty of money.'

Rae was interested by this last statement. 'Was that true? Did Brotherton have money?'

Sandra laughed. 'God, no. He just liked people to think that he did. As I said, he was a complete poser. If Katie'd been in her right mind, she would have seen through him right away. But she'd taken a big emotional hit after the death of her aunt and uncle and was very fragile. That toad spotted it and moved in on her.'

Rae wondered whether the commune had ever had any chance of succeeding with its leading light being such a dubious character. With Trent Baker in the picture and Andy Atkins lurking in the background, it must have been like living in snake central.

'Did she say anything else about this other woman? What she was like, for example?'

'I got the impression she was vivacious and a bit full of herself. Oh, and she had a temper. As I mentioned, Katie said she was wary of her. I really can't remember anything else. We spent most of the time talking about happier times back in our student days.'

Rae smiled at her. 'You've been really helpful, Sandra. My boss always says that it's the little details about people and their behaviour that help when you're trying to piece things together. It's a bit like a jigsaw. It's great when we get confirmation of something that someone else has told us, and that's what you've done.'

Sandra's eyes filled. 'I still can't believe it. She was a lovely person and my best friend for several years. I can't help feeling I let her down big time. Why didn't I put more effort into tracing her? The thing is, she sometimes used to talk about moving to the Welsh mountains. I kind of assumed that's what she'd done, and that's why we'd lost touch.'

'What I can tell you is that we think she fell in love with Paul Prentice, so maybe they had a few happy months together before this all happened. Didn't he talk about it when he visited you?'

She shook her head. 'Not really. It was a very short chat we had. He was on his way up to Berwick to see her remaining family. Maybe you'll find out more from them. I did like him, though. He seemed kind, considerate.'

'He was, by all accounts. He looked after her when she was really down. We know that.'

'So are the two murders linked?'

'We can't say for certain, not yet. That's all I can tell you at this stage.'

* * *

The train journey northwards from Durham to Berwick took a little over an hour, so Rae was there by late afternoon. She checked into her hotel, and then made her way to the address she'd been given for Katie's only surviving relatives, an aunt and uncle. She would need to tread cautiously here because she didn't know how close they'd been. After all, as Katie's only remaining family, why hadn't they put more effort into tracing her after she'd disappeared? Somerset Police had no record of any approach from them after their niece's disappearance. Nor had they made any attempt to claim the farm as their property, according to land registry records. It was all very peculiar.

Palace Green was in an old part of town close to the waterfront. It was a tiny house that had evidently seen better days, and its frontage had a tired look. She rang the doorbell and waited. She heard the slow approach of footsteps and the sound of a security chain being engaged. The door opened a crack. Rae could just make out the face of an elderly woman peering through the gap.

'Mrs Brown? I'm Detective Constable Rae Gregson from Dorset police. I'm here to talk about your missing niece, Katie Templar. We phoned you yesterday to make the appointment?'

There was a pause. 'Oh, yes,' she answered, her voice unsteady. 'I'm a bit nervous of callers since my husband died. Do you want to come in?'

'Yes, please. I have some questions for you so it might take half an hour or so.'

The door opened. Rae stepped into a dark and somewhat dusty hallway and from there into a small front parlour. It, too, was a bit dingy. Rae thought the whole place could do with some sprucing up. It could so easily be made into a lovely old home. Despite its small size the place had a lot of potential.

Once they were seated, June Brown said, 'I haven't seen Katie for a long time. How is she?'

'That's what I'm here for, Mrs Brown. She's been missing for twelve years.'

'Really? Twelve? I thought it was only a couple of years. I didn't realise that much time had passed. We never kept in contact with her, you see. We thought she'd moved away somewhere.'

Was she suffering from memory loss? Rae cleared her throat. 'I have bad news, Mrs Brown. We found Katie's body last weekend, buried on the farm she owned. We think some-one killed her.'

It took a few moments for the news to sink in. 'Oh, that's terrible. It's awful, the violence at the moment. It's on the news a lot.'

'This wasn't recent, Mrs Brown. We think she was killed twelve years ago, probably by someone she knew on the farm.'

June Brown tutted. 'My husband always said she'd come to a bad end. He refused to have very much to do with her, said she was ungodly. It goes to show, doesn't it?'

Rae couldn't believe what she was hearing. She'd pre-pared herself for a range of possible reactions from Katie's sole remaining relatives, but not this one. She took a deep breath.

'You said your husband died recently, Mrs Brown. He was her mother's older brother, wasn't he?'

'Yes. He didn't approve of Katie's mother very much. She was flighty. That's what he said.'

'What was your husband's job, Mrs Brown, just out of interest?'

'He was a Baptist minister. He was in the Church all his life. He was a good man.'

'When did he pass away?'

'Last year. It only seems like yesterday, yet time drags so.'

'Do you have any children?'

'Yes. My son, Roger. He lives in York. I didn't see him for a long time, but he's been to see me more often since Edward died. They didn't get on.'

Rae decided not to pursue the relationship between father and son, though June and Roger would probably prove to be Katie's only close relatives.

'When was the last time you saw Katie? Can you remem-ber? Someone told us that you went to her graduation in Durham.'

There was another pause. Rae could see the concentration on June's face. 'Yes. All three of us went. There was a bad row afterwards and Edward insisted on us coming home rather than staying the night as we'd planned. Roger refused to come with us. That's when he and Edward fell out.'

Rae thought hard. This wasn't going to be as easy as she'd hoped. She'd harboured thoughts of having a quick conversation, asking a few sharp questions and getting precise replies. Instead she felt that she was treading on a very fragile surface, one that might shatter at any moment.

'Have you had any other visitors asking about Katie over the years?'

'I can't remember. I left all that to Edward. He dealt with it all. There may have been some but . . .' June shrugged.

She looked so frail, so devoid of any spark. Had she always been like this or had her husband slowly sucked the life out of her? Rae wondered if he'd been an Old Testament purist, a fire and brimstone type. One of her neighbours had been like that when she was a teenager, full of bile against anything modern and anything that went against strict biblical teaching. He'd bumped into her once after her transition and had told her she was destined for hell and would burn in the fiery pit for all eternity. She still remembered her pleasure in replying, *In that case, I'll probably have you there for company, you evil, joyless, life-sucking vampire.*

'Did you ever get any post from Katie? Letters, documents, cards? That kind of thing?'

'Well, there's a box of stuff upstairs in a cupboard in the spare room. Edward used to grumble when anything from her arrived. I think it all went in there.'

'I'd like to look at it if I may. Would that be alright?'

June just looked tired and defeated. 'I suppose so. What harm can it do now?'

Rae slowly climbed the stairs behind June and was shown into a small single bedroom. June opened a cupboard and pointed to an old cardboard box on the bottom shelf. Rae pulled it out. She recognised the handwriting on the envelopes and postcards. All were in Katie Templar's thin lettering. One brown envelope, thicker than the rest, caught her attention so she lifted it from the pile and opened it, extracting the closely typed pages inside. It was the trust document for the farm, the very item that might pull everything together and explain the two murders and the subsequent years of acrimony. She'd struck gold.

CHAPTER 30: THE BACK-STORY OPENS UP

Friday morning

In a café near York's main railway station, Rae was sitting with Roger Brown, only child of June and Edward and, more importantly, cousin to Katie Templar. She'd phoned him the previous evening from her hotel in Berwick and asked if they could meet. He'd agreed at once and named a place where they could have a late breakfast, saying, rather intriguingly, 'There's a lot I need to get off my chest.'

He began almost at once. 'My dad was a man trapped in his own bigotry. Even if part of him wanted to understand me, he was fenced in by petty doctrines and church directives. It was the same with Katie. He made up his mind about her and wouldn't budge. Eventually this caused him to lose both me, his son, and Katie, his only niece.'

Rae took another mouthful of her scrambled eggs on toast. 'You went to her graduation I believe? That's what your mum said.'

He sipped his coffee. Rae noticed that his hair was showing a few flecks of grey. What was he? Late thirties? Early forties? He had olive skin and dark hair and looked as if he exercised.

'That was when it all blew up — for Katie and for me. I'm gay, you see. I'd tried to keep it secret from both my parents, but I was really struggling. It's possible he may have guessed as I was growing up because a few comments were made about my lack of interest in girls and he became more distant. I was fighting it myself back then, refusing to admit what was glaringly obvious to me.'

Rae gave a wry laugh. 'God. Don't I know that feeling. Years of trying to hide the big secret from the world, in case the world doesn't like it. By world, of course, we mean parents, brothers and sisters, cousins, friends and neighbours — the very people we should be able to be honest with. We worry that it'll cause rifts within our families, that we're somehow letting them down, that we're worthless. Being trans is no different, believe me. It's like being caught in a trap with no way out. It's an impossible choice. You either keep it hidden, holding all the stress inside so as not to upset those around you, or you tell them, and probably create anxiety, tensions and splits among those closest to you. For me it was a nightmare that went on for years.'

Roger nodded. 'Probably worse for you. You have my absolute admiration. It must be really hard being trans, even now. Anyway, the argument started just after the ceremony when Katie told us her plans and what she wanted for her life. Dad was totally dismissive and told her that her role was to be a wife and mother, as laid down in the scriptures. Katie was such a mild person normally, but she got really angry and tore his argument to shreds. I suppose he felt humiliated, but he had it coming. He then attacked her personally and accused her of having loose morals, saying she would end up in hell. I felt I couldn't stand by and let her take all the flak, and I chose that moment to tell them the truth about me and my sexuality. Maybe it wasn't the best time to come out to them, but Katie was being entirely reasonable, while he was downright nasty and vindictive towards her. I felt she needed me on her side. So then he tore into me, and that was that

— I got disowned. Apparently, he wrote me out of his will, though I've no idea who gets the dosh when my mother dies, probably the local dogs' home. I haven't broached the subject with Mum since I started visiting again. Anyway, I wouldn't touch his money with a barge pole, not after what he said and did. There won't be much anyway, not even after a lifetime of scrimping and saving, trying to make ends meet on the income of a Baptist minister. Mum's got that house on a fixed low rent for the rest of her life but then it reverts back to the Church. My guess is that they'll want to sell it.'

Rae sipped her coffee reflectively. When would be the best time to tell him that, as sole living relative, he was likely to have become the legal owner of Heathfield Farm in Somerset's Quantock Hills?

'Maybe we should talk about Katie,' she said. 'As I told you on the phone, last week we found her body on the farm. She'd been murdered, probably a good twelve years ago. That's what we're investigating, so anything you can tell us about her, and the farm, would be helpful.'

'I still can't believe it. We thought she'd moved to a smallholding somewhere. She mentioned something like that the last time I saw her. I think your man Paul Prentice tried looking for her.'

Rae filed away this snippet of information. It would need to be checked. Surely Prentice would have left some trail behind him during his search? Maybe he'd asked around after her.

Roger continued, 'I went down to visit the farm once, but I didn't like the atmosphere. It was poisonous, and Katie seemed really upset. I went back a few months later but she'd already left, and the place was in chaos — well, that's what I was told. Your news shows it in a very different light. Someone had killed her and, what did you say, buried her body in the woods? It's all beyond belief.'

Rae made a quick decision. 'Roger, your memories of the place might prove vital to us. I need longer than this quick chat. Could we go somewhere more private, do you think? Your home? Or I can ask for an interview room at the local nick. Which would you prefer?'

'Don't really mind, but our flat would be convenient. My partner's gone to work for the day.' He started to get to his feet, ready to leave.

'There's something else you need to know. Although we can't be totally sure of the current situation, there's a possibility that Heathfield Farm may have returned to Katie's sole ownership just before she was killed. I've got the original trust document in my possession and we'll need to go through it with a fine-tooth comb, with legal help. But if that is the case, it now belongs to her next of kin. That could be you.'

He sat down again, hard.

* * *

Rae's return journey to Dorset seemed to pass in a flash. She'd learned so much from the people she'd spoken to in Durham, Berwick and York, and she spent the hours sifting through the new information about the main protagonists in the commune and how it altered her perceptions of each one of them. It was just like a giant jigsaw puzzle, with the picture emerging in three dimensions. Each of the characters had been fleshed out and their role in the commune brought into clearer focus. But the ways they related to one another had also become more sharply defined. She'd travelled north in the hope of learning more about Katie Templar. She spent the journey south reviewing what she'd discovered about Tim Brotherton, Catherine Templeton, Trent Baker, Andy Atkins and Paul Prentice as well. And then, of course, there was the matter of the trustees, the small inner core that had, somewhat secretively, set the agenda for the commune's development. Finally, the legal conditions that governed the farm's ownership, as originally developed by Katie herself, with its two important clauses. Firstly, the return of the farm to her family in the event of Katie's death.

And then there was the escape clause, kept secret from the other commune members. This stated that if any class A drugs were ever found in the possession of, or distributed by, any one of the commune organisers, the ownership of the farm would revert back to the person of Katie Templar and the trust would fold. Roger Brown had been able to explain Katie's reasons for including this strange clause. The tragic death of her parents, when she was still a youngster, had occurred in a horrific car crash caused by a cocaine-fuelled driver skidding around a bend at high speed and losing control of his vehicle.

Rae looked out of the window as the train sped south. She didn't take in very much of the view. She was trying to imagine the effect Trent Baker's arrival must have had on the farm, with his history of intimidation coupled with continuous drug and alcohol abuse. Had that been the point when Katie had realised that the commune's time was really up? And was her murder the result?

* * *

Back in the main incident room at Wareham, the other three detectives were thinking along the same lines. They were examining copies of the all-important trust document that Rae had emailed through overnight.

'So, we have a motive,' Barry said. 'Doesn't this make it less likely that Brotherton killed her? He was there when the trust was set up and would have known about these clauses all along. He would have realised that killing Katie would result in the commune losing its home for good, but the other two might not have been aware of that.'

'Good point,' Sophie said. 'Although he was a trustee, I reckon Atkins's eyes would have glazed over at the legal wording in this stuff. And Trent Baker appeared on the scene later. He might not have known about it either. Whoever killed her, it looks as though they saw her as an obstacle to certain plans of their own. Those plans could well have included drugs.'

'Maybe we need to look at it from a different angle, ma'am,' Lydia said. 'Let's assume Katie didn't want the commune to fail. Maybe its basic ideas were dear to her heart. She wouldn't have wanted to trigger that clause — she'd have been pulling the plug on everything she'd planned for. But if someone was bringing in hard drugs, what alternative was open to her? To my eyes there's only one. Get the cops in. I wonder if that's what she threatened to do? Maybe she went further and was about to make actual contact with the local police. And that's when someone felt there was no alternative but to stick a knife between her ribs.'

Sophie and Barry looked at each other.

'Convinces me,' Barry said. 'It's neat, simple and explains everything. So, who was it?'

'Trent Baker's still at the top of my list,' Sophie said. 'He had a history of using hard drugs. We know he had a violent streak. But I wonder if he was helped by someone else. When he made that attempt on Catherine Templeton's life a couple of years later, it was done in a frenzy. In the case of Katie Templar, she vanished completely, without a trace. And someone circulated those false rumours of how she'd been seen leaving. It was neat and clever, and for twelve years it took everyone in until we found her body. Those aren't the actions of someone who kills in a fit of rage.'

'So who else helped?' Barry said.

She shrugged. 'Take your pick. Any of the three of them.'

'With respect, that's a cop-out, ma'am,' Barry said.

'Think about it,' Sophie said. 'Andrew Atkins is an untrustworthy schemer. According to his ex, he doesn't even bother to get involved in his own son's life. What does that tell you about his sense of responsibility? Tim Brotherton seems to have been all things to all people at different stages of his life. Is there a real person hidden somewhere behind all those facades? Look at what he's kept from his own partner. She knew nothing about his past. And we know he's a practised liar. Then there's Catherine Templeton. We know she's a liar too. I've never been convinced of the reasons she gave in court for Baker's attempt on her life. I wonder if something else was said between the two of them that night in the pub. I wonder if she said something, even threatened to expose him as Katie's murderer, that made him decide to silence her, but the attempt failed.'

'In that case, why didn't it come to light in the court case?' Barry asked.

'Because they both may have had too much to lose. I've read the court records and talked to some of the officials there. All the way through that trial there's a sense of something left unsaid, something running below the surface, hidden. Which would make sense if it was the two of them that killed her.'

'So, do we make a move on anyone? Bring them in for further questioning?' Lydia asked.

'Nothing formal yet. We'll wait for Rae to arrive and give us the complete picture of what she found. Anyway, we still have Prentice's murder to sort out, in case you've forgotten. It may not have been the same person that killed him and Katie.'

'You don't really believe that, do you, ma'am?' Barry said.

She smiled. 'Of course not. I'm just saying that to keep you on your toes. By the way, the forensic team are having another look at the knife that Baker used in his attack on Catherine Templeton all those years ago. Something suspicious showed up in the evidence used at his trial. And another interesting snippet came in from Polly Nelson just now. Someone got Heathfield Farm valued in the final month before the place was abandoned — a local Bridgwater estate agent took a look at it.'

'Do we know who arranged it?' Barry asked.

Sophie nodded. 'Oh yes. It was our friend Andrew Atkins. I think it's time you and I spoke to this group of lying, scheming tricksters again, Barry. Rae isn't due back until late afternoon, so let's get on with it.'

CHAPTER 31: LIKE A BEGGAR

Friday afternoon

Sophie and Barry drove to Bath through a midsummer rain-storm, the torrential downpour catching them just as they turned onto the Warminster bypass. The rain lasted ten minutes then disappeared as fast as it had arrived, and the streets of Bath were bone dry. They called first at Catherine Templeton's place of work, a small pharmacy in a row of shops along a side street not far from where she lived. She appeared, looking flushed and angry.

'Now what?' she demanded. 'Why are you bothering me at work? Can't it wait, for God's sake?'

This was a very different side to the Catherine they'd been shown a few days before. What was she so worked up about?

Barry waited a few seconds, watching her, before he replied. 'No, it can't. Is there an office we can go to?'

'No, there isn't.' She looked around, frowning, then glanced at her watch. 'It's nearly lunchtime. I'll ask if I can take my break early and we can talk at home. This had better be worth the interruption.'

It took less than three minutes to drive to her house. Catherine stared out of the rear window for the duration of

216

the journey, refusing to respond to any attempt at conversation until they were safely inside her front door. She turned to face them as soon as they were inside.

'So?' she said. 'What's this about?'

With Sophie remaining in the background, Barry began. 'Your car, Ms Templeton. You pointed it out when we last saw you. What you failed to tell us was that you'd only owned the red Ford for a week or so. Until very recently you had a white VW Polo.'

Catherine looked at him through narrowed eyes. 'So what? It didn't seem of major importance. Not to my mind, anyway.'

'When I asked you if you'd driven your car to Dorset anytime recently, you were clear in your reply that you hadn't. What I now need to know is did you drive to Dorset in the Polo? Or in any other car, come to that?'

There was a momentary hesitation. 'No.'

'Did anyone else drive it to Dorset? Did someone borrow it perhaps?'

She shook her head. 'I don't make a habit of lending my car to anyone.'

'I'm not asking about any habitual lending of your car. What about just the once?'

'No. I don't lend my stuff out to people, and certainly not my car.'

'So if it showed up on a CCTV camera at a petrol station in Dorset, it would mean what, exactly?'

During the lengthy silence that followed, Catherine looked as if she was about to explode out of barely restrained rage.

'Someone kept a spare set of keys for the car,' she finally said. 'I've been working weekends lately. Maybe it was borrowed without my knowledge.'

'By who, Ms Templeton?'

She glared at him for a full twenty seconds. 'Andy Atkins. I've known him for years.'

Barry nodded slowly. 'Would that be the same Andrew Atkins who was on the commune with you?'

She nodded.

'And Trent Baker's fishing trip companion on the day he assaulted you?'

Again, a slight nod.

'Is there anything else you want to tell me, Ms Templeton, while you have the chance?'

'No. Of course not. What are you implying?'

'Just that it all seems a bit more complicated than you've led us to believe. You've maintained a close enough friendship with Mr Atkins to trust him with a set of your car keys, even though you never lend it to anyone. It just seems a bit odd to us. He lives and works down in Dorset. Why would he come all the way up here to borrow your car, only to drive it all the way back to Wareham? And then, presumably, make the whole trip again to bring it back? All without your knowledge.' He watched her intently.

'Well, he bloody didn't, did he? If you must know, he spends occasional weekends here, staying with me. Satisfied now?'

'So, are you in a relationship with him?'

'For God's sake, what's it got to do with you? It's our lives. Jesus.'

Barry raised his eyebrows. 'You haven't answered the question.'

'Shit. If you must know, we've been on-off for a long time, ever since those times on the farm, though it's been more off than on. But recently we've been back on.'

'You told us all about your ruined date with Russell Poulter as if he was your new boyfriend. But it seems you were seeing Mr Atkins at the time.'

She sighed loudly. 'It wasn't like that. Why do you make it sound so grubby? Russ was just a dinner date. We'd only had coffee together a few times before that, and it was our first evening out. And that's all it was. Andy and I go way back. It doesn't mean we're an item or anything.'

'It puzzles me that he drove to Wareham in your car. Surely if he was here visiting you, he'd have his own car with him?'

She shook her head. 'He came by train.'

'Well, I'm glad we've got that cleared up. But there is something else we need clarifying. You said that you only joined the commune a few months before it fell apart. We've been talking to a lot of other people who were there at the time and that doesn't seem to be what they remember. According to them, you arrived within the first year of its existence. So why did you tell us otherwise?'

She was beginning to look frazzled. Barry thought of a juggler trying to keep too many plates in the air. Catherine wiped her brow with the back of her hand.

''Cause I was probably boozing and smoking too much dope. My memories are a bit hazy. It's as simple as that.'

'So what you're saying is that we can't rely on anything you've told us about those days, but we can rely on what you're telling us now? Is that right?'

'Oh, for Christ's sake. You're twisting everything. I'm the innocent party here — you should know that. I've a good mind to make a complaint about police harassment.'

'You're perfectly at liberty to do so, Ms Templeton. I've tried my best to be courteous in my questioning, but if you feel I've been too abrasive, you should go ahead. We've clarified what we needed to know, so we'll head off.' He waited a few seconds. 'For now.'

The two detectives left the house, its occupant watching them with a face like thunder.

'She's lying again,' Sophie said. 'No one in their right mind would take a train from Wareham to Bath. It's sixty miles but the train journey involves two long-winded changes. It can take four hours. He has a car, for Christ's sake. Why wouldn't he have used that? Which then begs the question, why did he borrow hers rather than using his own? What was he trying to hide? I think it's time we brought him in.'

She called Dorset while Barry drove onto the motorway, heading for Weston-Super-Mare. Sophie then phoned Tim Brotherton, asking him to wait for them at home. Tim had been ejected from the house he'd shared with Judy Price for the past six months. Apparently, it had been Judy who'd found him his new home, a small bedsit in a rundown part of the town. They found a parking slot close by and walked the few yards to Brotherton's new address.

They mounted the grubby stairwell to the second floor. Sophie shook her head. He'd thrown away a comfortable life with Judy Price for this. Some people just didn't recognise a true gem when they saw one. Too full of his own bullshit, that was Brotherton's problem. But was he a killer? She had her doubts. The doorbell was hanging from its mount with one wire exposed, so Barry rapped on the door. It was opened by a dishevelled Tim Brotherton, hollow-eyed and unshaven.

'Well, hello, Mr Brotherton. What a lovely sunny day it is. Can we come in for a chat?' Sophie had already pushed herself inside.

Barry wished he could manage that bonhomie combined with blatant mischief the way his boss did. It seemed so easy with her, but he knew there was no point in him even trying to copy her technique. He'd never get away with it, not with his more introverted personality. She sometimes appeared to be a bit of a bull in a china shop, although he knew it was all carefully worked out in advance.

'Thanks for letting us know you were moving,' she went on. 'I always appreciate a little bit of cooperation from people. It helps to oil the wheels and puts me in a cheerful mood. That's always a good thing.'

They entered a room that doubled as both living and sleeping accommodation. It had a sash window at the far end, with a sink set below it. A small hob cooker occupied one corner and the nearby worktop was dominated by a microwave oven that seemed to take up most of its surface. A small table and two upright chairs occupied the opposite corner. The divan bed doubled as a couch and was covered by an intricately patterned throw. Brotherton moved to the window and opened it a further couple of inches, pulled the two chairs across to the middle of the room and slumped onto the divan. He looked exhausted.

'I never imagined you in a place like this, Mr Brotherton. It'll just be temporary, I expect?'

Brotherton scowled. 'Yes. I've got myself on the list at a letting agency for something bigger. This was the only place that was available at the time. Beggars can't be choosers, can they? And that's how I'm being made to feel. Like a beggar.'

'I'm sure things will improve for you. We have a few questions, and I need you to be totally honest with us. This time. We have two murder cases and we're getting closer to solving them. Let's start with Paul Prentice, shall we? When was the last time you saw him?'

The silence seemed to last a long time. Finally, Brotherton said, 'A couple of years ago. He turned up on my doorstep with a load of questions. I was living in Taunton at the time. I don't know how he found out where I lived.'

'What kind of questions?' Sophie asked.

Brotherton shrugged. 'The same old stuff. What could I tell him about when Katie Templar left? We'd already been over it all, years before, at the farm just before we shut up shop there. He turned up unannounced then too.'

'So did you tell him the truth or did you spin him the same yarn you gave us?'

'I told you what I believed to be true, that she left early one morning and headed to the local bus stop. Look, I know I said it was me that saw her head off. I admit I should have said it was someone else.'

'Who?'

'It wasn't one person. It was three: Trent Baker, Andy Atkins and Catherine Templeton. They all said they'd seen her go.'

Sophie thought for a few moments. 'But you also said this was early in the morning. I got the impression she was heading for the first bus.'

He nodded. 'That's what they told me.'

'But were they often up at that time? The first bus was at, what, six thirty in the morning?'

'Andy was up then, quite often. He was in charge of the working part of the farm. We had a few cows that needed milking. As for the other two, well. I s'pose it was a bit unusual.'

'Didn't you think it was unusual at the time? Didn't you question them about it?'

He shook his head. 'No. Look, we knew she'd be leaving at some point, to join Prentice. It wasn't a surprise.'

'The thing is, Mr Brotherton, Andrew Atkins denies seeing her that morning. He told me that she slipped out during the night, and no one actually saw her go. So who am I to believe?'

He looked shaken. 'I can't believe it. All three of them told me the same thing.'

'So why did you tell me something different last week? Why did you imply that you'd seen her?'

He shook his head slowly. 'Misplaced loyalty. I was trying to protect them, even after all these years. I still want to protect everyone who was there in that commune. I put my heart and soul into that place and into supporting the people there. When you told me about the body, I just didn't believe it could have been her — Katie. I believed what they told me. Why would three people lie?'

Sophie looked squarely at him. 'Are you really as stupid as you sound, Mr Brotherton? Have any of them been in touch with you recently?'

'I went to see Catherine a few days ago. She was angry. Andy came to see me last month. It was the first time I'd seen either of them since we left the farm.'

'So you haven't seen Trent Baker?'

He shook his head. 'Why would I go looking for him? I didn't realise at the time just how nasty he is.'

'He was at the hospital last weekend, trying to dig for information about Judy. He's been seen several times during the past week sitting in a car across the road from the house you were sharing with Judy. How do you feel about that?'

Brotherton put his head in his hands. 'Christ. What the hell's going on?'

'You tell us, Mr Brotherton. You're the one who was meant to be on top of what was going on all those years ago. Or were you just wandering around with your head in the clouds?'

He didn't answer.

'Let's turn to the facts, shall we? I need to know more about the trust that had nominal ownership of the farm. In particular, some of the clauses that Katie had written into the deeds. Let's start with the one that gave her the final say in the appointment of trustees.'

Brotherton's expression was blank for a moment. 'Oh, the trust. I'd forgotten all about that. God, it all was so long ago. What do you want me to tell you?'

'Well, how did you feel about it? You were the group leader, after all.'

He shrugged. 'I don't know. I never really thought about it.'

Sophie looked at him closely. Was he still covering things up? 'But it must have been a nuisance, Mr Brotherton, surely? It meant your hands were tied to some extent. It would have prevented you from adding Trent Baker as a trustee during the final year or so.'

He appeared to be lost in thought. 'Maybe that turned out to be a good thing. He got added as a signatory to the bank account though. That was probably enough. It might even have been a step too far. Anyway, what do you mean *would have prevented*? It did prevent him, that's what I thought.'

Sophie shook her head. 'No. Because the board of trustees had already folded by then. Didn't you realise that? Come on, Mr Brotherton, get real. The ownership of the farm reverted back to Katie a couple of weeks before she died, when Trent Baker smuggled in some cocaine. That action would have triggered the reversion clause. You must have known. When she vanished, the farm was already back in her sole possession. You and all the others were close to being illegal squatters. Maybe you and the other trustees kept it from the others, even your pal Trent.'

'I never told anyone about a clause like that, even Trent. I must have forgotten about it myself. Are you sure about it?'

'Oh yes. We have a copy of the trust document and we've had a legal expert pick it to pieces. Coupled with a couple of witnesses to the fact that Baker had begun to bring drugs in.'

Barry stepped forward. 'Timothy Brotherton. I'm arresting you on suspicion of the murder of Katie Templar at Heathfield Farm in Somerset in July 2005. You do not have to say anything. But it may harm your defence if you do not mention when questioned something which you later rely on in court. Anything you do say may be given in evidence.'

At that moment, Sophie's phone rang.

Once Brotherton was safely stowed in the local squad car that had been waiting around the corner, Sophie told Barry the news.

'That was Matt at HQ. Andy Atkins was nowhere to be found when the hit squad called to pick him up early this morning. And it gets worse. Trent Baker has gone walkabout from his home in Bristol, despite the watch on his flat.'

'So what now? Should we arrange for Catherine to be lifted — if only for her own protection?' Barry was looking worried.

'My thoughts exactly,' Sophie said. 'She's gonna be one angry bunny, but we need her safe. I'll get on the phone to Polly Nelson.'

Barry's brain was working fast. 'It's possible they've been acting independently, but my guess is that this is a joint effort. Could they be trying to get out of the country?'

'It's possible, but I don't see how Baker could manage it — we've still got his passport. Even Atkins wouldn't find it easy, not with all the airport security we have in place nowadays. I just wonder if they're meeting up somewhere and planning to lay low for a few months. The question is, where? Where's a good place, somewhere between Wareham and Bristol, where they might be able to live under the radar for a while? It'd have to be close to a motorway in case they need to move on quickly.'

Barry laughed. 'You've answered your own question, haven't you?'

CHAPTER 32: THE SEARCH

Friday afternoon

The wooded slopes of the Quantock Hills seemed to have lain undisturbed for centuries. Moss-covered trees crowded together on the uneven slopes, bringing a perpetual gloom to the spindly brambles, ferns and nettles that tried to rise from the semi-twilight beneath the high canopy of foliage. It was cool and dank, the occasional clearings like oases of greenery in which wildflowers, grass and assorted shrubs made the most of the sunlight. Rabbits nibbled at the tufts and deer moved slowly across the clearings, only to vanish into the shadows beneath the trees. Even the birdsong was sporadic, and it was almost impossible to spot the birds themselves, up in the top layer of branches, hidden from the sight of anyone at ground level. The police search team, a party of only twelve, moved forward silently. Greg Buller's snatch squad was with them, up from Dorset, along with Gerry Baldwin and Floyd, the police dog, plus Sophie Allen and Barry Marsh. Everyone was dressed in black combat-style gear and boots. Two firearms officers were with the group, and the rest carried Tasers.

They'd started at the farm, checking the derelict buildings to see if anything had been moved since the forensic team had left several days earlier, but nothing seemed out of place. The silence was eerie. Sophie recalled what Rae had said about her unease when she'd first visited the long-abandoned farm. Maybe it was due to the way the light played on the forested slopes of the coombe, the dappled mix of brightness and shadow — mostly shadow. There was no doubt that the short vale had a strange atmosphere about it. Could renovating the farm change all that? Sophie didn't see why not.

The team began to move through the fields towards the place where they'd found Katie Templar's body. Beyond that, the woods were wilder and the slopes steeper. Sophie could understand why Rae had felt as she did about the Quantocks. The whole area breathed an atmosphere of loneliness and threat, and it was all too easy to imagine some nameless, malevolent force lurking in the shadows. Had it always been like this? Katie Templar had grown up on the farm, living here with her aunt and uncle after the death of her parents. Her jottings had suggested that she loved the place, not just the nearby fields and pastures but the woods and hillsides too. Of course, that was before violent death had come calling.

Greg Buller, the search co-ordinator, had decided to make an initial sweep of the area immediately around the farm then cover the north-east slope of the coombe during the afternoon. By early evening their numbers would be swelled by the arrival of extra personnel from Somerset, so the search area could be widened. Sunset wouldn't be until ten o'clock this early in the summer so, with luck, they would have the whole of the immediate area checked by the time darkness fell. It had to be done carefully. Andy Atkins was an experienced forestry worker who would know how to use the lie of the land to hide his movements. Moreover, he'd been a worker on the farm for almost a decade in his youth. He'd know every nook and cranny, every copse and thicket. Sophie was worried that the two fugitives would manage to slip through the net. She'd requested that officers from the local force check all local car parks, side roads and areas of waste ground looking out for unidentified cars, particularly any that matched the descriptions of the ones belonging to Atkins and Baker. But would they have been stupid enough to have driven to this area to hide, then left their cars on public display? It was unlikely. It would make more sense for them to have driven to Bridgwater or Taunton, and then taken a bus to within walking distance. Of course, all this assumed that the two runaways had come to this area in the first place. What if her and Barry's guess was wrong? They could have gone anywhere in the country. But the search had to start somewhere, and this seemed a likely location. Something still told her that she was right, that the two suspects were lurking nearby while they made long-term plans. All of this bother could have been saved if Trent Baker had been kept locked up for longer after breaking the terms of his parole. Maybe that had been too much to hope for, with Britain's prisons bursting at the seams.

* * *

'I still don't know whether I made the right decision. She might well blow a gasket when she sees me here. I mean, what exactly can I bring to this search effort in my state? I ask you!' Lydia Pillay was struggling to clamber out of Rae's car, hampered by her elbow crutches. Rae Gregson was at the rear, pulling a collapsible wheelchair out of the boot.

'Come on, Lydia. Now you're here, you may as well make the most of it.' Rae assembled the wheelchair and pushed it towards her. 'Your carriage awaits, ma'am.'

Lydia lowered herself into the wheelchair. 'Where exactly are we going, anyway?'

'I thought maybe the local tea shop first? I'm parched after that drive. I could do with a quick cuppa.' Rae pushed the wheelchair along the narrow pavements of Bishops Lydeard village centre, where she found a café and manoeuvred it inside. The interior was cool and dark, and smelled of strawberry jam. The solitary member of staff looked up briefly and then returned to her phone.

'How about a cream tea?' Lydia suggested. 'The smell of those scones is making my stomach rumble. Duty calls and all that, but we can delay our response for twenty minutes or so.'

'You know me. I always follow the orders of a superior officer,' Rae said, 'especially when food's involved.' She placed the order and joined Lydia at the table covered in chintz and set with pretty place mats.

'So how do we play this, boss?' Rae asked. 'I mean, they're only half expecting me to appear and that's a bit later on. I was lucky to get an earlier train than I thought. And as for you, well . . .'

'I don't know. Maybe I should have thought things through a bit more before insisting on coming with you. I don't reckon I'll be very much use, will I? Not like this.' Lydia gave a mirthless laugh. 'I suppose I can help with the co-ordination. Checking off maps and so on. Ticking lists. You know, all that vital stuff.'

The waitress brought their tea and scones, complete with small dishes of clotted cream and jam, all served in pretty chinaware.

'That smells divine,' said Lydia, closing her eyes in mock ecstasy.

'Those are lovely photos on the wall,' Rae said to the waitress. 'Did you take them?'

The waitress shook her head. 'My partner. He's trying to set himself up in a photography business but it's hard going. I display some of his best ones to help with the promotion. They're for sale and all were taken around here.'

'What, even the caves?' Rae said. 'I didn't realise the Quantocks had any.'

'Nor did I, and I've lived here all my life,' the waitress said. 'It was only after I started seeing Gary, my partner. He wanders around all over the place with his camera. Apparently they're the only two round here, and they're pretty small by caving standards. Serious cavers never bother with them. Who'd come here with the Mendips only an hour's drive away?'

'Can I have a closer look?'

The waitress took the two photos from the wall and brought them across. 'They're only a few miles away,' she said. 'You can see where they are from the photo titles. This one, Holwell Cavern, is bigger but I think the farmer who owns the land has blocked the entrance to stop people going in. This other one, Cothelstone Hill Cave, is pretty small. It's almost completely hidden in a small wood, as you can see. I always think it looks a bit spooky, but it makes a lovely photo, don't you think?'

'I'll buy them both,' Rae said. 'Forty quid the pair. What do you say?'

'Done.' The waitress smiled delightedly.

* * *

They left the car on the grass verge close to a five-bar gate. A farm track led around a low hill towards a distant set of buildings, but the two detectives were more interested in a faint path running up a shoulder of grassland, beyond which Holwell Cave should be situated.

'Are you okay?' Rae asked. To her this was just a gentle stroll, but Lydia still had months of treatment to go before she would be fully fit. Nevertheless, Lydia was setting a good pace for someone still on elbow crutches.

'Don't fuss, please. I'm fine. This is just what the doctor ordered, and it can't be more than fifty yards. Once we're on that high spot we should be able to see the cave area fairly clearly.'

'I don't think this path has been used for months. I haven't spotted a single broken blade of grass, let alone a footprint of any kind. And that gate we came through hadn't been opened for ages.' Rae was growing anxious. Nobody knew they were here, mainly because Lydia had refused to call in and tell the boss what they were up to.

'C'mon, Rae,' she'd said. 'Who on earth would ever think that two dozy women, one of them a cripple, walking a few yards up a hillside, were on the lookout for runaway thugs? It's a no-brainer.'

They reached the top of the rise and stopped. The area was deserted. They could see the rocky outcrop ahead. Lydia peered at it through her binoculars. 'The area's covered with nettles and brambles, and I can see some barbed wire. It doesn't look as though anyone's been in there for months. Let's get back.'

Lydia found the downhill return more of a struggle and she was clearly in some discomfort when they climbed back into the car. 'That settles it,' Rae said. 'It's the wheelchair for the next one, or you stay by the car.'

'It should be fine,' Lydia panted, still out of breath. 'The map shows a definite track running close to Cothelstone Cave, probably for farm vehicles. I don't think we should get too close, just have a general look-see.'

The area around the second cave proved to be much more heavily wooded than the approach to the larger one they'd just left. Rae parked the car and got out. A small stream tumbled down a narrow gorge with a dirt track beside it. Lydia had already got her breath back, but Rae took the wheelchair out of the boot and manoeuvred it into position.

'I'd just feel happier with you in it, Lydia. It means you can concentrate on the terrain as we pass and if we do need to make a quick getaway, we can move faster than if you were on your feet.'

Lydia sighed. 'Okay, Miss bossy-boots. No need to rub it in.'

They proceeded slowly up the narrow coombe. Lydia had her binoculars out and was carefully examining their surroundings as if she was looking for birds. The sound of trickling water gave the scene a peaceful air.

'There are footprints in that damp patch of mud over there,' Lydia said. 'Don't stop, just get a bit closer as you pass.'

Rae did as she was told. 'Two sets,' she said. 'Different sizes. Very recent. Shall I go on a bit further?'

'Yes.'

Rae walked on. 'Cigarette butt on the ground to our right. It looks very fresh. I'm getting goosebumps. Do you think we're being watched?'

'I don't know, but I'm starting to feel uneasy too. Do you hear how the birds have stopped singing ahead of us? It may be coincidence, but let's play it safe. Turn around and we'll head back.'

Rae turned the chair and headed back to the car, expecting a blow to the back of the head at any moment. She helped Lydia into the passenger seat, packed the wheelchair away and started the engine. It was a while before either of them spoke.

'Okay,' Rae said, 'how are we going to do this without the boss blowing a gasket? I'm terrified of getting the sack for putting us in danger. After what happened to you just a few months ago, she's going to be livid. I never really thought we'd find anything.'

Lydia looked at her glumly. 'Neither did I.'

CHAPTER 33: THE CAVE

Friday afternoon

Sophie spent some time looking at the two photographs. The search group was having a well-deserved break for refreshments, sitting inside the unit's control van, which was parked in the ramshackle farmyard.

'You say you bought them at a café nearby? I didn't know there were caves in the Quantocks.'

'Well, that's it, ma'am,' Rae said. 'Hardly anyone does. It was the waitress who told us they were local. We drove past them on the way here.'

Sophie turned to the search leader, Greg Buller. 'What do you think, Greg? Would it be realistic for them to hole up in a cave?'

He shrugged. 'At any other time of the year I'd say no. Caves are too cold, too wet and too dark for people to live in them for long. But we're just coming into high summer and it's been relatively dry for the past month. It's possible. Maybe it's worth giving them the once-over. We've drawn a blank here.'

'Start with the smaller one — Cothelstone,' Lydia said. 'We had a quick look at the hillside leading to the other one and it looked like no one had been near it for weeks. The entrance looks as if it's blocked too, not like the photo. Cothelstone is more accessible.'

Sophie looked at her askance but made no comment. 'Can we go with that, Greg?'

'Sure. Either way round, it doesn't matter to me. I'll get a team sorted and we can make a start in an hour.' He got out of the van.

Sophie switched her attention back to the map, saying under her breath, 'Don't underestimate me, you two. Greg might not have spotted what you didn't say, but I'm not so easily taken in. And that's all I've got to say on the matter. Now go and find yourselves something useful to do. Barry's around here somewhere.' With that, she turned her back on them and walked out.

'Phew. I think we got away with it,' Lydia said.

Rae said nothing. She had to work with Sophie every day, whereas Lydia could afford to be more relaxed about upsetting her.

Twelve search personnel were detailed to take part in the raid on the cave, with four of them working their way further up the narrow valley in a Land Rover and approaching from above. With meticulous co-ordination, their sudden swoop worked like clockwork. Rae and Lydia waited by their car, parked just where they'd been two hours earlier. They heard the voices of the returning team before they came into sight. They had two teenage boys with them, both clearly drunk. Greg Buller was carrying a plastic supermarket bag in which cans of lager and a half-bottle of vodka rattled.

'Not exactly the result we were looking for,' he said, as one of the lads lurched sideways and threw up in a nearby bush.

'We're performing our civic duty, Greg,' Sophie replied. 'Can someone take these two young reprobates home? Apparently, they live in Bishops Lydeard.' Her gaze homed in on Rae and Lydia. 'A job for you two, I think.'

Lydia was clearly about to object, but Rae dug an elbow into her ribs.

* * *

It took only another thirty minutes for the squad to regroup and initiate a similar swoop on the larger cave at Holwell. By this time, they'd been joined by a group of local Somerset officers who were also members of the Mendips Cave Rescue team, complete with some serious caving gear. Although this second cave was supposed to have been blocked by a huge wall of soil debris some thirty metres in, it had always been thought that the tunnel probably ran much further. If the two runaways had settled in the cave, they might have found a way past the obstruction.

Greg Buller waited until everyone was in their designated position, and then gave the order to move in. As the team reached the narrow cave entrance, it was clear that the corrugated sheet that covered it was slightly askew, with enough of a gap for a person to slip through. The upper strand of barbed wire had been untied from its post in such a way that it could easily be pulled aside and refastened.

'Whoever it is, they've come from up the hill,' Buller said. 'What about the farmer, Barry? Did he have anything to say?'

Barry shook his head. 'No. He says he hasn't seen anyone here for weeks. Maybe they arrived after dark.' He kept quiet about the farmer's report of the two young women he'd spotted that afternoon, making their way halfway to the cave before returning to their car. 'Could it be our two?'

'You lot know more than me. You've met them. What do you think?' Buller asked.

'Andy Atkins has lived in this area for most of his life and he's worked on several of the local farms,' Sophie said. 'He would know about this place. As for Trent Baker, well, no one knows what's going on in his head. And he's been in a prison cell for the past decade. This couldn't be much worse than a cell, could it?' She tightened the straps on her stab-proof vest. 'Are we ready to move in? Does everyone know what they're doing?' She looked at each of them, waiting for their confirmation. At least they'd had a chance to practice at the previous cave. 'Okay, Greg. Over to you.'

Buller led the way, accompanied by two armed officers from his squad. Barry moved in with two cavers and another four members of the uniformed team as protection. Sophie brought up the rear with two more armed personnel, who swept the beams of their powerful torches around the sides of the narrow tunnel. Another small group remained outside, spread across the hillside and keeping a lookout.

Initially, the walls of the cave were dry, but they soon spotted areas of moisture where water seeped in from the underlying rock. The team slowly and silently advanced, checking each gully and rock shelf. Sophie saw a bend in the tunnel ahead. The groups in front of her stopped, with a gap of several yards between each one. She watched Barry move forward and stand beside Buller, peering ahead. He whispered something to Buller and gave a nod.

There was a sudden movement forward at the front of the group and she heard Buller shout, 'Armed police. Stand up and put your hands in the air. Now.'

Someone shone a powerful light on the back of the cave. Two men stood, screwing up their eyes against the dazzle. Sophie stepped forward. Trent Baker. Andy Atkins. Rae had been right.

CHAPTER 34: THE KNIFE

Saturday morning

There it was. The knife. Safely sealed in a strong, transparent plastic wallet, still coated with dried fish slime and Catherine Templeton's blood, along with other bits of residue. Residues that had perplexed the analysts at the time of Catherine Templeton's assault a decade earlier, but now made total sense and provided that final piece of hard evidence. The forensic analysis a decade earlier had, of course, found large quantities of Catherine's DNA. How could they not? The blade had been coated with her blood, as had the handle. What had puzzled them then were the traces of another person's DNA, someone who had never been identified. Until now. Sophie had that particular ten-year-old profile laid out in front of her, along with the one that had arrived from the Somerset forensic lab, extracted from the bone marrow of the buried skeleton, which had been positively identified as being that of Katie Templar. Fortunately her dental records were still held in a Bishops Lydeard dental practice, even after more than a decade had passed. The two profiles matched exactly. She'd been killed with Trent Baker's knife. But what was the story behind the act? Sophie still didn't fully understand the complex interplay between the main protagonists. What had happened between them all those years ago? Financial pressures, loss of control and ownership of the farm, drugs, petty jealousies and rivalries, psychotic personalities and even an abortion. What a toxic mix.

She examined the knife. Its blade was about eight inches long, dulled by the stains that had dried onto its once shiny surface. But it was the handle that caught the attention. It was made of a dark wood, with engravings of intertwined snakes running along its length. This wasn't a knife that would be forgotten in a hurry, it would be too easy to identify for one thing. People would remember it and, equally important, who the owner was. This was the kind of knife an attention-seeking show-off would own and flash around to impress people. Who else but Trent Baker? Why on earth had he kept the knife after Katie Templar's murder? Why hadn't he at the very least cleaned it? Any sensible person would have disposed of it as soon as possible, maybe burying it well away from the body or throwing it in a waste bin in a neighbouring village. But then Trent Baker wasn't a sensible person. *Narcissistic, attention-seeking sociopath* would be an apt description of this man, someone so self-obsessed as to be incapable of logical reasoning. Someone who clearly got a kick out of destructive and violent mischief-making.

She faced him now, across the interview room table. 'You see, Mr Baker, we don't even have to prove that the knife is yours. That's already been done, ten years ago, during the trial for Catherine Templeton's attempted murder. So, for ten years we've had the weapon you used to murder Katie Templar safely under lock and key, vacuum-packed and kept in perfect conditions. We have witnesses who will testify that you frequently waved this knife about on the farm when you were drunk or high and wanting to intimidate people. What I want to know is this: why? Why did you kill her?'

'I didn't.'

'Your knife, Mr Baker. And we know you had an argument with her. Why not make it easy on yourself and tell us the truth for once?'

He didn't reply.

'Can you explain the money in your bank account?' Sophie asked. 'It's been there for, what, just over twelve years? Where did you suddenly come by that amount?' She glanced at her notes. 'Interesting that it was originally about a third of the money that went missing from the farm's account. Just coincidence maybe?'

He sneered at her. 'Fuck off, you cunt.'

He said nothing else, refusing to answer any more questions. Any detailed account of the events that led to the young woman's death would have to come from the other people involved, and how likely were they to cooperate? Sophie and Barry closed the interview and moved to the adjacent room, where Tim Brotherton sat, tapping his fingers nervously on the tabletop.

'I still can't believe it,' he said. 'I was convinced she'd left to join Paul Prentice.'

'You've told us that a dozen times, Mr Brotherton,' Barry said. 'What we need now are facts. Why she was killed, for instance. So let's go back to the time of her abortion, when she returned from London with Paul Prentice. Take us through what happened.'

Brotherton looked down, frowning. 'She was pale. She looked really ill. Exhausted. Even Paul looked depressed and anxious. I guessed something major had happened, but I wasn't ready for what they told me. I hated the thought of what she'd done.'

'But you'd abandoned her, hadn't you? Several weeks earlier? Didn't she find you sleeping with someone else? What did you expect, Mr Brotherton?'

'I don't know. Maybe I was too young and naïve. We all were, I guess. It was that day, more than anything, that made me realise how futile it all was. How our dream had gone sour.' He paused. 'How I'd let everyone down, but most of all her. I felt sick at myself.'

'Who was it you were having a fling with? The one that caused the break-up?'

'Catherine. Catherine Templeton.'

'And what happened to that relationship?'

He shook his head from side to side as if to dispel unwelcome memories.

'I was so ashamed of myself, I stopped seeing her. I drank too much. Paul left shortly afterwards to see if he could find somewhere for him and Katie to live. His job had been kept open for him apparently. Katie was going to join him once the situation at the farm had settled down, that's what he said. There was a lot of legal stuff to sort out.'

'Did it ever get sorted out, Mr Brotherton?'

He answered quietly, 'No. She was the senior trustee. I was still trying to talk her round when she left.'

'Talk her round to what?'

He looked miserable. 'To taking more of a backseat role. Handing responsibility over to me. Adding a couple more people as trustees.'

'Who?'

'Trent Baker and Catherine Templeton. He'd been pushing me to sort it out with Katie. He wanted to formalise his role in the group. The two of them were together by then. The thing is, with Paul gone and Katie threatening to leave, it only left me and Andy as trustees. Adding Trent and Catherine would bring us back to four. Well, that's what I thought. Then, one evening, Katie told us the ownership had reverted to her. She refused to endorse Trent as a trustee, claiming he'd brought hard drugs into the group. There was a huge argument, with her on one side and Trent and Andy on the other.'

'How did it end? Was there any resolution?'

Brotherton kept his eyes on the table. 'Not really. She said she was thinking of calling the police in because of the drugs. I just couldn't believe what was happening. I had no idea there were drugs coming in. I hadn't seen any. But she was adamant.'

'How did it all finish?'

'She walked out. I followed her and tried to reason with her, but she was having none of it. She told me it was over. When I got back to the meeting room it was empty. The others had gone.'

Barry thought hard. 'When did that meeting take place?'

'I think it was the evening before she left. My memory's a bit blurry, but I think that's when it was.'

'You mean the evening before she was murdered, Mr Brotherton. She never got an opportunity to leave.'

* * *

Sophie sat opposite Andy Atkins in the interview room, Barry beside her. She had an idea that he might break more easily than the others.

'Think of the position you're in, Mr Atkins. We have two dead bodies and you're heavily implicated in both murders. Your friend Trent Baker has already served a ten-year sentence for the attempted murder of Catherine Templeton with that vicious knife of his, and you just happened to be in the area at the time, on your supposed fishing expedition. Now we find the same knife was used to kill Katie Templar all those years ago and, lo and behold, who was present at that meeting at the farm, and supporting Trent Baker? You. He couldn't have done it alone. She was buried in a properly dug grave, several hundred yards away from the farm buildings. He would have needed help to get her body up there. You'd been working on that farm, on and off, since you were a teenager. You knew the layout intimately — the fields, the woods, the hedgerows. You would even have known how deep the soil was, how pliable. And as for Paul Prentice, we have all the evidence we need. We've even got a statement from the pharmacist in Blandford who treated the scratches you got from the dog. How do you think it's going to look to a jury? Do you seriously think you have the remotest chance of getting off? Because if you do, you're living in fantasy land. To cap it all, we traced the doctor in Bath who gave you the rabies jab the following day. He remembers you well, along with the conversation about bat populations. Come on. Get real. Tell us what happened.'

She sat back and watched him. His head was bowed so she couldn't see his eyes. His face was pale and drawn. Had he slept at all last night? She doubted it. He was an outdoor type, someone who needed open spaces and fresh air. His first night in the cells would have been a nightmare.

Finally, he spoke. 'I didn't do either of them.'

Sophie was about to speak but he held his hand up. 'I was there, but I didn't kill them. I've been set up as the fall guy, particularly for Prentice.'

'Who by?'

'It's complicated.'

Isn't it always, Sophie thought. But she smiled brightly at him. 'I'm all ears.'

CHAPTER 35: TRUTH WILL OUT

Saturday morning

'What is this all about? Why have you brought me here? I don't even live in Dorset, as you well know.'

Catherine Templeton was clearly angry, but she was managing to hold her temper in check. Just. Her cheeks were flushed, and her eyes were constantly darting around the room, occasionally settling on the two detectives sitting opposite her, neither of whom answered her questions.

'Don't think you can play your psychological games with me,' she suddenly said, showing a spark of her usual anger. 'This is ridiculous.'

Sophie shook her head. 'It isn't a game, Ms Templeton, not anymore. When someone is murdered or subjected to a violent assault, what might have been a game up to that point becomes tragically serious, as you well know, having come within a whisker of losing your own life a decade ago. Tell me, did it change your outlook on life, being the victim of a murder attempt like that?'

She watched Catherine closely.

'Of course it did. Have you any idea what it's like, watching and feeling someone stick a knife into you? Knowing your lifeblood is ebbing away? Feeling more and more distant from everything and seeing it all fade to nothing?'

'I haven't, no. The rest of us can try to imagine what it must be like, but it's almost impossible. Particularly if we haven't witnessed such an attack either. Unlike you.'

Catherine sat up with a start. 'What do you mean?' She leaned forward in her seat and glared at Sophie.

'Exactly what I said. You were there when Trent Baker killed Katie Templar in precisely the same way, two years earlier. And it must have shocked you. The blood. The look of total terror on her face as she realised what was happening. Tell me, does witnessing a violent death like that, close up, have a life-changing effect? Are you the same person afterwards? The evidence tends to suggest not.'

Catherine became indignant. 'I don't know what you're talking about.'

'You got blood on your clothes. One of the other women on the farm saw you in the laundry room, early the next morning, trying to wash the stains out. She went out when she saw what you were doing, so you never noticed her.'

'I'm not saying anything.'

'Look, we're not after you for Katie's murder, not if you help us out. It's got so many similarities to Baker's attack on you that we're satisfied he wielded the knife. But you were there. You watched. Maybe what happened shocked you. Maybe it wasn't what you'd thought would happen. But we need to know. If you don't tell me now, you'll be charged with murder, alongside Trent Baker. Do you really want that?'

Like the other two interviewees, Catherine stared down at the table. She shook her head. 'She was such a goody-goody, that woman. She acted as if she was some kind of saint. What right did she have to tell us what we could or couldn't do? Bloody Tim Brotherton had become totally withdrawn for some reason. When he did speak, he was all preachy too, as if he was some kind of messiah. He was worse than useless in that state. So we got her alone, to try and reason with her.'

'Who's we?'

'Me, Andy and Trent Baker.'

'About what?'

'The future of the place. There was some kind of trust that owned the farm and she was on it. So was Andy, but she and Tim always kept him in the dark about the decisions they made. Andy and Trent reckoned this was the best time to change things, what with Tim living in a dream world of his own. So we got her into the meeting room late that night, after a formal group meeting had finished. We thought she'd see reason. I always thought she was a bit of a softie, but she showed a different side that night. I didn't realise Trent and Andy were out of their heads on something. She refused point blank to add us to the committee. Then she told us that she was going to call the cops in. Trent blew a gasket and suddenly she was backed up against the wall with him lashing out at her. It was only when I saw the blood that I realised what he'd done. I didn't know he was like that. It was a total shock to me.'

'So, what happened then?'

'It was late, so no one was around. They got her body out and I cleaned up. That's when I must have got blood on my clothes.'

Sophie smiled at her. 'That wasn't so hard, was it? Aren't you glad you've got it all off your chest?' Catherine nodded. 'And everything you've told us is the truth?'

'Oh, yes. Absolutely.'

Sophie turned to Barry and raised her eyebrows.

His voice was low, almost kindly. 'Catherine, could you tell us how traces of your DNA came to be found on the remnants of a heavy wooden branch on Paul Prentice's campfire at Arne?'

She went white and started to shiver, pulling her thin summer cardigan more closely round her. 'I want a lawyer.'

* * *

Rae wandered into the incident room and saw Sophie and Barry standing by the window, talking. 'I'm exhausted. I hope all that driving you made me do was worth it.'

244

Barry merely laughed. Sophie said, 'What? Do you mean you ever doubted us, Rae? Shame on you! No, it may have seemed insignificant but that little bit of evidence from Catherine Templeton's neighbour was crucial. Haven't I always said that nosey neighbours are my favourite people? When we heard from Taunton that Prentice probably made a visit to Bath a few weeks ago, we had to check it out. So what was she like, this neighbour?'

Rae rolled her eyes. 'A bit snooty if you ask me. That's probably why she remembers him calling on Catherine. I mean, a tramp. Who can approve of someone like that coming to call on your neighbour, particularly in a place like Bath? No wonder she was at the window with her ear pressed to the glass. Not that she would ever admit to that, of course. Anyway, from what she overheard, it sounds as if Prentice was getting close to the truth about what happened to Katie. It was only a couple of days before he was killed. Is that what you think happened too?'

'Yes. He was probably getting closer to the whereabouts of the missing money as well. Remember his background in finance? He'd know what to look for. Maybe he dropped a hint about it. Our guess is that Catherine followed him to find out where he was based. Her work confirms that she was off ill the next day. It ties in with the statement from the guy at the hostel in Taunton that Prentice had seen someone he recognised and left in a hurry. We know Atkins visited Catherine that weekend. He probably drove to hers to talk things over and they decided to silence Prentice one way or another. They travelled to Arne in her car, she clobbered Prentice and he went after the dog.'

'So, was it Atkins that Jade saw, poking around the place a few days later?'

'We think so. It was after we'd released the first press statement, the one after Jade found Prentice's body. It mentioned that the dog was still alive. Our guess is that they thought we wouldn't be that bothered by the death of a down-and-out and that we wouldn't know who he was. But he must have remembered that the dog's collar came off in the struggle. That's why he was there, looking for it, before he started work that morning.'

Rae frowned. 'Do you really want Jade called as a witness? The defence barrister would have a field day with her being your daughter.'

'We know,' Barry said. 'It'll be up to the CPS. We'll use Pauline Stopley if we can. She saw him the night Prentice was killed, and the description matches. They'll only call Jade if they have to.'

Rae frowned. 'I don't understand. If Catherine Templeton was only a witness to the murder at the farm and didn't take part, why get herself involved in a murder now? I can't see her doing it out of love for Atkins. She's too indifferent to other people.'

'I think you've answered your own question, Rae,' Sophie said. 'My guess is that she's neatly swapped roles with Atkins in her account of what happened that night at the farm. I think it was her and Baker who killed Katie, with Atkins as the onlooker. And one or the other of them has manipulated him ever since. They're two very unpleasant people. That's why they fell out with each other. And once that happened, Baker had little choice but to try and silence her. He was the one who actually killed Katie, remember. When I read the transcript of his trial, I felt there was something unspoken, some kind of history between the two of them. Now we know what it was. Shakespeare got it right. *Truth will out.*'

CHAPTER 36: THREE DINNER DATES

Saturday evening

Judy Price had met Russell Poulter several times during the previous week, after bumping into him at Taunton police station where they'd both gone to finalise their statements. They'd started talking and something clicked. They'd shared a coffee and had then enjoyed a second evening in a pub in Weston, near to where Judy lived. This was their first visit to a proper restaurant, this time in Bath, close to where Russell lived. In fact, it was the very restaurant that had hosted Russell's ill-fated date with the thunderously angry Catherine Templeton.

Judy was feeling happy and relaxed, as if a great weight had been lifted from her shoulders. As indeed it had, with that bloody Tim Brotherton facing possible prosecution for conspiracy and the whole, sorry mess of her relationship with him finally put to rest. She looked across the table at Russell. He seemed like a decent guy — reliable, honest, considerate and eager to please. The detectives had all been full of praise for him when she'd asked what he was like. It was about time she found someone sensible to settle down with. Maybe this was him at last, the elusive man that she'd always known she ought to be looking for, rather than the arrogant, thoughtless and self-centred idiots she'd too easily taken up with in the past. She watched him as he tucked into his plate of lasagne. He wasn't pretentious. He didn't brag or boast. He didn't try to impress her with tales of his exploits. He didn't try to dominate the conversation but really listened to what she had to say. Judy had even met his mother a few hours earlier when she'd called at his house to collect him. Mrs Poulter had been dropping off some photos of a recent family wedding. Poor Russell had obviously been taken by surprise and looked as though he was praying for the ground to open and swallow him up. Obviously the last thing he wanted was his mother fussing over him in front of his new girlfriend. In fact, Mrs Poulter had been a proper sweetheart, with the same considerate approach to people as her son.

Suddenly aware he was being observed, Russell smiled and blushed at the same time, and Judy's heart softened further. What a find. So unlike the secretive and controlling Tim Brotherton.

Looking Russell in the eye she raised her wineglass. 'To us.'

'What's brought this on?' he asked. 'Do you want to share it with me?'

'I don't know. It's hard to pin down, but I feel kind of comfortable with you, you know? Maybe it was meeting your mum earlier. I thought she was lovely. And you're such a nice guy, Russ. You're easy to be with, easy to talk to, easy to like. I think I may be a bit tipsy already.'

He blushed again. 'I don't know what to say.'

She laughed. 'Don't say anything.'

Then she leant across the table and kissed him quickly on the lips. She could taste the sauce. Very nice.

* * *

Sophie Allen selected her clothes carefully. Possibly in her younger years she would have chosen black, but recently she'd become all too aware of the way in which it could age someone with her middle-aged skin and pale complexion. She opted for grey: a pair of well-cut grey trousers, and a mottled grey and cream top in an animal-print pattern. A cashmere cardigan, a pair of wedge-heeled sandals, a slate-coloured bag, and she was ready. She picked up her small overnight bag, walked to the car and set off, heading into the evening sun.

She was ten minutes late in arriving, deliberately so. She'd driven to Dorchester more slowly than usual, enjoying the mild, balmy air and the views of the rolling Dorset country-side. How fortunate she was to be living here. Sometimes she felt as if she were living in heaven.

Pauline Stopley was already at the restaurant, sitting at a table in a secluded alcove. She was dressed in cream and tan, and looked stunning. Sophie smiled to herself. Surely those were the same leather trousers that Rae had raved about when she'd interviewed Pauline? The former actress rose as Sophie approached and the two women embraced briefly.

'It's lovely to see you after all this time,' Pauline said. 'I'd given up hope of you ever taking me up on my idea of an evening out. You look as cool and elegant as usual. How do you do it, in your job? Oh, congratulations on the promotion, by the way. I guess you're set for higher things.'

Sophie smiled. 'Thanks. If you must know, when it comes to work it's almost always a case of swan syndrome. You know the one. Looking cool and elegant above the surface but paddling like fury underneath. I haven't had much of a chance to relax since I got the promotion. It's all a bit hectic. And as for higher things, well . . . I've always wondered about ending my career in academia.'

Pauline raised her eyebrows. 'Really? Doing what?'

'Criminal psychology, maybe. I've often talked about it, but I'm not sure whether I really want to do it. Maybe it's nothing more than a fantasy.'

'But it sounds great. I'm so impressed. Do you want a drink by the way? I'm just sipping my way through a gin and tonic.'

249

'Sounds good to me.' Sophie turned, caught the attention of a passing waitress and ordered her own drink. They spent the next few minutes perusing the menu. Pauline seemed to know the relative merits of most of the dishes, so Sophie followed her suggestions.

'This place can't be far from your flat, Pauline,' Sophie said.

'No. It's great. Within easy staggering distance, though it's a bit too far from Tony's manse. I don't bring him here. There are a couple of equally nice places on his side of town. How are your family, by the way?'

'All good. It's been very quiet at home today. Martin's out at Arne this evening with some birdwatching friends, doing the annual bat count. They'll end up in one of the pubs, no doubt. And Jade's been pottering around in her bedroom, getting ready to go out. I don't think you've met her, have you? Only our elder daughter, Hannah.'

Pauline frowned and bit her lip. 'Look, I'm sorry about all that. I have this reckless side to my character and sometimes it gets out of control.'

Sophie smiled, stretched her hand across the tabletop and placed it on top of Pauline's. 'Don't worry. I have the opposite problem. I'm far too controlled. Probably I'm far too controlling. My brain never seems to stop thinking ahead, scheming. I sometimes wonder if I should be worried about it, that it's some strange kind of malignancy that doesn't afflict other people.'

Their food began to arrive, and conversation switched to the relative merits of the dishes they were tasting, their respective calorie counts and the qualities of various wines.

'You can stay over at mine, if you want,' Pauline said quietly, almost nervously, as they sipped coffee at the end of the meal. 'You've had quite a lot of wine, don't you think?' She looked across at Sophie quizzically.

'Yes, that would be ideal, thanks. I warned Martin I might and brought an overnight bag. I left it in my car. It's in the public car park at the end of the road.'

'Great. That's close to my flat.'

'I know. That's why I chose it.'

'I feel a bit manipulated now.'

Sophie laughed. 'That's me. The arch-manipulator. Just you remember who's the boss.'

They settled the bill and left the restaurant. After they'd collected Sophie's bag from her car, Pauline slipped her arm through Sophie's and they strolled the hundred yards or so to Pauline's home.

* * *

George Warrander pulled up outside a low cottage in a quiet side road in Wareham and sat for a few moments before getting out of the car. He was feeling almost sick with anxiety. He glanced at the time, even though he'd checked it every minute since setting out from home. Seven o'clock, bang on time. He sighed. This whole thing was ridiculous. It could only end in disaster. What had he been thinking when he'd first arranged this date? He stood by the car, slowly shaking his head. This was such a bad idea on his part. He heard her footsteps and looked up. Her long dark hair shone in the evening light and her welcoming smile melted his tension away. She looked breath-taking.

'I saw your car draw up, so I just came straight out. You look a bit tense, George. Are you okay?'

He returned her smile and his heart began to stop pounding. 'Yes. I was just feeling a bit nervous. You know, given the situation.'

She smiled again, this time more mischievously. 'I sort of understand. But, hey, we only get one chance at life, don't we? Gotta grab opportunities when they arise, otherwise you're always left behind in the slow lane.'

'Well, that's one way of looking at things,' George said. 'I'm always a bit slow and cautious, to be honest.'

'Very sensible. Actually, I am too, really. I just say these things to see what effect they'll have. Shall we get going? It's only a ten-minute walk from here. Look, I'd love to be able to say that we'll split the bill, but I really don't have much money and this place isn't the cheapest around.'

'We've already discussed all this. I said it was okay.'

'I know you did. But can we both pretend that I'm paying my fair share, even though I'm not? That way I won't feel under any obligation towards you.'

She put her arm through his as they started to walk towards the town centre.

He smiled for the first time. 'In the circumstances, am I likely to try it on with you? I mean, I'd need to be suicidal, wouldn't I?'

She giggled. 'Bloody hell, yes. I'm just so in awe of you for going ahead with it. It reminds me of something I learned in physics about seemingly impregnable energy barriers and how they can sometimes be breached by a small number of random particles. It's called quantum tunnelling. Maybe that's what you are. A human quantum tunneller. Breaching barriers no one else would dare to attempt.'

He looked at her. 'I just felt something a few weeks ago when we were talking. I felt we kind of connected in some way, and you kept popping back into my head. Look, when I was in my last year at university, I met someone I really liked but I didn't act on it and she ended up with someone else. I regretted it for ages and kept wondering . . . The someone else turned out to be a vicious psychopath and ended up killing her. I was interviewed as a witness, and that's why I ended up joining the police.'

'That's so awful,' she said. 'So some good came out of it, despite the tragedy?' She suddenly stopped walking and turned. 'Ah, and I can guess who interviewed you. Her. The unmentionable one.'

George grinned widely. 'Oh, yes. And I've never regretted the decision I took to leave my safe, well-paid job as an economist and join the police. It's the best thing I've done.'

'Second best,' she quickly replied. 'You've asked me out on a date, remember.'

They continued to chat amiably as they strolled towards the Indian restaurant. Inside, they settled themselves at the quiet corner table George had asked for when he'd booked. He looked across the table at Jade Allen. She smiled back at him, and it took his breath away. Maybe this was going to work out just fine after all.

THE END

ACKNOWLEDGEMENTS

Several people have helped in the research for this novel, maybe more than they realised.

Margaret and I had a walking holiday in Somerset two years ago and spent three days on the Quantock Hills. We met up with our friends Jane and Barbie Hamlin, who live in Somerset, at the Dead Woman's Ditch car park. Some fifteen months later, while staying with them in Somerset, Jane lifted a small book off her shelf and said, 'This might interest you.' It was *The Abode of Love* by Aubrey Menen. I was gobsmacked. I'd just written the scenes about a twenty-first-century commune and here was a detailed account of a religious cult that was set up in the Quantocks in 1846. Jane and Barbie took us into Taunton and also to the main Quantock Hills visitor centre at Fyne Court.

I also need to mention the help of another friend who spent part of her childhood in the area around the Quantocks. Sylvie's recollections have been invaluable, usually given over a drink in one or other of Salisbury's fine pubs.

It's lovely to be part of a friendly group of authors. Those of us published by Joffe Books had a get-together just before Xmas 2018. It was great to talk over issues with Janice Frost,

Helen Durrant, Joy Ellis, Charlie Gallagher and the rest of the gang. Thanks to the boss, Jasper Joffe, and his team — they're wonderful. Special thanks go to the editorial team; Anne Derges has done another great job in sharpening up my original text.

THE JOFFE BOOKS STORY

We began in 2014 when Jasper agreed to publish his mum's much-rejected romance novel and it became a bestseller.

Since then we've grown into the largest independent publisher in the UK. We're extremely proud to publish some of the very best writers in the world, including Joy Ellis, Faith Martin, Caro Ramsay, Helen Forrester, Simon Brett and Robert Goddard. Everyone at Joffe Books loves reading and we never forget that it all begins with the magic of an author telling a story.

We are proud to publish talented first-time authors, as well as established writers whose books we love introducing to a new generation of readers.

We won Trade Publisher of the Year at the Independent Publishing Awards in 2023 and Best Publisher Award in 2024 at the People's Book Prize. We have been shortlisted for Independent Publisher of the Year at the British Book Awards for the last five years, and were shortlisted for the Diversity and Inclusivity Award at the 2022 Independent Publishing Awards. In 2023 we were shortlisted for Publisher of the Year at the RNA Industry Awards, and in 2024 we were shortlisted at the CWA Daggers for the Best Crime and Mystery Publisher.

We built this company with your help, and we love to hear from you, so please email us about absolutely anything bookish at feedback@joffebooks.com.

If you want to receive free books every Friday and hear about all our new releases, join our mailing list: www.joffebooks.com/free-books

And when you tell your friends about us, just remember: it's pronounced Joffe as in coffee or toffee!